Only Between Ourselves

Only Between Ourselves

Spiderwize
Remus House
Coltsfoot Drive
Woodston
Peterborough
PE2 9BF

www.spiderwize.com

A CIP catalogue record for this book is available from the British
Library.

The views expressed in this work are solely those of the author
and do not necessarily reflect the views of the publisher, and the
publisher hereby disclaims any responsibility for them.

All characters in this publication are fictitious and any
resemblances to real people either living or dead are purely
coincidental.

ISBN: 978-1-911596-18-9

Only Between Ourselves

Elisabeth C. Thompson

For Sabine
and the
Museannie

The past is still, for us,
a place that is not yet safely settled.

Michael Ondaatje
(Canadian novelist)

Chapter 1

Most families have secrets. Ours was no different. Over the years I had colluded with the cover-ups, more from a desire for self-preservation than anything else but I had paid the price. I was plagued by dreams; insightful, cathartic or just plain scary they were a reminder of a past I would have preferred to forget.

As I sat in my chair by the French windows, sun streamed in to the lounge infusing every part of me with a delicious warmth, gilding the flecks of dust floating above the floorboards, making them shimmer and spin. Balmy hints of varnish reached me as I contemplated the crossword. Staring down at the clues I realised the transition from quick to cryptic had been a mistake.

I stifled a yawn, attempted an anagram, moved letters about in my head; the dream dodging failed. Words merged together, melted away and the dreams stalked me again; tiptoeing behind me like children in a game of creeping Indians they tapped my shoulder. I was young once more, no longer a child and yet not quite a woman ... it was summer, I was in the garden. My mother was calling me.

"*Geneviève.*" I recognised that tone of voice. It did not bode well, "*Viens, vite.*"

Having reached an age when the urge to defy outweighed the will to comply I feigned indifference.

Louisa stopped skipping. She approached me, rope trailing behind like the lacy train of a wedding dress. "Maman's calling, Genie."

I continued to scan the book resting across my knees, not moving a muscle, heart pounding. "I know."

Louisa did not understand. An instant response was required when our mother called. She had learned the consequences of dilly-dallying. Flipping plaits over shoulders, she fingered the daisy chain I had made for her earlier and tried again. "Aren't you going in, then?"

I closed the book and uncrossed my legs, "In a minute," I said. Easing the red and white check of my Gingham skirt into a funnel I tipped the last of the daisies onto the grass and stood up, curling my toes into the cool green strands before slipping them reluctantly back into sandals. It had been a golden summer with just enough rain to keep the flowers and lawn at their best. There had been a bumper crop of gooseberries; the apple tree was rosy with fruit.

"She'll shout if you don't hurry up," Louisa said, her freckled forehead crumpling into a frown. "I don't like it when she shouts."

"She won't be shouting at you; she hardly ever shouts at you. Anyway, I'm going in now. See?" I walked towards the sandstone steps that led out of the garden and trod up the foxy brown curves as if tomorrow would do, heading for the back door with an exaggerated swagger.

Louisa giggled. "I'm coming too." She dropped her skipping rope onto the path making the handles click together like castanets. "Wait for me."

I always did.

A distant door slammed shut. I felt my hand being tugged. "Are you awake?"

"Lou," I said. "What's wrong?"

As my mind spun between fantasy and reality I realised it was not Louisa at all. Cradling wrist against waist I remembered why I was nodding in my chair when I should have been outside weeding and feeding.

I had been going away. The trip had been planned for a while. I had not seen the girls in months, much longer than usual and I had been feeling guilty. I treasured the camaraderie we shared and the way time went into reverse when we were all together. It was only natural. Kate and Diana were my oldest and dearest friends. Conversely, I did not want to see my mother. This was to be a duty visit, nothing more; my insurance policy against a troubling conscience later.

Nothing matched in the room but I had everything I needed. The furniture had been collected over the years as and when I could afford it. I knew each piece intimately; the little side table brought back from the tip and treated to a makeover, to several makeovers. I recalled the day I spent stripping it of polish only to decide it would look better painted. After a while, I began to dislike the shade of blue I had chosen and re-painted it white. I was still not satisfied and a few weeks later I reached for my rubber gloves and stripped it back to bare wood again; this time I varnished it and had a piece of glass cut to the exact size for the top so that it made a practical coffee table.

My chair had been rescued from a charity shop and re-covered at night school; the sofa, a gift from a generous friend and beside it, a second-hand display unit with cupboards beneath … but the curtains were new. They were the colour of sovereigns and just kissing the floor, the sumptuous folds held back by tassels it had taken me weeks to find in the right shade. The room had a comfortable familiarity to it. It was my safe place, my sanctuary and mine alone. No-one could take it from me.

There was a time when my life had not been so ordered, when even washing my face had been a struggle; when Arthur left and my world had imploded.

I had never understood how he could have done that to me after years of investment in our relationship and having given me no hint of dissatisfaction with our life together. "But I'm your wife," I'd said as if that trumped any argument he might put forward. "What about Cerys? She won't understand. You can't leave us. We're a family."

"It's no good, Genie. I have to go."

"What have I done wrong? I can be a better wife, I know I can. Tell me what to do."

He had taken my hands, avoided my eyes. "It's not you," he had said. "I'm sorry. I didn't mean for this to happen."

"What *has* happened?"

"I don't know how to tell you."

He had found a way of course and the pain I had felt at his confession had been unbearable; even so, I had tried to persuade him to stay. My tears had left him unmoved. I had cajoled and begged. He had simply walked out of the door. I never saw him again.

It took years to re-configure my life. When he had gone I would have struggled without the girls. At first I would pick over our marriage in forensic detail, hurt myself even more; I wanted to understand, to see if it had been my fault, if it could have been prevented, but after the initial wave of grief had passed I realised I had to rid myself of the habit or go under. I learned to live with the situation. The pain softened with the years. Cerys had been a powerful motivation for life. My little girl had needed me to be strong. I reckoned I must have pulled it off. Cerys had turned out fine.

The child sighed. "I'm not Lou," she said. I shushed her as my mind drew me back in.

I had prepared a list … a necessary antidote to senior moments. 'Gifts for the girls,' it had prompted. I remembered locking the front door behind me and making for the bus stop with my raincoat, a talisman against April showers, thrown across my shoulders like a cape.

The bus smelled of wet coats and diesel. I had missed the shower but muddy footprints carpeting the gangway to the back seat told a different story for some of the other passengers.

Tucking elbows to ribs I squeezed into the seat next to a young man, back curved and neck thrusting forward like a hungry tortoise. My bag brushed against his knee. I apologised. He ignored me, edged nearer the window and contemplated the outside world with a fixed stare. I sat still, trying not to invade his personal space, the bag perched on my knees like a pet pug. I returned to the list; chocolates for Diana without a doubt but what should I get for Kate … a bottle of wine?

When the bus stopped in town and relieved itself of its passengers I was the last one to get out. A scented candle, maybe, Kate liked candles; tickets for the theatre; a cashmere scarf? The driver revved the engine as I lingered by the door, its mechanism hissing with the effort of concertinaing itself open. I used the handrail to swing myself forward and jumped off the step with a balletic bounce.

The cherry tree immediately caught my eye. It was standing in a nearby garden, the candy floss of blossom an echo of my youth and of the garden my mother had so carefully tended, nurtured, loved; perhaps more than she had loved her children.

Nudging my glasses into a more comfortable position, I stretched up to see if I could reach a posy of the cream petals to hold to my nose. My height had always been a disappointment to me. Louisa had grown into a reasonable five foot five; I claimed five foot two, but five foot would have been nearer the mark. They were almost within reach when a lorry bowled past wafting them away from my grasp.

I leant forward to try again and misjudged the edge of the pavement. My toe stubbed the kerb. I tripped. My hand flew out to save me but instead of breaking my fall it had taken the full weight of my body. My wrist cracked under the strain. I winced as I remembered pain spreading through my body like knot-weed through a border, making it impossible for me to breathe let alone think sensibly.

She stroked my hand in a soft, child-like way. "Wake up."

Everything seemed to go into slow motion after that. My bag fell onto the pavement; gloves tumbled after purse. I saw my keys sail into the gutter.

I knew straight away that it was a serious injury. The pain had been accompanied by nausea, which for a moment had threatened to overwhelm me. I took a deep breath and swallowed hard. As I sat there, dazed and embarrassed, a young man crouched at my side. "Are you ok? Shall I call an ambulance?"

I looked up at him, noting his unease and the patch of stubble left carelessly under his chin. "I think I might have broken something. So silly of me, not looking where I was going," I babbled. He made the call and retrieved my belongings, replacing them in my bag, setting it on the pavement close by.

I had fallen opposite the library doors. It was only a few seconds before two members of staff hurried out to offer their assistance.

"Are you all right?"

"I think so." I felt light-headed. I saw the girl through a haze; celestial eyes, golden hair, unnaturally pale complexion, the collar of her cardigan flapping behind like wings … and then there was the voice of authority.

"That was a nasty fall," he said. Short and stocky, an identification tag pinned to the pocket of his shirt, he exuded confidence. "We saw it from the window."

"I've called an ambulance," the young man explained. He was pre-occupied, glancing down at his watch. "Look, I've got to go. I'll be late for work. Can you take it from here?"

"No worries."

"I've hurt my arm," I said in a small voice.

The voice of authority looked at my arm but he didn't touch it. "I'm a first aider. I think it's your wrist. Come inside and sit down while we wait for the paramedics. They shouldn't be long."

I wanted to thank my Good Samaritan but he was nowhere to be seen. "He's gone," I said, surprised he had been spirited away so fast.

"We'll look after you." The angelic voice had been gentle, reassuring and then the girl tucked a hand under the elbow of my good arm and shepherded me over to the library. I realised with surprise and relief that my glasses were still in place and undamaged. I struggled to see anything without them.

"Gran …" she was not going to give up. I could feel her breath on my cheek.

Gentle hands helped me onto one of the padded benches I'd seen accommodating the Thursday knitters. I was relieved it was a Tuesday. I felt ridiculous and painfully aware of being observed by several pairs of eyes as it was.

Someone offered me a drink but the voice of authority rejected it straight away. "It looks like a bad break. She may need surgery."

"Surgery …" his comment had alarmed me. "I'm supposed to be going away tomorrow."

"Let's wait for the professionals."

Another thought occurred to me. I would not be able to collect my granddaughter from school. "Could someone ring my daughter? My phone's in my bag." I had been shaking at that point and starting to panic. "Where is it? Did anyone pick up my bag?"

"I've got it here." The girl passed it over to me and held it still while I plucked the phone from its depths. I sat there feeling like Edward Scissor Hands wondering how I could make my fingers co-operate. Another volunteer helped me to find my daughter's number. My teeth had been chattering far too much by then for me to have made the call. She had broken the news to Cerys. The voice of authority informed me that I was in shock but I had already worked that out for myself and then there was a flurry of activity as the ambulance arrived outside.

A young woman in a high visibility jacket approached me. "Hi, I'm Sandie … and you are?"

"Genevieve McBain."

"May I call you Genevieve?" I nodded despite thinking it was a trifle too familiar. "Did you bang your head when you fell? Lose consciousness at all?" I managed a shake of the head. "Is there any chest pain?"

"No, it's just my wrist."

"And how's the pain on a scale of one to ten?"

"It doesn't hurt so much now … as long as I don't try and move it, probably a five."

"I can give you morphine."

"I'm fine." I did not want to be out of it if there were decisions to be made.

"Right, well I'd like to put your arm in a sling before we set off. It'll be more comfortable for you, are you all right to walk?"

I had risen to my feet on rocking horse legs. "I think so," I said. I recalled checking the route to the doors, determined not to trip for a second time.

Sandie took hold of my good arm to assist me. "Let's go."

It was then that I realised I had no choice but to be paraded in front of the handful of people milling round the library foyer and a line of staff well-wishers who had morphed together amoeba-like to produce an informal guard of honour. I turned to mumble my thanks. I must have made a sad spectacle. They were probably thinking I should not have been allowed out alone at my age. There was a time when I might have agreed with them. I knew better now. It had been the stupidest of accidents. It could have happened to anyone.

"Mum sent me to ask if you'd like fish for your tea."

My mood lifted as I caught sight of Cerys through the library window. She was hurrying along the pavement checking her phone like a city trader keeping track of investments. "My daughter's just arrived, can she come too?" I asked, wary of suffering the trauma of a hospital visit alone.

"Mum," she had been breathless with anxiety and haste, "What have you done?"

I tried to make light of things. "It was a silly accident … two left feet as usual …"

"She's taken a tumble," Sandie said, her smile overly cheerful. "Are you coming with us?"

Cerys nodded and waited for me to be sorted out before she climbed into the ambulance. "How on earth did you do it?"

"I wasn't concentrating. I'd come into town to get gifts for the girls ..."

"Well, that's the end of your trip," she said. "You won't be going away now; you're bound to need a plaster. There's no way you'll be able to manage a case."

There had been an undertone of concern to that statement. I knew she meant well but I wasn't ready to be dictated to. "We'll see," I said.

Sandie was busy taking my blood pressure. "You'll probably need help for a while. It's not easy getting dressed with an injured wrist and then there's driving, cooking … even making a cup of tea …" it was at that point I realised my plans might have to be put on hold.

"It's a good job I'm only next door," Cerys said. "You're going to need help with everything. Still, at least you didn't break your glasses."

Breaking my glasses would have been preferable, if more expensive, to losing the use of an arm for several weeks; after all, I did have a spare pair. Breaking my glasses *and* my wrist would have been taking bad luck to extremes.

"Do you want fish?" I could sense her fidgeting at my side, waiting for an answer.

It was barely a ten minute drive to the hospital and not long before I had been deposited in a wheelchair and pushed into a cubicle to await assessment like a guy on bonfire night awaiting the flames. We sat there in silence listening to the informal exchanges in the neighbouring bays. Silly accidents seemed to have been the dish of that day.

"It's my knee, doctor. I was doing the kitchen floor … I slipped …"

"We need to clean it up."

"But they were anti-bacterial wipes."

I had imagined the smile on the other side of the screen. *"Just to be on the safe side … you won't need stitches … the nurse will sort you out and then you can go."*

The curtains parted to reveal a young doctor, shirt sleeves rolled up to the elbow, stethoscope dangling from his neck like hippy beads, the voice recognisable from the kitchen floor incident. "What's happened here?" I appreciated his pleasant manner. I liked the way he had addressed me directly.

"We think she's broken her wrist," Cerys said before I could utter a word.

He smiled politely at my daughter and then looked at me, brown eyes thickly fringed with lashes; bright, intelligent eyes, full of solicitude as he waited for my reply. "It was just carelessness. I suppose I'll need an x-ray," I said in an effort to regain some control.

He nodded as he examined me with gentle hands. "How did you do it?"

"She fell over in town."

I took a deep breath. "Actually I tripped up the kerb outside the library. Not looking where I was going; my mind on other things. Will I need an operation?"

"I can't say until we've seen the x-rays. Let's look on the bright side. It could have been your hip."

I had been grateful to him for putting things into perspective. At least I could walk.

It was a straightforward break. No surgical intervention necessary. When I was finally allowed home, my wrist strung up out of harm's way, I was exhausted. "I think I'll have a rest," I said. "Thanks for coming with me."

Cerys had been gracious and understanding. "That's ok. There wasn't much going on at work anyway."

"We didn't have to wait long, did we? You hear such horror stories about A and E."

"We must have got through in record time. Do you want something to eat?"

I thought I had taken up enough of her day as it was. "I'm not hungry," I said.

"It's nearly time to fetch Becky from school. She's going to be surprised when she sees your plaster; a cup of tea, then?"

I had never been known to refuse a cup of tea. I smiled my thanks and checked the garden from my chair. Everything was growing like mad. "I'm going to have trouble keeping the garden tidy," I said.

"We'll all help. Becky will love it. Have a nice rest, I'll send her round when we get back."

I rocked my neatly encased arm like a babe in arms and remembered how at first I had thought six weeks sounded like a long time. It had passed pleasantly enough. Although I had missed being able to cycle or drive, the rest of my life had gone on much as usual ... apart from the clothes. Zips and buttons were out. Tee shirts and track suits were in.

"Is it ok or do you want something else?" the child asked in a weary tone.

I lifted my head from the back of the chair and met my granddaughter's eyes; round, blue, so reminiscent of my sister's. "Sorry, Becky, I was dreaming. What did you ask me?"

She sighed. "Do you want fish for tea or something else?"

"Fish will be fine."

"Ok. What were you dreaming?"

"It was about your Great-aunt Louisa and then my accident."

"I've never met her, have I?"

I considered her fresh-face, her sweet smile. Wisps of brown hair curled round her ears and tickled her chin as it escaped from the pony tail to which her mother insisted it must be tethered for school; most days she would pull out the hair bobble and transfer it to her wrist as soon as she left the playground, but not today it would seem. "You met Great-aunt Louisa once but you were only a baby."

"I don't remember that."

"No, you were too young. You do look a lot like her, though."

"Can we get your photos out later?"

"I don't know. Haven't you got a piano lesson?"

She pulled a face. "I wish it was still the holidays."

"Come on, now. You love your music. I can tell by the way you play. My grandpa played the clarinet. He was very good. You must get it from him. I missed out on the musical gene." She knew I had trouble holding a tune when humming along to the radio.

"I like playing," she said emphasising the playing, "I just don't like the lessons." She adopted a careworn expression. "I wish I was older, then I could choose; I'd play whatever I wanted, when I wanted and if I didn't want to, no-one could make me."

"If you don't practice you'll soon forget."

"I think I need a break."

She made me laugh. "How old are you?" It was not really a question but she took it as such.

"You know how old I am, Gran. It was my birthday last week, remember? You gave me a card with a big pink ten on it."

"So I did. Don't wish your life away, Becky. It has a habit of whizzing by all on its own and then before you know it you end up like me, stuck in a chair with other people cooking your meals and only your dreams for company."

"You don't have to stay in the chair," she said prosaically. "You've only broken your wrist … your legs are all right and I'm your company"

"That's true and very good company you are, too. I'm just being silly."

"When I had appendicitis I sat in a chair at our house and Mum brought *me* food. All sorts of things I'm not usually allowed. Cookies, strawberries, millionaire's shortbread," she said. She grinned at the memory of all the delicious goodies her mother had provided to tempt her appetite.

"Hmm, millionaire's shortbread; lucky you," I said. I rested my head on the back of the chair and closed my eyes again. "You'd better go and tell your mum about the fish."

"After my lesson … can we look at them then?"

I opened one eye. "Oh all right. After your lesson and after we've eaten," I agreed, adopting a firm tone, "But only if your mum says so and you're quite sure there's no homework."

Chapter 2

There were three albums in all. I kept them in a drawer under my bed alongside other bits and pieces I did not want on permanent display. Looking through them was a ritual I had initiated with Becky before she started school.

On the days I looked after the child while her mother was at work and the weather had made trips to the park impossible, we would thumb through the albums to pass the time. As she grew older, she would ask more questions. More of my memories had to be retrieved and shaken out like old clothes from an attic trunk.

Cerys had never been particularly interested in the photographs but in my daughter's daughter I had discovered an ally, someone who loved the old stories almost as much as her grandmother loved telling them. She knew them intimately and woe betide me if I varied the tale or missed something out. Our journeys through time had been a godsend since the accident. The hours flew by as we reminisced.

One by one I removed the albums from the drawer and laid them out on the bed. I sat back on my heels and considered my wrist. Only one more day of the plaster, then I'd be able to get on with my life and make that trip, but I wanted to be sure my arm had regained its strength before I tried to do too much.

Cerys was always telling me I was trying to do too much. The only problem was that I wasn't sure how much 'too much' was. My intention was to keep going until my mind or my legs, or both, gave way. I looked after my health. No-one could argue with a regime of chocolate and red wine. I took other precautions; my five a day, those crosswords, the bike. I felt free in the saddle, letting the adrenaline flow and my thoughts roam uninterrupted as I pedalled away.

I got to my feet as I heard the back door close and Becky's voice curl up towards me. "I'm back, Gran. Mum says I have to be home by nine."

"In my bedroom," I called.

I heard her tripping lightly up the stairs and then she appeared at the door, hair wafting to and fro like the threads of a bead curtain. The pony tail had gone. "Have you got the photos out?"

I pointed to the bed. "Bring them downstairs, would you?"

We sat side by side on the sofa and I opened the first album. "This is a picture of my mother," I said.

"Tell me about Lettie."

"You already know about her."

"I know but I want you to tell me again. Why was she called 'Lettie'?"

I knew the rules. I repeated the explanation that had been trotted out parrot-fashion so many times before. "Because her name was Violette, because she was French and very pretty ... like you and because she didn't want to be called Grandma, Gran or Nana."

"Why didn't she want to be called, Grandma or Nana?"

"She said they were ugly English words. She thought she was too young to be anyone's grandmother." That was my mother's character in a nutshell. Cosseted and put on a pedestal by her parents she would say and do whatever she liked without a care for other people's feelings. Throughout her life she had used her good looks and wilful nature to get whatever she wanted.

Becky nodded. "Tell me about the blue camomile teapot."

"If we're going to do all that again I'll need a cup of tea."

Before I could move she had jumped up. "I'll get it. I've been practising for my badge at Brownies. I know where everything is, even your Mr. Darcy mug."

"Thanks, it's a bit of a struggle for me with this arm. Don't bother with the pot. Just put a teabag in the mug. The kettle should have enough water in it. Mind your fingers," I warned.

I stayed in my seat, not wanting to dent her confidence in her abilities. "I've done it," she called a short while later emerging from the kitchen with the mug clutched between both hands and walking slowly like a waitress carrying a birthday cake with all the candles lit.

I blew at the top of the mug a little too ferociously, making the tea roll like the Solent in a force five. It slopped over the side of the mug onto the table. "Gran," she said in a disapproving tone.

"Sorry." I handed her the mug while I mopped up the tea with a Kleenex. She handed it back and I took a tentative mouthful. "Delicious. Thank you." I looked at her expectant face. "Right, the teapot, well, I've known that teapot for as long as I can remember. It lived in the pantry of our house when I was a little girl."

"I love the pantry bit."

"I'll do that first. The pantry was quite small, about the size of a cloakroom. It had rough plaster walls and a square window no bigger than one of your exercise books ..."

"It faced north," she said.

"It did and it was covered with a mesh screen to keep out flies. There was a tamarisk tree in the garden. Some of the branches lent against the wall of the house right by the window. The sun hardly ever shone through; it was shadowy in there and cool with the stone floor and marble shelves."

"The shelves were stacked with food."

"Yes and Lettie's herbal remedies. There was *Verveine,* for a good night's sleep, *Tilleul,* to calm the nerves and *Eau de Melisse* for a queasy stomach."

"What about the other things?"

"You mean the brown bottles?"

"Yes."

"I didn't know anything about them except that we weren't allowed to go near them. Lettie was very firm about that."

The bottles, ribbed glass with the corks forced into their necks standing proud like top hats at the races, had been stored on a narrow shelf near the pantry ceiling. My mother had warned us never to touch them. We had been told they were poisonous; they certainly looked menacing. I would count them every time I went in there to check that none had gone missing and that the corks were still in place, worried that one day they would pop out and the bottles would issue evil fumes into the air which would make us ill … or worse.

"Why did she need medicine in the pantry?"

"You had to pay to see a doctor in those days and pay for your medicine, too."

She nodded. "Now the glass jars," she said.

"Ah, those jars, well, they were full of preserved fruit. My favourites were the plums and pears. They had such tight lids. I couldn't open them when I was your age. You had to push up a metal lever to break the seal and they were stiff."

"Kilner jars," she said. She looked pleased with herself for remembering.

"Yes, that's it. There was a larger jar at the back of the bottom shelf, rather like your spaghetti jar. It was full of lily petals preserved in clear liquid, probably alcohol of some sort." My mother had been a great believer in gin. Becky allowed me another sip of tea but I could tell she was impatient to hear more. "Did I ever tell you about Lettie and the gin?"

She frowned and looked grave. "I don't *think* so, but I know about gin. It was called 'mother's ruin'. People in Victorian times drank it a lot. They gave it to their babies to keep them quiet."

"How do you know that?"

"Miss Reid told us in year five. It was History in Action week. We had to dress up like Victorian school children."

"I'd forgotten."

"Mum and Dad have a glass of wine sometimes … if Dad's not at the restaurant; you have to be eighteen to drink alcohol now you know."

"Hmm, well, Lettie liked a glass of gin while she cooked Sunday lunch."

She fiddled with her hair, twirling it round and round her finger as if spinning wool, unimpressed with the mundane. "Tell me about the precious things," she said.

"There was a big mahogany cupboard in the dining room. It had glass doors fastened by a brass lock and key." I had a vision of the crystal glasses, eight of every type, chiming to each other as my mother unlocked the doors. "Lettie kept all the precious things in there. Louisa loved the liqueur glasses …"

"She called them fairy glasses …"

"That's right."

"… and you liked the champagne glasses best," she said.

"I did. They had wide bowls and such slender stems; they seemed grown-up to me, sophisticated …" I paused remembering that there were only seven of those. The eighth had met with a tragic accident one day when I was helping my father with the washing up. The stem had come away in my hands. It had fallen to the floor and rolled slowly over to his feet. I'd watched, glued to the spot, clutching the bowl wrapped in a cloth like a Christmas pudding, prickles of fear shivering up and down my spine as I wondered what would happen next. "You've wrung its neck," he had whispered. "Quick, give it to me."

Plucking the severed stem from the floor he'd whipped the cloth from my hands before my mother realised what had happened. He knew retribution would be swift. She had berated him in French, which had been bad enough but not as bad as if she had boxed my ears. That was a story I did *not* want to share "... and there was a decanter," I went on swiftly, "as well as the trifle bowl and an oriental coffee set my grandmother had passed on to us."

"The one decorated with Japanese ladies."

"Geisha girls in beautiful dresses ..."

"With chopsticks in their hair," she said triumphantly.

"I'm sure they weren't really chopsticks ..." I said "... but that's what they looked like to me when I was little. It was such delicate porcelain that the cups and saucers were almost transparent."

"The saucers had chrysanthemums painted all over them."

"They did and we were never allowed to touch them, let alone sip from the china it was so fragile."

"What else was there?"

"Silver spoons and a cake slice, a bonbon dish with tiny feet on bandy legs, several china bowls decorated with exotic birds and her diamond rings of course."

"What happened to them, Gran?"

"I expect she sold them."

After I left home various items had disappeared from the house; furniture, a family of ebony elephants, all her jewellery. None of it had come my way. All I had in the jewellery line was some bling on a budget. "I'm not sure if I've ever mentioned this, but once in a while Lettie would pour some gin into a little bowl, drop her rings into it and then brush them with a toothbrush as if they were a set of false teeth. When she'd dried each one with a silk hanky and the diamonds sparkled like stars, she'd hang them on hooks in the cupboard where they stayed for safe-keeping until she took them upstairs to the ring tree beside her bed. Afterwards she would pick up the bowl and polish off the last few drops of gin in one go."

She gave a squeak of disgust. "You've never told me that before. I think you made it up."

"No, cross my heart; she did really, and if she'd had a bad day a neat gin was guaranteed to put her in a good mood … but I really wanted to tell you about the lily petals."

She scrunched her forehead. "What lily petals?"

"The ones in the spaghetti jar. At least that's what I think they were. They *looked* like lily petals, but who knows," I said with a Gallic shrug of the shoulders.

She gasped. "You didn't eat them did you?"

"No, they were healing petals. You see, one day I hurt my big toe." She looked blank. "Surely I've told you about my big toe?" She shook her head. I glanced down at my bare feet and wriggled my toes, nails gilded with polish. "I've never liked wearing shoes. When I was little I used to run around everywhere in bare feet."

"I do that."

"Well, let this be a warning to you, young lady. One day when I'd finished all my jobs and I was allowed out to play in the garden, I scraped my toe on a stone. The pain was awful. I rushed into the house crying, dripping blood everywhere. You'd have thought I'd chopped off my leg, there was so much blood."

She looked concerned. "What did Lettie do?"

"She told me off of course and in French which was very scary."

"It was an accident."

"I shouldn't have been playing outside in bare feet. I knew that ... and I was making a fuss. We weren't allowed to make a fuss about anything but worse than that I'd made a mess in her kitchen, that's really why she was cross. She cleaned me up and noticed I'd torn a chunk from my toe. It was hanging off the end of it like the flap on a letterbox."

"Eugh ... that sounds horrible."

"It was horrible and it hurt so much ..."

"Did it hurt as much as your wrist?"

"Almost as much ... anyway, Lettie sorted me out. She told me to sit still while she disappeared into the pantry. It wasn't long before she came back carrying that big jar. When she unscrewed the top, the liquid inside smelled suspiciously like gin but I didn't dare say so. She wrapped my toe in some of those petals and I had trouble sitting still then, I can tell you. They felt most peculiar. At first they stung a little and then they felt wet and cold but comforting at the same time."

"Didn't you have elastoplasts?"

"These were nature's elastoplasts."

"How did they stay on without the sticky bits?"

"She tied up my whole foot in a crepe bandage."

"How did you walk with your foot in a bandage? How long did you have to keep it on?"

"It's always questions with you, isn't it?"

"Mum says you don't learn unless you ask questions."

"Quite right, well, the next morning Lettie took off the bandage and the lily leaves and, do you know what?"

"No. What? Had it gone black?"

"No, there wasn't a mark on it. Not even a scratch."

"No scab?"

"There was nothing but lovely pink skin."

"Didn't it hurt any more either?"

"Not a bit. It had completely healed."

She thought she could explain this amazing phenomenon. "Lettie must have been a witch." I didn't comment. There was a brief respite while she pored over some more photographs and then the questions began again. "What about the camomile?"

"The camomile, well, that seemed to be good for everything. The minute we complained of stomach ache or a headache, out would come a tin full to the brim with yellowing flower heads. Lettie would throw a handful of them into the big blue teapot, cover them with boiling water and then we'd have to wait for the *tisane* to infuse."

"How long did it take?"

"Oh, not long, about five minutes. "*Voilà*, she'd say when the time was up."

Becky grinned. "*Voilà*," she repeated. "I can't wait to go up to senior school so I can learn French."

"It was a nasty bitter drink even with the spoonful of honey she added; Louisa and I were always sorry we'd even hinted at having aches and pains when the teapot came out."

She screwed up her nose. "It sounds disgusting. Did it work?"

"It certainly stopped us complaining. There were much nicer *tisanes* … ones I actually liked. Mint, for example, or lime flowers."

"We haven't done all the other food."

"Cheese, jars of pickles. Lettie made delicious fruitcakes. There was a big jar of Horlicks, too. In winter we had a mug every night before bed. It didn't stay fresh for long stored in a big jar. If the lid wasn't screwed down tight, the powder would get damp and go hard and then Lettie would break off lumps for us to chew so that it didn't go to waste. It tasted heavenly. I could suck it for hours."

"Like rock?"

"Exactly like rock. We didn't often have sweets so it was a big treat. Then there were the tins of ham, the last of the Sunday roast …"

"I know, I know, resting on a blue and white plate under a muslin tent."

"... and an enormous tin, full of coffee beans; actually it was more like a drum than a tin. The top was glass so you could check how many beans were left without opening the lid."

"We don't have coffee beans. Mum buys instant. She says it's quicker."

"It is, but there's nothing like the smell of freshly ground coffee. That was Louisa's job. She had to grind some of the beans every morning." For a moment I was transported back to the kitchen of my childhood home and the sinister growling of the grinder as my sister's small arm forced the handle round and round while the powdery grounds fell into the tray beneath.

"We've got loads of herbs," Becky said happy to have her own story to impart. "I counted them. There are thirty-five little bottles with shiny black tops in Dad's special cupboard."

"I don't think Lettie had that many and they weren't in bottles either. She picked them from the garden, gathered them into bunches, tied them together with raffia and then hung them up in the pantry to dry,"

"Did they smell nice? Dad's cupboard smells nice," she said.

"They smelled delicious; spicy and wholesome, just like your dad's cupboard, I expect." Her shoulders drooped. "What's the matter?"

"Dad's always working late. I hardly ever see him. He's at the restaurant most of the time. We don't do fun things together like we used to."

"Never mind, it won't be for ever," I said. "It's just while he gets things running smoothly." She sighed and picked at the hem of her skirt folding the blue cotton into tiny pleats before releasing them and then starting all over again. I wondered if I should coax her into revealing more and decided against it. She would volunteer the information as and when she was ready. "Shall I tell you about the jam now?" She nodded. "Well, every summer we'd have a big jam-making session, blackcurrant, redcurrant, strawberry, rhubarb and ginger, even gooseberry ... but never marmalade. Lettie didn't like that and anyway we didn't have an orange tree in the garden." I waited for her to tell me that orange trees didn't grow in England but for once she had nothing to say. "The preserving pan was huge, far too big for us to manage," I went on. "When I think about it now, it was quite dangerous; it swung around like a crane when she lifted it off the stove. It could have tipped up; we could have been scalded." I tried harder. "Imagine a huge volcano of sticky stuff cascading down all over us as we disappeared under the hot gooey mess," I said.

"Yuck," she said.

"Thanks goodness it never happened. When the jars had cooled Lettie would seal them with shiny cellophane circles. Louisa and I would pop cotton mob caps on the top of each one, fix them in place with elastic bands and then we'd write out their labels in our best handwriting and stick them on the jars, making sure they were straight. Lettie was fussy about them being straight. Everything had to look, just so, for her. After she'd checked we'd done it right, she'd let us line up the jars in the pantry. We always thought, with their mob caps in place, they looked like housemaids waiting to greet the master on his return home from travelling."

"Like in Downton, you mean?"

"Like in any grand house in the olden days with lots of servants," I said.

"I wish we had a pantry like that."

"You wouldn't have liked it in winter if you'd had to walk on that stone floor in bare feet. No-one needs pantries these days. We've all got fridges and freezers. People don't bother pickling food or making endless jars of jam like Lettie did. We had a big garden and grew our own fruit and vegetables. It's all different now. Houses and gardens are smaller, people lead busier lives; mums go out to work."

She turned back to the album. "Lettie's always laughing in the pictures. I bet she was fun."

I resisted the urge to contradict her. "She certainly loved having her picture taken," I said. That at least was the truth.

"I wish I'd known her," she said wistfully. She checked her birthday present watch with its glow-in-the dark wrist band. "Nearly nine."

"Time you went home."

"Can we look at them again tomorrow?"

"I'll have to consult my diary," I said pretending to take a book from my pocket. "Hmm ... I think I'll be free."

"You hardly ever go out."

"Actually, Miss Clever Clogs, I am going somewhere tomorrow."

"Where are you going?"

"That's for me to know and for you to find out."

"Tell me."

"Just the hospital, that's all. This bad boy is coming off," I said tapping the plaster.

The cloud lifted. She giggled. "That's better," I said. "See you tomorrow."

Chapter 3

"I expect you'll be pleased to get your arm back in action," Cerys said as we waited our turn at the Fracture Clinic the next morning. In leggings, tunic and boots up to her knees, she looked more like a principal boy than my daughter. She had her father's nose and my hair, although she straightened that every morning, a process I had never been able to understand. I had always loved my curls. She seemed to hate hers.

"I certainly will," I said. "I'm fed up with walking everywhere. I've missed the bike rides."

"I wanted to talk to you about that. Don't you think it's time you got rid of the bike?"

"No," I said. I knew I was no Victoria Pendleton but I was still capable of cycling a few miles at a sedate pace followed by a lime and soda at the pub afterwards with the rest of the club. "The exercise is good for me and besides, I like all the banter; they're a hilarious bunch." She looked as if she was about to say something else and then changed her mind. "I really need to make that trip up north," I added. "It's been three months now, with my wrist."

"Becky enjoys going through the albums with you."

"I enjoy it too."

"When are you going to tell her the truth about Lettie?"

I was searching in my bag for the magazine I had taken with me anticipating a long wait. I did not look up. "I don't want to, not yet."

"She has such a rosy view of everything."

"She's only a child. Let her dream. Ah. Here it is." I pulled the magazine out and nudged my glasses back into place. "Do you read the letters? I always read them first in case someone I know has written in."

"I don't buy magazines," Cerys said. "I never have the time to read them."

"Mrs. McBain?" The nurse was standing near a row of cubicles clutching a file in her hands.

"Mum. That's you."

I glanced at my watch. "It can't be. My appointment's not for half an hour yet."

"I'm sure she said, McBain. I'll ask, shall I?" She stood up before I could stop her. "Did you say McBain? Genevieve McBain?"

"That's it ... Mrs.McBain."

"Come on, Mum." She grabbed my good arm and tugged me into a standing position. "Do you want me to come with you?"

There was no way I wanted a minder, especially one who was prepared to be so critical. "I'll be fine, you stay here," I said. I dropped the magazine onto the seat and tossed her a provocative smile. "You can catch up on your reading."

The nurse beckoned me into an empty cubicle. "In here," she said. It was set up with an examination couch, two chairs and a trolley containing all sorts of stainless steel equipment. Implements of torture sprang to mind. A small basin with a levered tap was fixed to the wall. "Have a seat," she said. She soaped her hands, rinsed them and turned off the tap with her elbow. I watched her dry her hands with a handful of paper towels which she promptly discarded. The pedal bin clanged shut and she turned her attention to me.

"Now then, let's see how it's healed." She chattered about her husband's troublesome knee as she worked on my arm. We had moved on to her next-door neighbour's wedding by the time it was free of the plaster. It felt strange. It looked strange, much thinner and paler than the other one. I did not recognise it as mine "There we are, good as new, Mrs. McBain."

I stood up, preparing to leave. "Thanks. It's Ms McBain," I said, quietly. "I'm not married."

"Oh, I'm sorry." She rifled through the file on her desk. "It says *Mrs*. On your notes."

"It doesn't matter."

"Oh but it does. They're very hot on that in here, making the patient feel comfortable and all that. I'll get them to change it in the office. I'm going to refer you for physio but in the meantime don't forget the exercises I showed you and try not to trip up again. You need to be careful at …"

I sighed, knowing what was coming next, "… at my age?"

She uttered a sheepish, "Sorry."

"I'll do my best."

She followed me out of the treatment cubicle. "Well, here we go and on to the next one." She raised her voice slightly. "Mr. Hardcastle?" She put a hand to her mouth. "Can't get that one wrong, mister is mister whatever," she whispered.

"Yes."

"How are we poor females supposed to know if they're married, or not?"

"Some women don't care," I said, before I could help myself. "If they want a man they take him regardless and some men are too weak to resist." She looked surprised at my venom and I was ashamed that I still harboured a grudge against my husband after all these years. I had thought the

29

sense of betrayal well buried in the permafrost of my subconscious; it would seem a residue lay near the top waiting to be released, ready to contaminate the air if anyone so much as scraped the surface. There was warmth in my cheeks as I turned away and she rediscovered her professional smile.

A young man on crutches swung himself into the corridor in front of us, the plaster on his left leg covered in graffiti. "Right here," he said. "That knitting needle trick you told me about didn't work. I can't wait to get this thing off and have a good scratch."

"Charming," she said, "In we go." She held the curtains open for him and then let them flounce behind her like the skirts of a dancer mid jive as I moved away.

I walked slowly back to the waiting area trying to take control of my emotions. Why did it still hurt? I felt as if shards of barbed wire were piercing my flesh, making my breathing shallow and jagged. Cerys stood up as soon as she saw me. "All ok?"

"Yes, free at last," I said, forcing air in and out of my lungs as best I could. "What a relief. They've referred me for physio." I looked at my wrist. I tried to move it. It did not want to bend. She noticed.

"I expect the muscles are weak after all this time. Is that it, can we go now?"

"Let's have a coffee first," I said. "You're not in a hurry, are you?"

"No, I've got time."

The cafe was on the ground floor of the hospital near the entrance doors. Hidden away in the middle of a shopping mall, it was set up with huddles of chrome and glass tables married to surprisingly comfortable chairs, their faux leather seats slung hammock-like between the chrome frames.

The self-service counter was stocked with sausage rolls, cheese sandwiches and iced buns. I saw one token green salad. The vending machines contained nothing but sugary drinks and chocolate bars. "So much for healthy eating," I said beginning to regain some composure.

"I suppose they have to stock what sells," she said. "When are you going away?"

"As soon as I can get organized, I spoke to Kate last night. She can put me up; it's only for one night ... probably after the weekend."

"It'll be cheaper mid-week."

"I'd like to go as soon as I can; it's already been too long, Monday if possible. I was going to ask you to book me a ticket online."

"I could go with you, if you like. Kit's due some time off, that's if he doesn't decide they're short-staffed or something else crops up to keep him at work like it usually does," she said, a slight edge to her voice.

"I expect he's looking forward to a few days off. Becky says he's been working really hard."

"He has, or at least he *says* he has," she said. I hoped there had not been a falling out between them. It was probably nothing. They often argued. I decided a head in the sand approach would be best. "Do you want me to come?"

I did not want her to go with me. It was my cross to bear, not hers. Cerys hadn't seen her since she was a baby and that's the way I wanted it to stay. I did not want her tainted by my mother's twisted views and critical attitude. "I'd rather go alone. She won't recognise you. She probably won't even know it's me. Kate says her eyesight's bad now ..." I took my purse, leaving my bag on one of the chairs, jacket draped over the top of it like a yurt, "... coffee?"

"Filter, please." I headed for the counter and picked up a tray. She was right behind me. "Don't try and carry that, Mum. I'll do it. So, when are you going to tell Becky?"

"Tell her what?"

"You know what."

"I think I'll have herbal tea," I said.

"When, Mum? She needs to know."

"I haven't decided. What would be the use? They couldn't have a meaningful relationship; how about a snack, my treat?"

"No thanks. That's not the point. What if she dies? How will you explain that away?" I paid for the drinks and we headed back to our seats. "It could happen any time, Mum."

"I know that. Look, I don't want to tell Becky the truth until she's much older. She'll want to know about everything. She won't be fobbed off. You can't imagine the questions she asks me. Do you think she's ready for all that?"

"Children are much more aware now. Becky will understand. So, you're going to carry on with the fairy tale?"

"That was the general idea, yes." I poured peppermint tea from the miniature teapot into the large cup and saucer we had collected from the counter, thinking Mad Hatter thoughts and hoping this was the end of my interrogation. I inhaled the minty fragrance. "Mmm … this smells good."

"What about me, then? I'm part of the story."

"You were never involved. It didn't affect you."

"How can you possibly say that?"

She seemed hurt by my words. I did not understand. "You were only a toddler; you barely knew him ... or her."

"I wasn't a deaf toddler."

I looked at my daughter … really looked at her and knew I had presumed too much. I nudged my glasses up my nose and summoned up a smile but it turned into more of a grimace. "No, I'm sorry. I should have realised."

"You'll have to do it some time."

"I know I will ... but not yet."

Chapter 4

Becky arrived half an hour earlier that evening. "How's your wrist, Gran, let's see." I pulled back my sleeve to reveal the wasted arm. She stroked it, her touch as soft as dragonfly wings on my skin. "It looks like one of those baguettes Mum gets from the supermarket; you know the ones you put in the oven and pretend you've made yourself."

"Thanks but I don't *think* I'll be putting it in the oven."

"You could sit in the sun, though. That'll help; lots of vitamin D. It's good for bones and things. Victorian children got rickets because they didn't have enough vitamin D," she said authoritatively.

"I'll bear it in mind. Top marks for your teacher. She seems to know how to get you to remember things. Are we going to look at these photos now?"

"Yes please. I've been wondering … did Lettie speak French all the time?"

"Not all the time, but quite a lot."

"I know how she answered the phone."

"Go on then, tell me."

"Well, instead of saying the number or just, hello, she'd say, *ici, le faive two four faive neuf dooble faive*," Becky said screwing up her face as she struggled to get her tongue round the Franglais.

"Very good; my friends loved it. They'd call, put down the phone and call back again just to hear her voice."

"Didn't that make her cross?"

"You bet it did." I did not want to explore that avenue. I turned over a few more pages. I pointed to a picture of my mother in a fur coat. "What do you think of her coat in this picture? She was at her friend's wedding in France, just after the War."

Becky peered at the photo. "That's the *fur* coat," she said disapprovingly.

"In those days everyone who was anyone had a fur coat," I said. "I loved it. It was soft and silky, warm to snuggle up to on the hard wooden pews when she took us to church. It smelt lovely, too."

Becky wrinkled her nose. "It can't have. It was made from a dead animal."

I shook my head. "It smelt of her perfume and the peppermints she kept in a secret pocket in the lining in case the incense caught the back of her throat during the service and made her cough."

"My throat feels funny."

"Perhaps you need a drink." She shook her head. "I hope you're not getting a cold."

"Miss Reid's got a cold. She had a box of tissues on her desk today. What's incense?" she said and sniffed loudly.

"It's a special spice they burn in some churches. The priest carries it around in a bowl on a chain …"

"Like a cereal bowl?"

"More like a large sugar bowl with a lid, very ornate, decorated with a filigree pattern."

"Filigree, what does that mean?"

I sighed. "This is worse than Perfection."

She giggled. "That's one of your quiz programmes, isn't it?

"One of my favourites," I said. I wasn't going to admit that I only watched it so that I could ogle Nick Knowles.

"Filigree, how can I explain? It's a delicate lace-work pattern ... a pretty pattern of spaces cut out of whatever it is you want to decorate."

"Oh. You mean like those paper snowflakes we made at Christmas."

"More or less; the bowl's called a censer and the priest waves it about during the service. It gives off a lot of smoke and an aromatic scent. It's supposed to add extra significance to the whole ceremony, make it more holy."

Becky sniffed again. "What does it smell like?"

"Sort of sweet powdery flowers, I suppose."

"It sounds nice."

"It always makes me cough, like it did Lettie."

Becky had moved on. "I like this one," she said, pointing to a picture of a garden full of flowers and a cat sunning itself on a rockery. "What was the cat called?"

"You know his name."

"*Bijou*, that means jewel. He's got very fluffy fur."

"He was a very beautiful cat ... a Blue Persian and they are fluffy. Lettie had to comb him every single day or he got a fur ball in his stomach which made him sick. He had lots of tangles. It took her ages to tease them out."

"Is that why he's got a cross face?"

"I expect so," I said.

"Why was he called *Bijou*?"

I had no idea why my mother had chosen that name for the cat. I had never asked. He was just *Bijou*. "Probably because he was gorgeous and he had a good pedigree. He was an 'aristocat' I expect that's why."

"I bet the garden was pretty. There are lots of flowers in it, like yours. We haven't got any. Mum says she can't be bothered with the weeding."

I thought of all the gravel and decking in my daughter's garden and felt sorry for the little girl. I had enjoyed gardening as a child. "You have some nice shrubs and the bird bath," I said.

"Yes, but I wish we had flowers … roses. I'd like some roses and then I could make perfume with the petals."

"The garden was Lettie's pride and joy. She loved gardening but some plants weren't allowed to grow there."

"Which ones do you mean?"

"Well, apart from the usual weeds, you know, nettles, dandelions and things, she couldn't stand bluebells."

"Why didn't she like them?"

"Because they were blue; Lettie didn't have anything blue."

"I like blue. It's Mia Bailey's favourite colour."

"Mia?"

"She's the new girl at school. She used to live in Spain."

"Oh, I see. Lettie had some funny ideas. She reckoned blue was unlucky. It was just Lettie being Lettie. Her favourite colours were red and green. If she found any bluebells in the garden she'd dig them out with her fork, throw them in the wheelbarrow like a farmer tossing hay, wheel them round to the back garden and tip them onto all the other weeds and leaves and things she'd piled up in a corner waiting to be burned on a bonfire when the mound got high enough."

"Why didn't she take them to the dump in her car?"

"She didn't have a car. In those days people burned leaves and weeds in their gardens. Autumn always smelled of bonfires. We had privet hedges down the front path which had to be clipped back each year and sycamores and elms in the back garden. There were hundreds of leaves to burn."

I could almost hear her mind whirring. "What about the compost heap. You must have had a compost heap."

"We did but you can't put weeds on a compost heap and anyway, it was full of grass cuttings and vegetable peelings."

"Where did you live when you were little?"

"We lived near here at first and then we moved up to Liverpool when Louisa was about five."

"Why aren't there any pictures of your dad in the albums?"

"Lettie tore them up after they separated."

"That wasn't very nice."

I had often felt the same way but I refused to make a judgment on my mother's actions. I could remember the acrimonious discussions. I had never forgotten my father's drinking and my mother's violent tempers. It was unsettling to be reminded of all that. "People handle their disappointments in different ways. Lettie chose to blank him out and we were expected to do the same. We never talked about him after he left."

"I don't know what he looked like."

I had rescued one photograph of my father. She had never seen it. I thought now was the time to put that right. "I do have a picture of him if you'd really like to see what he looked like. I hid it so that Lettie wouldn't find it and throw it away with the others."

"Oooh, yes please. Was it in an old biscuit tin under a loose floorboard in your bedroom?" she asked, wide-eyed.

"It was in my bedroom but not under the floorboards. I kept it in a shoebox wrapped in tissue paper under a pair of ballet shoes."

"You never said you had ballet lessons."

"I didn't. One of Lettie's friends gave us the shoes. She knew Louisa and I enjoyed playing at dressing up. The shoes didn't fit us for long but I loved the silky ribbons you were supposed to tie round your ankles. I kept them for ages."

"Have you still got them?"

"No. Lettie gave them to some scouts who came to the house collecting jumble." That experience had taught me a valuable lesson. I was horrified when I came home from school and found the empty box in my wardrobe. I checked in the tissue paper. The photograph was still there. If she had found it … I didn't want to imagine what might have happened to me. After that I made a conscious effort to try not to show a preference for any of my other belongings in case she decided to deprive me of those too. "The photo's upstairs. I'll go and fetch it."

Chapter 5

The young man in the photograph stared at the camera with a serious expression. I had forgotten how alike we were. I took a minute to observe his features. It had been a while since I had seen them.

His eyes were dark like mine and soulful, his face clean-shaven. His hair was debonair brushed back from his forehead in crinkling waves. He had gifted me those, too. He had certainly been a good-looking man. What had happened to make their marriage turn sour? I had not been my mother's confidante and too young to understand why things had been the way they were when he left.

I remembered my mother refusing to go out with him because she didn't like his friends and disapproved of his drinking; what had come first I wondered, the dependence on alcohol or her disapproval of the company he kept? He was my father but I knew very little about him.

I heard footsteps on the stairs. "Have you found it?"

I sat down on the bed. "This is him, James Caesar McBain. Everyone called him Mac, except us of course. We called him, Papa."

Becky took the photograph from my hand. "Well, he looks all right."

I thought for a moment remembering my conversation with Cerys and decided she was old enough to hear a watered down version of the truth. "He wasn't always very kind to Lettie."

She stared hard at the photo. "Was Lettie always kind to him?"

I was taken aback. I had been at pains to give her a positive view of her great grandmother. I wanted her to love the illusion. Had the child read between the lines and gleaned a grain of the truth? "What do you mean?" I said.

"Well … sometimes … if one of my friends is mean to me, I'm mean to them."

"Oh Becky, that's not very nice."

"It's not because I don't like them or anything. It's just that I get angry. I don't like what they've done. I want to pay them back."

"I don't know if I approve of that," I said. "Paying people back can lead to all sorts of trouble."

I was not prepared to pick apart my parents' relationship although I had often speculated about it myself. Clearly neither of them had been mature enough to ride the waves of a stormy relationship. "I don't think it was like that for them. I think they just grew apart. Let's go back downstairs."

The photograph she selected next was a formal one of me in a summer dress carrying a basket of flowers, little sister Louisa cross-legged at my feet. "You look nice in this one," she said.

"Yes … I've always loved flowers. Lettie taught me about gardening."

"Like you've been teaching me?"

"Just like that; I don't know what I'd have done this summer without you to help me out."

Her cheeks flushed with pleasure. "That's all right, Gran. It was fun. Did Lettie have a sunhat like yours?"

"No. Sometimes she wore a scarf to protect her hair from the embers if she was lighting the bonfire but she didn't think much of the English weather. She was used to hotter temperatures where she grew up. She complained about it all the time. "

"Didn't she wear sun block?"

"I don't know if there was such a thing then. When I was young we didn't worry about getting sunburned; we'd never heard of melanomas, or factor thirty sun screen. You could count the days on one hand when it got really hot each year. Babies had sunhats and old men watching cricket. If you were on the beach you might see some of the men tie a knot in each corner of their handkerchiefs and turn them into sunhats … we didn't have tissues then, everyone had a cotton hanky instead; dainty ones decorated with embroidery for the ladies, large, plain ones for the men, but that was about it."

"Mum makes me wear a hat in summer. I have to take one to school."

"It's probably very wise with all this global warming going on. Anyway, when the chores were done, Lettie would lie in a hammock in the hot sun smothered in coconut oil, burning her skin to a deep tan."

"She must have had sunglasses."

"She did wear sunglasses; the most glamorous ones you could imagine. They were decorated with chips of glass masquerading as diamonds." She was about to interrupt again but I pre-empted her. "Pretending, that's what I mean; imitation diamonds all over her sunglasses. I can see her now, lying there, like Greta Garbo ..."

"Greta ... who?"

"Greta Garbo. She was a famous film star from the nineteen thirties and forties ..." I sniffed the air "… I think I can smell the oil of citronella Lettie used to chase away wasps."

Becky giggled. "You are silly, Gran. I'm scared of wasps."

"Lettie wasn't scared of them. I don't think she was scared of anything. She fell in love with a handsome young soldier and married him without a second thought. She made her home in a foreign country, learned a new language well enough to set up her own business and managed to bring up two children without the help of her husband or family at a time when that was considered bad."

"I think she was a pioneer … and a witch," she said.

"She certainly had the pioneering spirit, always pushing the boundaries." My mother had taken no notice of what the rest of the world thought, or did. If she felt she was doing the right thing that had been enough for her.

"Did you miss your dad? I miss mine. He's hardly ever at home."

I gave her a hug. "I did miss him a bit, but Louisa missed him more. She was the baby of the family and he'd spoiled her."

I wondered if that had been another reason for the breakdown of my parents' marriage. Could my mother have been jealous of her daughters, of their youth and his attentiveness? Louisa had escaped the worst of her fits of temper and acts of unkindness due to my father's interventions. He had tried to protect us both. I had done my part to shield my sister from our mother's impatience and rage. After my father left there had been no-one to do that for me. I was flagging but I could sense she wanted more. "Did I ever tell you about *Bijou* and the wasps?"

"No. Did he get stung?"

"He didn't get stung and he wasn't afraid of them either. He would search them out in the garden and when he caught one he'd pat it about with his paws as if he was plumping up pillows."

"I wish I'd seen him," she said. "Did he sit on your knee?"

"Goodness me, no, he was quite a superior cat, far too important to sit on anyone's knee."

"Did he have his own basket?"

"He had a cushion with his name embroidered in the middle in gold thread. Lettie made it for him. She was always sewing. That's how she earned her living; making clothes for other people. We were expected to make things, too. I made all these cushions," I said, leaning forward so that she could examine the tapestry designs on the cushions behind me.

"I like the one with the cat's face on it best."

The round cushion was propped up on the arm of the sofa. It was purple silk with a cat's head appliquéd on the top of it in black velvet. Yellowish green eyes stared out of the black face. String whiskers flopped down like an old man's droopy moustache. They fell either side of the satin tongue which poked out of the embroidered mouth in a curious fashion. She stroked the whiskers.

"Lettie made that one."

"She was clever, wasn't she? I'd love a cat," she said and sneezed ... a bit like a kitten might.

"I know. It's a shame about your mum's allergy. Are you sure you haven't got a cold?" She shook her head. "You'll have to wait until you have your own house and then you can have a whole army of cats if you like."

"I'll have to get a job first. I'll need money to buy their food."

"Of course, that's very sensible. *Bijou* had his own special food. No cheap cuts of anything or tinned food for him. Lettie made sure he had fresh fish or steak every day. It was my job to poach the fish in milk and serve it up to him on his dish which was kept in an enamel bowl under the pantry shelves with his brushes and combs."

"I've got a special plate. I made it at school. I painted a dinosaur on it."

"I know you did, you showed me. It's very artistic. Every day, after she'd brushed him, Lettie would let him go outside into the garden. He'd saunter about with his tail in the air like a king inspecting his kingdom and then roll about in the catmint until it was flattened into a comfortable throne so that he could sun himself on the rockery and doze."

"It can't have been sunny all the time. What did he do if it rained?"

"Ah, well, that was a different matter. He hated getting wet. He wouldn't set a paw outside the back door if it rained unless he was desperate. If he had to step on the soggy grass or he trod in a puddle while he was out he'd sit by the door and miaow and miaow until someone let him in."

"Didn't you have a cat flap?"

"I don't know if there were such things then. Anyway, after that he'd make another fuss until Lettie took notice of him."

"Then what did he do?"

"He'd hold up a paw and stare at her with his head at an angle, looking haughty and impatient like this ..." I said, putting my head on one side and staring at her with a funny expression "... and he wouldn't stop making these odd growling noises until she'd dried him off to his entire satisfaction."

She chuckled. "I wish I'd seen him. Did he go hunting for mice?"

"No. He was too grand for that, or too lazy."

She turned some more of the pages and sneezed again and then sniffed loudly. I passed her a tissue. "I think you have caught a cold."

"It was raining on your wedding day; where's that picture of your wedding? The clothes all look so funny. Why didn't you have a wedding dress?"

I sighed and removed her fingers from the album. It was no wonder I had so many dreams with her giving me the third degree every time we looked at the photographs. I put it to one side. "We don't have the time for that now. You'd better get off home. We'll do the rest of it another day."

Chapter 6

I didn't see much of Becky over the weekend. My assistant had been banned from helping because of her cold. I left the packing until Sunday evening. It had never been a favourite task; all that sorting, folding and trying to remember every last little thing that might be needed. It was only one night, I kept telling myself. It would hardly matter if I forgot something.

I was pleased when the phone rang. There was a slight delay before I heard my sister's transatlantic drawl. "Hi Genie … how are you?"

"Lou, it's great to hear your voice. I had a dream about you the other day."

"What was I doing?"

"Oh ... just being you. How are things?"

"Ok. I wondered how you were getting on with your wrist."

"Really good, the plaster's off. I'm free to carry on as normal now. I was just packing; going north."

There was another pause … a longer one this time. "I don't know why you still put yourself through that."

"Because I want a clear conscience at the end, that's why. You do your bit."

"It's only money."

"You could use it yourselves or give it to the boys ... donate it to charity."

"Don't they say charity begins at home? As long as I don't have to see her I'm happy to pay for her care."

"And I'm happy to visit once in a while. Kate says she doesn't do much now. Her eyesight's going."

"She'll find that hard, something she can't control."

"She couldn't control Papa," I said. "He didn't hang around. If he had things might have been different ... for all of us. I was looking at his photo with Becky. It made me think."

"He had the right idea, she's one crazy cookie. I don't blame him for disappearing. I did my own disappearing act if you remember."

"Getting married at sixteen is hardly disappearing."

"I wasn't there for you, though, was I? America's a long way from Liverpool."

"I was glad to see you happy. Carter's the best thing that ever happened to you. How is he?"

"Still wheeling and dealing. He's taken the boys up to the cabin for some shooting."

"They're hardly boys."

"They are to me. How's Cerys?"

"She's fine."

"And that adorable little Becky; how's she?"

"She's fine, too."

"It's so unfair you had a daughter, then a granddaughter and I ended up with three boys and not even the sniff of grandkids."

"I'm sure your time will come."

"It had better hurry up. I'm not getting any younger."

"You're not as old as me."

"I feel it sometimes."

"None of them got girlfriends yet?"

"Billy was in a relationship for a while. I told you."

"Oh yes. That was sad."

"He's still cut up about it. That's one of the reasons Carter took them all away."

"Is she out of hospital?"

"I don't know. After the accident her parents asked Billy not to contact her. She might never be able to walk again. It seems a bit harsh. He wasn't even there when it happened and he was prepared to stand by her even though she was in the car with another man."

"What happened to him?"

"Search me. He disappeared without trace."

"She might get back with Billy."

"I doubt it. Money talks over here and they've got plenty. Billy wasn't in their league."

"What about Seth and Clive?"

"Oh they're too busy enjoying themselves to settle down."

"Clive's only just left college."

"He's been working for twelve months now."

"It can't be a year …"

"Seth's looking to buy some property. Do you think that's a good sign?"

"It could be."

"I sure hope so. When are you leaving?"

"Tomorrow morning. I'm getting the train from London at eleven."

"Call me when you get back."

I decided to ring Cerys after that. I had planned to drop in next door to say goodbye but now I had left it too late; I only had time for a quick call. "Are you all ready?" she asked.

"I am, nearly. I've just the last minute things to put in my case."

"Becky's cross with me. She wanted to come and help. Apparently you told her you don't like packing."

"Fancy her remembering that. How is she?"

"She's still a bit snuffly."

I heard Kit's voice. I was surprised after what she had told me about him working all hours. "Kit's home," I said.

"Yes, briefly. He's making bread. Becky's helping."

"That's good. They should do more things together. Tell her I rang, give her my love."

"I will. I have to go, Mum. Have a good trip."

I was anxious not to miss the train the next morning and I woke every hour until it was time to get up. I left the house before Becky had even considered getting ready for school.

Cerys had booked me a seat on the Liverpool train. It was waiting on the platform when I arrived at Euston. I found the seat, stashed my case and settled down with the magazine I had tried to read at the hospital.

The train was a fast one. Scenery flashed past without me being able to recognise a thing, I yawned. I felt my eyelids droop. I tried to resist, shifted my position, opened my eyes wide and stared outside in another attempt at dream dodging but my subconscious, like Nanny, knew best. I was about to take my medicine without a spoonful of sugar to help it down. I slept and the dreams snuck in.

It was my wedding day. I was dressed in the silk two-piece my mother had made for me. She had decided a conventional wedding dress would be too expensive. My views had not been canvassed. The ring had not arrived. I was starting to panic. My mother-in-law was being unhelpful. I heard my voice. "Did it come in today's post?"

"No." I saw her lips snap shut as if one word uttered was more than she was prepared to give.

"The jeweller said he posted it weeks ago." Agnes Ryder's eyes were steely but she said nothing. "How can we get married without a ring?" I felt like weeping. Agnes shrugged but offered no suggestions. "What am I going to do?" My voice echoed back to me in time to the clatter of the wheels on the track, "going to do ... going to do ... going to do."

Lettie's face appeared and then her body floated over to join it. She was fiddling with her finger, "*You must 'ave mine,*" she struggled but the ring would not move, "*Zut ... savon Geneviève.*"

"She needs soap. I'll get it …" I said the words out loud and woke myself up.

The dreams seemed to pick on the most painful episodes in my life and replay them. My wedding day had not been ideal. I looked about me to see if any of the other passengers had noticed my outburst. The only person nearby was a young woman, eyes closed, a file of abandoned notes on the seat beside her. She was plugged in to earphones, mouth half-open, lips quivering as gentle breaths eased their way in and out. I sat up straight and willed myself not to drift off again. It had not been a good dream and yet not quite a nightmare. Despite my best efforts, my head started to nod and I picked up where I had left off.

Lettie was smearing soap all over her finger, "*Non ...ce n'est pas possible ... it will not budge. It will 'ave to be yours, Agnès.*"

Agnes Ryder looked as if she were about to choke. "*Mine?*" she said, in a tone worthy of Lady Bracknell. Suddenly the room was full of people muttering and pointing fingers. With everyone else's eyes upon her she had no choice but to comply. She tugged the wedding ring from her finger and handed it to a face-less Arthur. He seemed to vacillate between light and shade, turning this way and that like a pavement sign in a draughty arcade. Her eyes bored into me, her expression one of twisted disdain. I was shrinking, becoming smaller and smaller like Alice after the entire 'drink me' potion.

I stirred and fell into a deeper sleep. The scene changed. I saw myself in the room I had slept in as a child. I was writing a letter to my aunt in France.

Chere tante Jeanne, I hope you are well. I know you haven't had much news from us recently and I have so much to tell you. When Louisa got married Maman was alone, so I left my job in town and after a while I found a post at a local laboratory. I have now worked my way up to analyst and it is very interesting work but when Arthur comes home, nothing will hold me back.

We met in London. He is a Lieutenant in the navy and I didn't like him at first but after our second meeting I began to think he was much nicer. He went away for three months and we wrote to each other every week. We've been seeing each other regularly ever since and last December he wrote telling me he was on leave. We got engaged. A month later when he was on leave again, we were married very quietly. It pelted with rain and I had to borrow his mother's wedding ring because mine had not come back from the jeweller (he sent it there to be sized) and Maman could not get hers off her finger, despite the soap.

We are so happy. He is terribly good and devoted. I'm sure you will like him when you meet. Perhaps you will write him a note in English. He is worried in case when he sees you, you will not understand him as he knows very little French.

There is one snag, though. His mother and I don't "hit it". I haven't heard from her since Arthur went back but I expect she will come round eventually. He is an only child you see and I don't think she likes the idea of him marrying. He is quite a bit older than me, too. He is going to come out of the navy soon and we will get a house, but for the moment I am still living with Maman.

Please give a big hug to Bon-papa from me and take one for yourself,

Geneviève

The train slithered to a halt. I awoke with a start. I didn't identify with the young woman writing the letter. I could not remember being so naive, so in love, so full of hope. It reminded me that I had made a lifetime commitment. Arthur had claimed to do the same but despite all that it had gone wrong. "I thought we'd be together forever." I heard his voice and recalled his pained expression as he had issued those words. "I've tried to fight it, Genie, God knows I have, but it's no good. My feelings for her are too strong."

Why had he let it happen? Why could I still hear him making his excuses? I felt my eyes fill up. I had cried then and many times since.

There were no words to describe my feelings as I had watched him leave. I was dry-eyed and numb by then, but still uncomprehending. Panic soon set in. How would I manage without him? I didn't want to bring up our daughter alone. I didn't want to live without him. If Diana had not happened to call round that evening quite by chance I could not say what I might have done in my state of utter despair.

She found me in the sitting room clutching a bottle of Aspirin, Cerys screaming in her cot. We went home with her, away from the empty house and the unpleasant scenes; away from all the memories; away from my life as I knew it. We never returned. I couldn't face it ... or him. My husband was dead to me, but only me; he was very much alive to someone else. I had no memory to honour, just the pain of rejection to suffer. It played itself again and again like a tape on a loop until I nearly lost my mind.

The girls acted as go-betweens. They packed up the house and supervised its sale. Kate let us stay with her in London while we became accustomed to our new status as a one-parent family; she was often away on buying trips which gave me a gentle introduction to managing alone. After a while I discovered I could live without him. Another few weeks and I felt strong enough for us to strike out on our own.

I looked out of the window and tried to regain a little composure. Crewe; it would not be long before Lime Street station. Even after all these years, just the thought of being so close to where it had happened made me hyperventilate.

I thought of Becky to cheer myself up. I knew she didn't like it when I was away. She had asked to come with me. I had promised to take her one day but not when she should have been at school. I told her it would have to be during the holidays. I remembered her asking me about her grandfather. "I've been wondering …" she had said.

I had folded my arms and crossed my legs. "Here we go. Whenever you say that I know you're going to ask me an awkward question. What is it this time?"

"…what happened to Grandad Arthur?"

"You know what happened to him. He had a brain tumour. He died."

"I know that but you said he didn't move away from Liverpool with you and Mum. Where was he?"

That was a tricky one. I thought I had a suitable answer. "He went to follow his heart." I hoped that would be enough to satisfy her curiosity. I should have known better.

"What does that mean … exactly?"

I had neatly side-stepped the question. "I'll tell you when you're older."

It was inevitable I should be thinking unhappy thoughts. It happened every time I made this journey. The cards my mind posted were not of sunny days and cherished memories. No magical landscapes or smiling faces. They were cards of devastation and broken dreams. The past unnerved me. It was not a safe place to be. Perhaps Louisa had the right idea in staying away.

The only pleasant part of the visit was meeting up with Kate and Diana. They knew everything about everything. I had no need to pretend with them and no need to explain; no need to keep secrets for there were none to keep. They gave their support willingly even though I had no right to expect it. I would always be grateful to them for that.

The brakes kicked in. The train slowed, shuddered for a while and then groaned as it tried to resist their pull. It stopped alongside a row of advertising boards, panting like a dog on a restraining leash. I stood up, fighting the desire to stay in my seat and wait to be taken straight home again. The doors hissed open. I set my mouth and stepped out onto the platform.

Chapter 7

"Genie, whoo hoo … over here ..."

It was the girls. They were both standing at the barrier, waving; Kate, tall and slim, exuding style in tailored slacks and linen blouse, her kohl-rimmed eyes an enigmatic grey; Diana, fresh-faced as usual, her fly-away hair doing its own thing and trademark earrings swaying in time to her body's rhythm. She was dressed in a simple cotton skirt and t-shirt, several rows of beads lying across her generous bosom in ever decreasing circles. "Here I am again. It's so good to see you both," I said before accepting their hugs and kisses and giving them mine in return.

Salty sea air filled my nostrils as we left the station. Seagulls mewed above the traffic noise. We linked arms dawdling along like teenagers out on the town, taking up more of the pavement than was seemly, ignoring fellow pedestrians and forcing them to edge out of the way. The bag of ferrets in my stomach stopped fighting as we caught up with each other. Kate was first, "How are you Genie, how's the wrist?" Now that her long blonde hair had lost its colour she wore it short and chic. It suited her.

"I'm fine thanks. The wrist's on the mend."

"Have you been out in the garden much?"

"I've done what I could. It's been a bit difficult with only one arm. Becky's been helping."

"How is she? Still asking questions?"

"She never stops."

"We're going round to Windgather, first," Diana said as she snatched the case from my grasp. "The car's round the corner."

"Have you got any news for me ... anyone getting married, splitting up ... what gossip from the grapevine?" I said.

"Kate has some news," Diana said. She rolled the beads between her fingers in a nervous fashion. It was a suck of the thumb gesture, a reassurance that all would be well. I guessed it was not good news.

Kate frowned at her. "I wasn't going to say anything until later."

"No point putting it off," Diana said. She clicked the remote on the car keys and the lights of an Alfa Romeo flashed at us. "Here we are. I brought Chris's car. You can't get much in my Mini. The back seat is like a parcel shelf and the boot's just ridiculous."

"I'm surprised it's still going," I said, smiling in a half-hearted fashion. I tried to make sense of her previous comment. Something had happened to Kate and it was bad. Was she ill? She looked fine. "What is it, Kate?" I asked as Diana stashed my bag.

"I had to have some tests," she said.

A horrifying thought hit me. "It's not the big ..." I couldn't bring myself to say it.

"Not the big C?" Kate said, her manner offhand. "I'm afraid so ... breast cancer."

"No."

"Don't look so shocked, Genie, it's just another challenge life has chucked my way."

It was hard to shift the shock from my eyes. How could she be so calm? She was suffering from a life-threatening condition. She had led a charmed life until now. She was the cleverest and most ambitious of us three. No money worries, a job she had enjoyed in the fashion industry and no marriages or divorces behind her ... and now this. How would she cope, how would we cope? "Why didn't you say?" I nudged my glasses unnecessarily closer to my eyes. "I could have gone to a hotel or something."

"I wanted you to stay with me."

"When did you find out?"

"It was only a few days ago."

"She's being very brave about the whole thing. I know I'd be dripping all over the place. Kate hasn't broken down once since she had the diagnosis."

"That's what you think," Kate said. "I don't like to make a show of myself in public. Anyway, what's the use in crying? It wouldn't do me any good. I've got to stay positive. That's what it says in all those brochures they give you at the hospital. Thankfully, it's only a small lump. They've caught it early. I'll go in next week, they'll take it out and that will be that."

She made it sound so simple. "You're having the op next week? I do wish you'd said something. I could have put this off for a while."

"No, you couldn't. I didn't want you to. You haven't been to see Lettie for ages. She can't go on much longer and then how would you have felt if you hadn't seen her? I'm not dying ... well, not yet anyway."

"No, of course you're not." Diana's tone was robust. "Right, let's get this show on the road."

The Spires' house was a rambling four-bedroomed semi with a sea view in a residential district a few miles to the north of the city centre. I knew the area well. I should have done. It was where I had spent most of my formative youth.

The house was untidy. It had always been untidy but what it lacked in neatness it made up for in warmth and welcome. Diana and Christian had raised four children in the house and remnants of their schooldays still remained. There were family photographs on the walls, school photographs; long hair, short hair, grimaces, toothy grins, toothless smirks. Books littered the tops of cupboards and spilled out onto the floor; a doll's house was trying to hide in a chaotic corner. Knick-knacks of every sort lay in the most unlikely places. Windgather was a bag lady of a house.

The door opened as Diana parked in front of the garage and a tall burly man appeared, scuffed boat shoes slopping up and down as he ambled towards us. "Hail daughters of Eve," he said in a voice familiar with being thrown to the furthest corners of an auditorium. "Welcome to our humble abode." A striped Rugby shirt hung over his jogging bottoms in an unsuccessful attempt at disguising a generous belly. It was dusted with flour. A delicious aroma wafted out of the house. Everything seemed uncannily normal at Windgather. I laughed in spite of Kate's devastating news. He had always managed to make me laugh. "Chris, it's good to see you; what's cooking?"

"Watercress soup and home-made bread; enter my portals, enter, I beg of you," he said walking backwards and waving his hands about in a dramatic fashion. "My brownies are nearly ready to emerge from the oven, but first I demand a kiss from the beautiful maidens." He stopped at the door, opened his arms and offered up a generous chin shadowed with designer stubble. Kate and I obliged. He turned to Diana. "But soft! What light through yonder window breaks? It is the east and Diana is the sun," he said taking her in his arms and kissing her passionately.

She chuckled when she managed to escape his clutches. "He never changes, does he? Go on through, Kate. I'll leave your bag in the hall, Genie. Do you need to freshen up?"

"Yes, but I know where it is," I said, not wanting to be even more trouble. "You don't need to escort me."

"I think I do," she said as she bowled me along with an encouraging arm. "When Chris has been cooking he leaves a trail of disaster everywhere. There's probably brownie mix all over the sink."

"I heard that," he called. "How dare you? Cake mixes are taboo in my kitchen."

"It's like having another child in the house," she said.

"Well, he *is* your toy boy."

"Hardly, there's only six months between us. Anyway, I wouldn't change him, however much mess he makes."

She followed me into the cloakroom, which unlike the rest of the house was almost clinically clean. She shut the door and leaned her shoulders against it. "I need to have a quick word."

My heart sank. "Is it worse than she thinks?"

"I don't know but underneath that cool exterior, she's really worried. Chris and I have decided to keep everything as normal as possible for her. We have to keep her spirits up. We're her safety net."

"Yes, I see. I feel so guilty landing a visit on you both now this has happened."

"Don't be. Seeing you is part of normal. We have to be relaxed, do what we usually do. Visiting Lettie is what she needs. A few trips down memory lane won't hurt her at all. I'd better go. I don't want her to think we've been talking about her." She opened the door and moved outside. "Oh and by the way …" she whispered "… she's calling the cancer Iris."

Chapter 8

We managed to ignore the subject of cancer all afternoon but after dinner at Kate's that night as we relaxed in her garden with a glass of wine, I felt the time was right to find out more.

Dusk was falling, night was staging a take-over. I imagined urban fox about somewhere, hunting. "It's dreadful the way they've started attacking people," I said, voicing my thoughts out loud. "Foxes, I mean ... and their calling cards are disgusting."

"There was a family under next-door's shed last year but they seem to have deserted us."

"It's probably just as well," I said. We sat there in silence for a while listening to the gentle sighing of the trees. "Why didn't you tell me, Kate?"

"You'd broken your wrist. I knew you were due to visit soon. I wanted to tell you in person. No long embarrassing silences on the phone."

"How did you find out?"

"It was a routine mammogram."

"Oh yes. Another of those little pleasures they reserve for us over sixties."

"Don't knock it. I'm glad I opted to carry on with them. The mammogram might have saved my life."

"I suppose that's worth brief torture. Are you glad you came back when you retired?"

"Yes, especially now; there's a state of the art oncology unit at the Royal. I don't want Iris to be the sole topic of conversation while you're here. Tell me about your latest adventure."

"There's nothing to tell. I haven't planned anything as yet. I've been rather stuck with my wrist plastered up. I couldn't do much at all."

"You could have checked the internet, done some research."

"Have you ever tried typing with one hand? It takes forever. I couldn't even switch on the lap-top. I had to wait for Cerys to come round. She's been a life-saver."

"I'm glad I never had children … especially now."

"Why do you say that?"

"I would have felt dreadful if I'd passed on a faulty gene. Can you imagine the guilt?"

"Don't they tell you?"

"Not unless you ask for the test."

"So … you don't want to know."

"What's the point? I won't be passing it on. Anyway, I'm sure I haven't. No-one else in the family has had breast cancer."

"Why do they think it's happened to you?"

Kate shrugged. "Years of smoking, maybe, constant stress. Too much wine at too many parties over the years … who knows? It's probably just sheer bad luck."

"You don't over indulge."

"I've had my moments. I'm not going to beat myself up over it. Iris is here uninvited and she has to go."

"She has. So … how's my charming mother?"

"Not good. It's not going to be much fun tomorrow."

"It's never fun."

"She's deteriorated a lot in the last few months. She gets up every day but she sleeps a lot. You'll be lucky if you get more than a few words out of her and most of those will be in French. You'll be able to understand her, but it's hard-going for me with my school-girl vocab. Mrs. Dukes hasn't got a clue what she's on about half the time. She's very patient with her. Those flats were a lucky find."

"That was down to Lou," I said. "I'm only going because I know I should."

"There's no, should, about it. I was saying to Di the other day, I don't know why you bother. She doesn't deserve it the way she treated you. I've always admired how you dealt with that … the way you carried on in spite of everything. I'm using you as my inspiration."

"How do you mean?"

"For the way I handle Iris."

"I don't remember having a choice. What else could I have done?"

"I don't have a choice either, that's what I mean. Enticed her to a sticky end?"

"I don't think I'm the murdering type."

Her eyes glittered. "I think I could be, given the right circumstances."

"Well, let's hope they never come up. I don't want to be visiting you in prison. What would I say to your god-daughter?"

"Cerys is all right. She'd understand. She's not as soft as you."

"Thanks. So I'm soft, now, am I?"

"It was a bad choice of words. It was a compliment. I should have said … um …compassionate. I tell you what though, if that husband of yours hadn't died of a brain tumour, I might have had to deal with him myself."

"This whole conversation is too dark for me," I said. "Iris must be warping your mind."

"Iris is first on my list," she said.

"You wouldn't go to prison for that one."

"No, but as things have turned out if I *had* done away with Arthur I wouldn't have had to serve my time, with Iris lurking, waiting to finish me off."

"Don't say that. It's never going to happen. Your time's not up yet. We're still going on the Orient Express. I'm not letting you off that one."

"Seventy sounds so old, doesn't it?"

"It sounds old but I don't feel it. Do you?"

"Sometimes," she said, "With Iris hanging over my head. We've got a couple of months to go yet. I'll tell you when I get there."

"It's so unfair."

"I have to admit to moments of the, 'why me?' mind-set. It feels like I've been forced to join an exclusive club I never wanted to join and now someone's signed me up for life."

"Are you scared?"

She stared at the geraniums adorning her decking, some of them on the point of bursting into a glorious vermilion show and then at me, her expression solemn. "The question is, scared of what?" The bantering tone had gone. "I'm scared of putting my trust, my life, in the hands of a bunch of strangers. I'm scared of the treatment being far worse than Iris; I've had no symptoms so far but I guess chemotherapy is going to be grim. I'm scared of losing my hair, not that there's much of that left now," she said tweaking the short layers. "I'm not scared of dying, if that's what you mean. My life has been good overall. I suppose you could say I'm reluctantly reconciled but I'm not going to give Iris an easy ride."

I didn't want the evening to end on a sombre note. "I'm glad you said that," I said. "I'm sure it's the best attitude to have. I'll be right beside you. When the treatment's over and you're feeling better, let's party." Strong wafts of a heady perfume filled the air. I breathed it in, twisting in my seat to appreciate the white flowers dredging the mass of foliage which camouflaged the fence. They were no bigger than the stars beginning to appear above us in the night sky and just as abundant. "Is that your jasmine?"

"It's glorious isn't it? I often sit out here with a glass of something and watch the sunset," she said in reflective tone. "I'm glad you're here."

"I'm glad I'm here."

"I'm sorry to land this on you."

"I want you to land it on me. How often have you had to be there for me?"

"I know, but still ..."

"This is pay-back time." I fingered the empty glass. "Any time you need to talk, I'll be there for you, even if it's in the middle of the night." I stood up. "I'd better get off upstairs. Being so old, I need my sleep; although now, I'll probably have nightmares about being murdered in my bed."

"I hope not." She followed me inside. "Sleep well, Genie. See you in the morning."

The bedroom had completely altered since my last stay. The purple ceiling and toffee walls had gone. It had been re-decorated in pastel shades. She had chosen the palest of greens for the cotton bedding. Not a colour I would have chosen myself but an attractive pairing with the stripped pine floorboards and lemon sorbet walls.

There were no curtains at the window. The regency striped drapes had been supplanted by a Roman blind in neutral calico. I wondered what her mother would have thought of all the changes to the house; the re-decoration, the loft conversion, the decking outside. She had never been one to spend money unnecessarily.

I unpacked a few essentials and got into bed. The duvet reminded me of the peppermint creams that were one of my mother's specialities; fragrant with a crisp sugar coating on the outside and soft and satisfying inside. I tucked myself into the delectable softness and fell asleep almost at once.

The dreams followed me.

I knew I was in a hospital. I was not ill. I could hear sobbing and then a woman's voice, a soft Irish brogue. "She's passed away, poor little thing. It was very quick."

Her words were gentle, understanding but I did not understand. I could see a baby lying in a cot; pale, still, quiet … too quiet. I walked over to get a better look and wondered why I felt so sad. "Whose baby is it?"

A nurse took my hand and I realised it must have been her voice. She was wearing a nun's habit, her face moon like and smooth. Her eyes were full of sympathy as they glistened and oozed onto her colourless cheeks like rock pools ooze into sand. "Yours, my dear, she was your baby. There'll be no more suffering now. She's safe in the arms of Jesus."

I heard a primeval shriek. It reverberated in my chest. My brain froze. I was wide awake, sitting bolt upright in bed. There was a knock at the door.

"Genie, are you all right?" Kate's voice was concerned, apprehensive. She peered in. "I heard a scream." She switched on the light. The cream silk of her dressing gown slid noiselessly across the floorboards as she approached the bed with a spectral glide. Despite my fright, I admired her elegance. My dressing gown was towelling, customised with tea stains and frayed round the edges. "Is it a spider?" she asked.

I dabbed at my eyes. "No spiders," I said.

"I didn't really frighten you with my murderous thoughts, did I?"

"It was that dream about Sadie. Why am I having that dream again? I haven't had it for years."

She sat on the bed and put an arm around my shoulders. "All my talk about death and destruction I suppose. I'm sorry."

"She would have been fifty at Christmas."

"I know."

"Sometimes I wonder what she would have looked like."

"Probably like Cerys."

"Jackie's having a big bash up at the tennis club," I said recalling with shame my twinge of jealousy when Diana had told me about the party. "I should have been pleased for her. It wasn't her fault my baby died. She has every right to celebrate her own daughter's milestone birthday."

"Yes. I wasn't going to say anything. Do you want to go and visit her grave before we see Lettie? We'll need to leave a bit earlier if you do."

I nodded. I very much wanted to do that. I thought of all the years she hadn't been there. I found it hard to imagine my baby as a woman. I tried not to think of her as a woman. I kept my memories close. I did not speak of her unless someone else mentioned her name. She was safe in my heart, preserved for ever as she had been, that tiny baby, my first born. I cherished the memories. In sharing them I felt they might be diminished, devalued in some way. I was fearful of letting that happen, of her slowly fading into shadow. I was wary of sharing those memories but I did not want her forgotten. I had no intention of squandering this opportunity to visit her grave.

I felt guilty again, concentrating on my own needs. "This isn't right," I said. "I should be offering you words of comfort, not the other way round."

"That's what friends are for. We'll share the words of comfort. It'll be my turn next."

"Thanks, Kate."

She turned to go. "Try and get some sleep now. I'll see you in the morning."

Chapter 9

I shilly-shallied the next day. Kate was first up and after tea and toast had been cleared away I sat at the table, chin in hands, much as I used to sit at my school desk all those years before. My hair still corkscrewed round my glasses in a similar fashion but the curls were no longer a lustrous brown. Streaks of silver ran through them now.

I stared into space as I had often done then, daydreaming when I should have been listening to the pearls of wisdom my teachers had tried to impart. The stinging from a well-aimed shard of chalk would soon bring me back down to earth.

No chalk this time, just a few words from Kate. "Sitting here won't get the job done."

I jumped at the sound of her voice. "I thought you were still upstairs."

She joined me at the table. "We're expected at around ten thirty. If we're going to St. Saviour's first, we'd better get a wriggle on."

I nodded. "No point taking anything with us."

"None at all; I took her chocolates last time and she gave them to Mrs Dukes, right in front of me."

"What about flowers? She loves those."

"Well … you can if you like but the place is never short of flowers. I think they must have a deal with the crem."

"How macabre," I said.

"Not really. They cheer up the flats. What good are they lying on all that gravel getting soaked and blown about?" She patted my shoulder as she stood up. "Come on, the sooner we go the sooner we can meet Di for lunch." She waved her car keys at me and moved towards the door.

I felt bad for needing a push. I knew I would have to man-up. All this remembering was doing me no good at all. I straightened my back and gave my glasses a tweak. Rising slowly to my feet I stamped about a bit to shake the creases from my linen trousers. I smoothed down my top, at the same time trying to tighten my stomach muscles in a pathetic attempt at reducing its Humpty Dumpty-ness. The top was a new one and my current favourite; *matelot* stripes with a boat neck, it had an attractive jauntiness to it. The youthful look had appealed to me; it gave me confidence every time I chose to wear it, but conscious of no longer being *gamine*, I had made sure it was long enough to cover my matronly curves before I bought it. I heard Kate calling. It was no good; I could put it off no longer. Taking hold of my bag, I followed her outside.

The churchyard felt the same. It looked the same, peaceful and safe. Sun shone through the trees surrounding the plot projecting dappled sunlight onto the headstones. Sadie's grave was marked by a small grey slab, insignificant in comparison with some of the other more grand memorials; angels guarding marble tombs, sturdy crosses decorated with garlands, even a granite book lying open for all to read except that the words had been blurred by the passage of time.

It lay silent, flat and solid. *Sadie,* it stated. No dates; no flowery words, simply who she had been. It was sufficient for those who had known her during her short life. The grass around the grave had been clipped; the whole graveyard had an air of collected calmness. A ceramic pot stood at the centre of the slab playing host to a bunch of yellow pansies. As final resting places go I could not have found a prettier setting for my baby.

Inevitably the memories crowded in as I stood there. Six months was not long. She had just started to become a little person when the virus struck. It was a swift end to a short life. I had felt despair as I stood exactly where I stood now; alone then as now, apart from Kate. When it happened, I had expected to be struck down at the grave-side. Kate had kept me company during that vigil and for many of the bleak hours that followed.

Arthur had been away on business. He had claimed the message had arrived too late for him to arrange a flight home. I had believed him. It was only after he left that I wondered if this had been entirely true. I reckoned he would not have been able to use that as an excuse these days with mobile phones and the internet giving immediate access to every part of one's life, not to mention the sinister tentacles of Facebook or Twitter. I was not a devotee of either despite Cerys and even Kate and Diana trying to persuade me of the benefits. He had hardly got to know his little daughter before her life had been snuffed out.

I had expected no comfort from his mother and none had been forthcoming. She had not attended the funeral, claiming to be too involved in caring for her husband who had succumbed to a bout of influenza a few days before, but she had written me a note of condolence which he delivered in person a few weeks later. We had clung to each other for support. I had thought at the time he must have made her do it.

Simon Ryder was different. He was a supportive father-in-law and a lovely man. He had appeared to be completely under the influence of his wife but on a couple of occasions I had witnessed a stubborn act of rebellion on his part which had resulted in her melt-down and then an immediate falling in with his wishes. I was genuinely saddened when he died from a massive stroke shortly after Cerys was born. I missed his wise words when my marriage fell apart. I could not help wondering if he would have been able to help when Arthur left, influenced his son's decision; even dissuaded him from going.

My mother had not been interested in Sadie. She had not wanted to be a grandmother. "*Elle est loin d'être jolie,*" she had said on meeting her for the first time. It was unkind of her to make a negative comment about my daughter's appearance and although I was used to her insensitive remarks that one had hurt. I kept Sadie away from her as much as possible. It was difficult living in the same house but I had managed it somehow. I walked miles with the baby in the pram. I visited friends, patrolled the park. When it rained, I went to the library or sat in the station waiting room with her; in those days, they lit a fire for travellers in cold weather. I recalled the smell of the coal as it burned, heard the crackle of the wood set to coax the fire into life. I was in love with my baby. To me she was beautiful whatever my mother might have thought.

The reason for Diana's absence could not be challenged. She had gone into labour on the morning of the funeral and she was waiting for her daughter to be born as I stood there staring down at the newly disturbed earth with unseeing eyes. I did not grasp the bitter irony of the situation until much later. As I was bidding a final farewell to Sadie, Diana was greeting her first-born, Jackie. We were all conscious of the fact that Jackie had become a permanent reminder of my loss and our friendship had been strained for a while … until Cerys arrived.

I had tried to rationalise my baby's death with the thought that any baby's life in those days had been precarious. If it had not been viral pneumonia it could have been whooping cough, polio or measles. Even chicken pox had been a killer. I made sure I took advantage of all the vaccinations available for Cerys and had persuaded Cerys to do likewise for Becky.

Kate put an end to my musings. "You ok?"

I nodded. My sense of loss was not acute. I felt sad but detached. My memories were jumbled, time had muted the pain. "Thanks for putting the pansies there."

"It wasn't me. I presumed you must have asked Di to do it."

It was a reasonable assumption. I did ask Diana to put flowers on the grave from time to time, Sadie's birthday, Easter, Christmas. Her house was nearest the church. "No. Someone must have made a mistake; put them on the wrong grave. They are pretty, though. I would have chosen pansies for her. That's *pensees*, in French; it means 'thoughts'. Did you know that in the Victorian language of flowers, pansies mean loving thoughts?" I said.

She smiled. "How sweet … your head was always full of useless information."

I sniffed and blinked hard, suddenly ambushed by intense pathos. "Hay fever," I mumbled.

"That's odd," she said casting a sceptical glance, "According to the radio the pollen count is low this morning."

I shrugged. "Let's go."

We drove through the town and down familiar leafy lanes into a road of Victorian mansions. Some of them had been converted into student accommodation with bicycle racks where a lawn should have been. Others had been left to age disgracefully, their once haughty facades now tired, paint peeling and weeds sprouting from the most unlikely crevices.

We reached the sheltered accommodation with five minutes to spare and drove round the back to the car park through an arch of sycamores. The building had risen from the flames of a derelict house. I noticed it had been recently decorated. Cream stone-work, the fire escapes and front door painted in Farrow and Ball's Dutch-inspired Hague blue. The contractor's board stood propped up against a wall, left as an invitation to treat.

"Bluebell blue," I said.

"I remember the bluebells," Kate said as she parked the car, "And those bonfires ... and your poor tortoise."

"It was such a shock when we found him."

"She didn't know he'd hibernated in there."

"Or so she said."

"She wouldn't have done it on purpose, surely," Kate said.

"Maybe not, who knows? I'll bet she doesn't like the new paint."

"I do."

"Me too, it looks very smart."

"She never goes out now. She won't have seen it. Ready?"

"As I ever will be," I said. I had visited my mother many times over the years. I knew what to expect; each time it was an ordeal but I had to be adult about it even though the thought of seeing her made me feel child-like and vulnerable. "Let's just get it over with." I got out of the car and walked the short distance to the front door. I waited for her to catch up and then pressed the buzzer. It echoed inside, long and loud like a bee in a bottle.

Someone, no more than a girl, appeared almost at once. Her sallow skin and raven hair made me think Eastern Europe. The pronounced cheekbones and pouting lips were as nature intended, no discernible stroke of a make-up brush or smudge of eye shadow; not even a lick of lip gloss. She contemplated us with peridot eyes. They were clear, guileless as they met mine. "Hallo ... you come for ...?" Her forehead sank into a frown as if she expected the answer to be problematic. Her face held a haunting beauty but she seemed unaware of her charms as she opened the door wider and stared at us.

I braced my shoulders. "Violette McBain," I said.

She smiled and beckoned us in with energetic hands. "I tell Miss Juke you here. Come, come."

"She's new," I said as I stood in the hall beside Kate and looked around as if seeing everything for the first time.

"She's been here a few weeks now," Kate said. She gave me a wry smile. "The flowers are lovely again."

It was a pleasant entrance hall. The laminate flooring was uncarpeted and the walls empty, apart from a giant poster of the London skyline at night. There were flowers everywhere; in troughs along the window sills, on stands beside doors and on top of the reception desk.

"They are. Lovely," I said. My neck felt like an elastic band at snapping point. I put up a hand to ease the tension. "How long's she going to be?"

She looked at her watch. "It's only just gone half past. She'll be here in a minute. You know how efficient she is. She won't want to waste any time. Let's sit down."

"I'm still feeling guilty that you have to do this with me when you'd probably rather be doing something else," I admitted. "I really appreciate it, you know."

"Shut up," she said and then grinned at my startled expression. "The counsellor gave me permission to say whatever I like now I'm living with cancer. Apparently it's part of owning yourself, or something."

I almost giggled but it came out as a hiccough. "You'll have my undivided attention as soon as we've got this over with, I promise."

"Ms McBain, Miss Grieves. How are you both?" Mrs. Dukes was out of breath as she bustled in, kitten heels tapping on the floor like cap guns. "Sorry to have kept you waiting." Her hair was cut short over her ears and sculpted to her head. She was wearing a grey suit over the white blouse which looked as if it had been applied to her torso with spray paint. "Mrs. McBain's dozing," she said, extending a hand first to me and then to Kate. "The hairdresser came to wash her hair this morning. I'm afraid it's rather tired her out. We like our residents to look their best for visitors. Come on through." She made a big show of rattling her keys before opening the door to my mother's flat. "Her appetite's not good but we're making sure she drinks plenty," she said. "Especially her tipple of gin every evening, she never refuses that." She gave a trill of laughter. "Ring the bell if you need me."

I watched her leave and felt the energy drain out of me. Kate gave me an encouraging nudge. We entered the small sitting room and found my mother asleep in her armchair. "It's really hot in here," she whispered. "I'm not surprised she's having a snooze."

I slipped off my jacket and approached her chair. I tweaked my glasses to settle them more comfortably on my nose and brushed some stray curls from my cheeks, putting off the moment when I would have to engage with her. I took a deep breath and touched her arm. "*Bonjour, Maman*," I said.

I noticed that the curtains had been changed from a geometric print to a bright floral pattern and wondered if the charity had received a generous bequest. I reckoned Mrs. Dukes would be disappointed if she thought my mother had any money to leave. She had managed to fritter it away on the regular trips abroad and her expensive life-style. If Louisa and Carter had not come to her rescue I dread to think where she might have ended up.

Her eyes opened. They were clouded in the still handsome face. Unlike the girl at the door, her face had been primed with foundation and rouged with blusher, a touch of lipstick making an effort to plump up the thin lips. It reminded me that she had never gone anywhere without lipstick. She made time to renew it regularly throughout the day. After each application she would fold her lips to seal it in and even it out.

Sometimes a crimson streak would stray into her mouth leaving a vampire-like smear on her teeth. This had always made Louisa giggle. I would not have dared. I had felt her hand warm my cheek too many times for such trivial misdemeanours. She had considered Revlon the Rolls Royce of brands. Once, when the local chemist had none in stock, she had subjected the poor man to a diatribe of French vitriol. His startled expression would have been comical had I not known as she swept out of the shop, that I would be her next victim.

In the past she had preserved her chestnut locks with henna dye but that was no longer an option; her hair was still thick and well-styled but it was now hail-white. A hand reached across towards me, joints distorted with arthritis, nails short and varnished pink. "*C'est toi, Geneviève?*"

"*Oui, c'est moi,*" I said, taking the hand. I kissed the papery cheek. It felt cool and unresponsive.

"*Tant mieux.*" The hand pulled away and the eyes closed. "*Louisa n'est pas là?*"

"No. Lou's in America."

She sighed, "*Ah oui.*"

"Kate's here."

Kate approached the chair and sat down on the seat opposite mine. "Hello Mrs. McBain. You're hair looks nice."

My mother moved restlessly in her seat but did not open her eyes. Kate and I exchanged glances. It was a few minutes before she spoke again. "*Geneviève?*"

"I'm here."

"*Je t'ai attendue depuis longtemps ...*" She was becoming agitated. She pointed in Kate's direction. "*Va t'en,*" she said with an imperious wave of her hand.

"*Maman,*" I protested.

"Does she want me to go?" Kate said. "It's all right. I'll wait in the kitchen."

Lettie's eyes scanned the room hopelessly. "*Elle est partie?*"

"Yes. She's gone. It's just you and me, *Maman*."

"*Je voudrai te dire quelquechose…*"

"What is it? What did you want to tell me?"

Her voice was weaker now, hardly discernible as she mumbled away in French. I leaned a little closer to her chair. "I can't hear you, *Maman*."

"*C'était important …*"

"It was important … was it something you needed?"

She shook her head impatiently. She tried to sit up straight and winced in pain. "*Ay ooey,*" she complained.

I moved her cushions, tried to make her more comfortable. "*Si vieille,*" she said. I felt compassion for her in that moment. She was old. Even she could not turn back the hands of time, however much she railed against it. Her tongue clicked on her teeth, "*Fatiguée.*"

"You're tired. Do you want me to go?"

Her fingers clutched at me with surprising strength and her eyes flickered. She tried to raise her head again. "*Reste là,*" she said. I stayed where I was, as instructed, waiting for her to remember. She relaxed her grip and started muttering to herself again, shaking her head and frowning.

I looked out of the window. I could hear a mower spluttering into life and then it appeared, guided by a young woman in jeans and builder's boots. It droned up and down the lawn leaving tidy stripes behind it like sleeper-less tracks. "The gardener's here," I said.

"*Voila, c'est ça …il est là …*"

"It's not a man," I said. "You've got a lady gardener; she's making a good job of the lawn. Does she come every week?"

"*Non … non … ce n'est pas ça … c'est lui.*"

"What do you mean *Maman*, who is it? I stood up and looked outside. "There's no-one else out there."

I realised now what Kate had been trying to tell me. My mother was rambling in French and making no sense at all. She was probably reliving some episode from the past. I sat there for another few minutes as the murmuring continued and then decided it was time to leave. "Get some rest now. I'll come and visit you again tomorrow. You can tell me all about it then."

Her eyes were still closed as I got up to go. She waved me weakly away. "*Tu va voir. Il faut dire a Louisa qu'il est toujours là.*"

I shook my head in frustration. I had no idea what she meant. What would I see? What should I tell my sister? Why would we be interested in the gardener? I decided she was too tired to make any sense and gave up attempting to understand. I would find out the next day. There was a chance she might be more lucid then. "*A demain, Maman,*" I said. I kissed her cheek and went to join Kate.

"What did she want?"

"I don't know. She said she had something important to tell me. She couldn't remember what it was and then she kept muttering in French and going on about the gardener. There was a girl cutting the grass."

"I heard the mower."

"She wanted me to tell Louisa about it. I think she was seeing things. Her mind's going."

"I told you. Perhaps she imagined it was one of her men out there. Maybe she thought he was the gardener, you know, like the gamekeeper in Lady Chatterley; grand passions and all that."

I shivered. "That's not funny."

"No. I'm sorry."

"Why would she want Lou to know that? I don't want to think about it. She was very tired. I said I'd come back tomorrow. Her mind might be clearer then. She might have perked up a bit. Do you mind if I stay another night?"

"Actually I want you to. You gave me an idea last night. I've decided to throw a party."

"You feel like throwing a party ... now?" I said, amazed she could even contemplate such a thing with the operation looming.

"I do. I want to have an 'Iris Out' party. I'm not going to feel much like partying when I come out of hospital, especially if I have to have chemo."

"Are you sure you're up to it?"

"Of course I am," she said fiercely. "I refuse to let Iris take over my life. I'm always ready to party. Let's get out of here. There's shopping to be done."

"I thought we were meeting Di for lunch."

"We are; shopping, Di, lunch and then partying."

I laughed in spite of myself. "You are quite mad," I said.

"You're a long time dead, Genie."

Chapter 10

I rang Cerys to tell her about Kate and explain that I would be staying longer than anticipated. She was fond of Kate. We had spent a lot of time together in the early days.

"Oh no … how is she?" she said.

"She's dealing with it."

"It must have been an awful shock."

"She's focusing on the op and making a good recovery."

"Send her my love. Tell her I'm thinking of her. Becky's been asking when you'll be back," she said.

"You can say I'm going to a party, but don't make it sound like too much fun; say it's just for grown-ups. I don't want her to think she's missing out."

"She won't be. We're going to the cinema tonight."

"All of you?"

There was a slight pause. "Not Kit. He's working."

"Oh, I see." Kit often worked evenings and weekends. There was nothing unusual in that but I had a feeling she was far from pleased about it. "That's all right isn't it?"

"Of course," she said a little too quickly. I knew my daughter. Something was wrong. "I've told her it's a 'girls only' night."

Kit was always so busy these days. The last time I'd seen him I had suggested he relax a bit more, spend more time doing family things or he'd burn out. "It can't be done,

Genie," he had said. "Not at the moment. I can't afford to let up with that new restaurant opening round the corner. We need to hang on to our customers. I don't want to risk any glitches." I hoped I was imagining things and that it was nothing more than a heavy workload that was keeping them apart. I did not want to contemplate something more sinister.

"How's Lettie?"

"Old, tired, much as I expected really. I said Becky could look at the albums while I was away. I left them out for you."

"I don't know when we'll have the time."

I knew she would rather not but Becky enjoyed them so much I hoped she would do it for her. "Perhaps you'll make time."

"I'll see how it goes."

I remembered what she had said to me at the hospital. It was foolish of me not to have realised how hurt she had been at the break-up of my marriage. Her father had left and she had never seen him again. We had moved to the other end of the country and he had died before arrangements for visiting rights could be put in place.

If their marriage was going through a difficult patch, Kit should be made aware of the emotional damage a cheating husband could inflict on a family. He would not want to hurt his own daughter in the same way Cerys had been hurt. He loved Becky far too much for that. We had a good relationship. I would have to explain it to him sometime.

The party was a good one. Kate had invited all sorts of people, most of whom I did not know but that did not seem to matter. We were all Kate's friends and we knew why we were there. There was no shortage of food, drink or laughter. The only thing lacking was sleep.

When we arrived at the flats the following morning, I was feeling fragile. Mrs. Dukes was hovering in the hall.

"She's taken a turn for the worse," she said which was immediately sobering.

"What do you mean?" My head ached. I should have remembered that just enough red wine was medicinal, too much, a mistake. I knew what Mrs. Dukes was trying to say. I needed to understand the sort of time frame we were dealing with; absorbing facts through a cloud of cotton wool was not ideal.

"I'm not sure. The doctor's with her, now."

"Has she had a stroke or something?" Kate said.

"I don't think so. She kept asking for the priest after you'd gone yesterday. We didn't understand at first and then she said it quite clearly. "Send for *Pere Michel*." He pops in from time to time. He's very good with the old dears. Anyway, he came at about six o'clock and stayed with her for at least an hour. She seemed fine afterwards. She had a good night but she wasn't interested in breakfast this morning. She just wanted to stay in bed. When we took in her elevenses we couldn't wake her. That's when we called the doctor. I was just about to ring you ... oh ... here he is, now. What news, doctor? This is Mrs. McBain's daughter."

The doctor was a small thin man, his face pinched, his hair grey and taking short back and sides to the extreme; he had glasses and a permanent frown. Curving his lips in a distant fashion, he shook his head. "She's very frail, I'm afraid. Her heart's getting weaker. There's nothing much I can do. It's only a matter of time. I don't think it will be long."

I stared at him not knowing what to say. Kate stepped in. "Thank you doctor," she said.

We exchanged glances as Mrs. Dukes saw him out. "What was he trying to say, minutes, hours, days?" I said. I nudged my glasses up my cheek. I felt nervous of what was to come and unsure as to how I should feel. "I'll go and sit with her."

"I'll come with you."

"No. Will you phone Cerys?"

"I will, but I'm coming straight back. What about Louisa?"

"Oh yes. She should be told. I haven't got her number with me. Ask Cerys to do it."

Mrs. Dukes joined us again. She must have overheard our conversation. "You can use the phone in the office," she said.

"Thanks, but I've got my mobile in the car," Kate said. "See you in a minute, Genie." She left us and Mrs. Dukes took my arm. She escorted me to the flat as before and patted my shoulder as she left me to tip-toe into the bedroom alone.

I repeated the mantra of the previous day. "*Bonjour Maman.*" My mother did not stir. It was still unnaturally warm in the flat. I felt too hot. I wanted to open the window but for some reason it did not feel right even though I knew that in much simpler and more innocent times, if a death were expected, a window would be left open to let the soul fly free. I perched myself on a chair near the bed and stayed put, waiting. My mind wandered as I sat there.

I was about eight in my daydream. I wanted to go out and play but my mother had insisted I do some needlework first. It was fine crocheted lace to be sewn along the edges of the new sheets and pillow cases. Tedious, time-consuming work but Lettie had liked everything to be *comme il faut,* even the sheets on our beds. I didn't have a thimble and the needle constantly bruised my finger as I pushed it through the stiff cotton, over and over again. It found its way between my lips as I sucked away the pain.

Another memory burst into my head, a rare sunshine memory. I was in France staying with my aunt and grandparents. We spent most of the summer holidays there. It had been a happy time with laughter and music. I remembered my grandfather playing popular tunes on his clarinet, a glass of wine to hand and my grandmother, sleeves rolled up to the elbow, scattering seeds for the chickens.

My grandfather had a neatly trimmed moustache and a twinkle in his eye. The iridescent tinge to the back of his waistcoat had fascinated me. My childish mind had wondered how my grandmother had managed to turn fish scales into a silky material. I knew she was an accomplished needlewoman like my mother. She made all his clothes. As a devotee of fairy stories and other mythical tales I had finally decided she must have used the Rumplestiltskin trick. If straw could be turned into gold, fish scales could easily be transformed into fabric in a similar fashion.

He would sit in his throne-like chair by the back door puffing away on a cigar with one or other of us on his knee and then laugh as we squealed in delight when he blew smoke rings in the air to amuse us.

We would pick fresh fruit for breakfast. I did the picking because at that stage I was much taller than my sister. She would hold the basket *tante Jeanne* had given her to gather the raspberries and red currants which grew in profusion in their hotchpotch of a garden.

Louisa loved picking the hairy gooseberries which were easier for her to reach but donned a hat and then a cardigan, however hot the weather. She feared being spiked by thorns or stung by nettles. My grandmother would lend her a pair of gloves and with a full set of protective clothing she looked more like a bee-keeper off to the skeps than a small child harvesting fruit.

I turned to gaze at my mother. We had experienced an odd relationship. I had been neither a daughter nor a friend. We had little in common. Yes, she had taught me about managing a house, gardening, cooking, caring for animals. Yes, she had kept me clothed and fed. She had challenged my views and made me very aware of hers. It was the more intangible components of a mother daughter relationship that had been missing; the shared humour, affection, loyalty; the feeling of being appreciated and loved, the mutual support. Those had all been lacking.

Her breathing was irregular. It was pitiful to watch her chest heaving up and down in an effort to keep life going. I wondered why I did not hate her. It would have been so easy to hate her. I did not feel anything very much except a sense of sadness at her passing. I wanted it to be over.

"I've done it," Kate said as she came quietly into the room. "Cerys says she's coming up in the car."

"She doesn't have to. What's the point?"

"She wants Becky to see her."

"Oh no," I said, alarmed at the thought of putting Becky through our ordeal. "There's no need. It's enough that we're here. She's too young to witness this. It's no place for a little girl."

"Well, she's taking her out of school and she's coming, whether you like it or not. Becky will cope. It's life, Genie. Death is just a part of life. You can't protect her for ever and Cerys has every right to be here anyway."

I fiddled with my glasses again. I knew I did not have exclusive rights to my mother's death. That wasn't what was bothering me. I felt the need to confess. "It's not that. You don't understand," I said. "Cerys wants me to tell Becky everything and I don't want to, not until she's much older."

"She can't make you."

"No, but it's not just Becky who doesn't know what went on. I haven't told Cerys the truth either. She only has a sanitised version."

"Oh, I see," Kate said. She stroked my arm. "Let's not worry about that now."

Chapter 11

Cerys explained later how pleased Becky had been to miss school. Apparently she had bounced out of the gates keen to find out where they were going.

"We're going to see Gran," Cerys had told her.

"You said you didn't want her to catch my cold."

"It's nearly gone. I don't think she'll catch it now."

"Is Dad coming?"

"No. He's too busy."

The same old excuse. I didn't say anything when she told me that but his attitude was beginning to concern me. She could have done with his support.

"Everyone stared when Mrs. Jones came to fetch me. We were in Drama," the child had declared. Cerys said she had felt bad to begin with. She had made her apologies and promised to make it up to her but Becky had not seemed bothered. "I don't mind. Gemma Stokes was bossing everyone about anyway."

She had wanted to know why they were visiting me. Cerys had anticipated that question. She had rehearsed her reply. "Auntie Kate's ill. Gran wants us to help cheer her up."

"What's the matter with her?"

"She has to go into hospital for an operation."

"Like my appendix?"

"A bit like that."

"Will she be nil by mouth?"

"I expect so."

I couldn't resist a smile when Cerys relayed all the questions to me. My granddaughter seemed to have an insatiable thirst for knowledge and a desire to know the minutiae of every situation.

"Will we see Di, too and Chris? Will I be able to play with the dolls' house? Lucy's told me all about it. I really want to see the dolls' house."

Diana and Christian had called in to see us on their way back from holiday in France a couple of times; once with their granddaughter, Lucy. Becky must have remembered. She had got on well with her despite the disparity in their ages.

"Why does Gran keep going up to Liverpool?" she had asked next. "Why doesn't Auntie Kate ever come to visit her?"

She had never asked me that one. Kate had visited me several times in the past but she was too young to remember. As I made regular visits up north to see my mother and invariably stayed with Kate it made no sense for her to come down south to visit me.

Cerys must have had trouble keeping her mind on the traffic with that little voice constantly in her ear. She had admitted to feeling exasperation at the constant stream of questions and I was certain her attempts to stem the flow had not met with much success.

I could understand why she had not wanted to be led down an aisle of queries, having to pick suitable replies at random from the shelves of bottled memories. What if she had selected the wrong one and revealed something she should not? She knew I was not ready to tell all for the moment, or at least what she thought was all.

The child had one last question and as usual a pertinent one.

"Mum …"

"What now?"

"Is Auntie Kate going to die?"

Mrs. Dukes had been popping in and out of the flat at regular intervals. "Would you like a cup of tea?"

"That would be good," Kate said. "Would you like one, Genie?"

"Just water, please."

She nodded and disappeared. I had lost track of time. "It must be nearly two o'clock," I said.

Kate glanced at her watch. "Half past; are you hungry?"

I shook my head. "How long do you think we'll have to sit here?"

"As long as it takes, I suppose. She seems quite comfortable."

I leant over the bed. My mother's eyes were closed. Her head lay still on the pillow, her chest barely moving. "I think she's slipping quietly away."

"Cerys will be here soon."

"I still wish she wasn't coming. I'd rather have dealt with everything on my own."

"Lettie *is* her grandmother. Perhaps she needs to be here."

I sat down and stared at the dressing table, the glass top smooth as an ice rink, comb riding side-saddle on a brush, ceramic dish playing host to all those little misfits in transit to a permanent home; safety pins, tweezers, a variety of buttons. The poignancy of the empty ring tree affected me. My eyes were drawn to the bed again. Kate was right. Cerys needed this. I felt guilty for a second time. "I didn't think of that; how selfish of me."

"You haven't got a selfish bone in your body. You can't think of everything. Your mother's dying."

"That's the thing. She doesn't *feel* like my mother. She never behaved like a mother. We had a strange relationship.

She gave us our dos and don'ts of course, but I ended up more of a skivvy than a daughter and then I was a nanny for Louisa. Mothering me didn't come into it with her."

"They had different views on childhood back in the day," she said. "We were all expected to be useful. We weren't supposed to have opinions or likes and dislikes. We weren't expected to share ..." she made quote marks in the air, "... *quality time* with adults. That's just how it was." She returned her gaze to all that was left of the Lettie of old. "She was very ... Lettie ... in those days."

"I wonder what she thought about everything."

"Perhaps it's best you don't know I'm sure she was sorry for some of her actions. I don't believe people when they say they have no regrets. We'd better be careful what we say. She could be listening to us discussing her life as if she's already moved on. Why didn't you tell Cerys?"

I wasn't ready to go into that; it would be time enough when it was all over. "It didn't feel right. Let's talk about something nice. The garden," I said.

"It was magnificent, wasn't it? She loved her flowers."

"Not the bluebells."

Kate smiled. "No, not them; you'll have to think about flowers."

"I thought we weren't going to do that?"

"Sorry."

"What do you think she was trying to tell me yesterday?"

"It was probably nothing, just the ramblings of an old lady."

My mind meandered back to Cerys and Becky. "I wonder how long they'll be."

"That's anyone's guess. It depends on the traffic."

"I hope they find this place all right."

"It's not hidden away. Has Cerys got GPS in the car?"

"Oh yes. Becky loves it. Especially when it says, '*You have arrived at your destination.*' She can take it off to a tee."

"She's a funny kid."

"I worry that she spends too much time on her own. I see a lot of me in her. She loves reading and what an imagination. She'll be surprised we're not at your house. She knows that's where I'm staying. She wanted to come with me, you know ... to see where you lived."

"My chance to be a fairy godmother, I can grant her that wish," Kate said with the wave of an imaginary wand. "I expect Cerys will have explained."

"I know when we're done here that I'll have to say something about what happened. I didn't want to before, but now I've no choice. I'll have to find a way of telling her more of the story."

"What, let out the big secret ... horror of horrors."

"Don't mock."

"I'm not. I know it's a big deal for you but she won't see it that way, believe me."

"I hope you're right," I said but I wasn't convinced. I glanced across at my mother again. "She doesn't even know her great grandmother is still alive. How do you think she'll take that shocker?"

"That's a tough one. I expect she'll be keen to see what she looks like. I would be."

The door opened and Mrs Dukes appeared with a tray. "Here we are, drinks," she said softly. "And biscuits. You've both missed lunch." She put the tray down and went over to take Lettie's pulse. "She's still with us ... just. She looks so peaceful, doesn't she? Such a beautiful face."

"Do you think she can hear us?" I asked.

"I doubt it, but you can never be sure. They say the hearing is the last thing to go. I expect she can sense she's with family and friends. Death has its own timetable you know. I always think of it as like having a baby. It will take however long it takes. She's not in any pain. I'll sit with her if you want to go out for a breath of air."

I shook my head. "No. I want to stay. You can go if you like, Kate."

Kate was equally determined. "I'm staying, too," she said. She handed me the glass from the tray. "Here, drink your water."

Mrs. Dukes busied herself checking the bedclothes. She stroked the pillows and tweaked out a crease. "That sun's bright this afternoon. I'll close the curtains a little, take the glare off."

A short while later the door opened again. It was the girl who had let us into the flats the day before. "Visitors," she said. "Mrs. and Miss?" The inflection in her voice turned the statement into a query.

"It must be Cerys and Becky," Kate said. "Shall I go and explain?"

"Would you? Just the minimum, don't go into too much detail."

"Stop worrying," she said.

"Thank you Frankie," Mrs. Dukes said. "I'll come too, dear. You might need me."

We were alone again, my mother and me. It was peaceful in the room, the silence broken only by her shallow breathing and the ticking of the bedside clock. I was mulling over Mrs. Dukes' comment about birth and death. I remembered my mother telling me how when she went into labour with me, my father had gone to fetch the doctor only to return too late. I had arrived unceremoniously on the kitchen floor in his absence causing untold inconvenience. I felt as if a strange bonding was taking place. For the first time in my life I shared an affinity with her; it felt like I was there to give birth to her death.

A vase of white lilies stood on a table by the window giving off hints of fragrance every now and then. I walked over to examine them. I stroked the waxy petals. It crossed my mind that lilies were not on my mother's hit list and although she had never tried to grow them in her garden, she had quite liked them. She had thought them elegant flowers, suitable for weddings or funerals. The coffin would be draped in lilies. I would make sure of it. She would have everything as *comme il faut* as I could make it.

I stared out of the window and noticed how good the grounds looked after the gardener's visit the previous day. The lawns were immaculate, the hedges trimmed into shape; if only relationships could be pruned back when they got out of hand. How much better life would be if it could be mown and clipped every so often to maintain a bit of order. It would save a lot of heartache. I wondered what Becky would make of the news that Lettie was still alive. She had never asked about when her great grandmother had died, or where. I had never suggested that she might still be alive; sins of omission … but I would not be going to confession. Perhaps my mother had asked to see the priest to confess her sins. I had no time to expand on that theory. The door opened behind me. I turned to see Kate leading the way into the room, Mrs. Dukes whisking along behind. "Here we are," she said.

Becky ran past her to give me a hug. Cerys held back as she contemplated her grandmother's features and then she hugged me too. I led Becky towards the bed. "Here's Lettie," I said.

She considered the yellowing face, the closed eyes and bloodless lips. I could sense the shadow of death drawing nearer. "May I give her a kiss?"

I looked at my daughter. She nodded. "If you want," I said, "Gently, now."

She deposited a light kiss on my mother's cheek and then gasped and took a step back as the eyes flicked open for a second, "*Louisa, c'est toi?*"

"She thinks you're Great aunt Lou," I whispered.

"*Geneviève, t'es la aussi?*" she murmured.

I took her hand in mine. I was surprised at how warm it felt. "*Oui, je suis ici Maman.*"

She didn't open her eyes again. "*Bien, c'est bien*," she breathed and with a slight shudder and a sigh, she left us.

I moved away as Mrs Dukes approached the bed. She lifted my mother's wrist, felt for a pulse and then shook her head. "She's gone."

In the feather-like silence that filled the room I slipped over to the window, twisted the handle and pushed wide the casement in the hope that after a turbulent life, she had at last found peace and her soul could fly free.

Chapter 12

It was cool in Mrs. Dukes' office. A slight draught encouraged the blinds to sway back and forth. They caught the frame from time to time, the tapping like the drumming of a weary woodpecker. It was a relief to be able to breathe easily after the oppressive atmosphere of my mother's room. I was surprised at how unemotional I felt. I had expected to feel something at her passing; sadness, relief ... triumph even ... but not indifference.

A circular rug in front of the desk denoted no-man's land between inmate and commandant; tea cups chinked on saucers but conversation was stilted. Cerys and Becky were sitting side by side on the cushion-less sofa like tailors' dummies, shell-shocked, silent. Kate was in an armchair adjacent to me. "We need to discuss the funeral," I said.

Mrs. Dukes was on to it. "Shall I ring Fr. Michael for you? I can recommend several good undertakers. Will it be a small family affair or something grander?"

"A small family affair," Cerys said before I could reply.

I thought this an ironic comment considering the circumstances. "A small family affair ..." I whispered in Kate's ear.

"Don't even go there," she whispered back.

"No," I said out loud. "I mean, yes. A small funeral, just immediate family ..." I glanced at Kate "... and close friends."

"It will be a burial, of course." Mrs. Dukes took a gold pen from her desk drawer and scribbled something down on the note-pad placed at right angles to her phone.

There was a pause as they waited for my response. I could not imagine ever wanting to visit my mother's grave. "I think a cremation would be more appropriate," I said.

She looked up from her note-taking. "Well, you can discuss the finer details with Fr. Michael. Can I give him your phone number?"

"No. You'd better give him mine. We'll deal with all that," Kate said.

I knew what she was thinking. There was little point in discussing further arrangements with Mrs. Dukes. Her role was over but I did not want to appear churlish. I rose to my feet. "If you could let me have those undertakers' details before we go ..."

"Of course, here you are, my dear," she said handing over several glossy brochures. "There's nothing much to choose between them. They all offer a good service."

I gave each leaflet a cursory glance and selected one at random, showing the room what I had chosen.

"The Co-op, right, do you want me to call them?" she said.

"That would be good," I said. "Thanks."

"I think we should go now," Kate said. "You've got my number if you need to speak to us again. Ms. McBain will be staying with me until after the funeral."

Mrs. Dukes nodded; we all shook hands ... and that was that. I was not sorry to be leaving the flats; at that moment, I felt strangely happy although I did not want to admit it. Kate was staring at me. "Are you ok?"

"I'm fine," I said. "Glad it's finally over if that makes sense."

"Yes," she said.

"I'm not looking forward to the funeral. I hope Cerys and Becky are ok. Cerys has never liked funerals."

"Does anyone?"

"I suppose not."

We drove back to the house in convoy. Cerys bustled Becky upstairs straight away. "I'd better go and check on them," I said. "Becky's had a double whammy."

Kate headed for the kitchen. "I'll put the kettle on."

I couldn't hear voices as I approached their room. I knocked tentatively and opened the door. Becky was sitting on the floor, a pile of books at her side. "Are you all right?" I asked. She glanced up and nodded without even the hint of a smile.

Cerys was unpacking her case. "I hope the funeral *is* on Friday," she said as she took out the black jacket she had brought with her in anticipation. "I don't want Becky to have any more time off school." She picked at several pieces of cotton littering the collar. "I knew I shouldn't have thrown that towel in at the last minute."

Becky caught my eye, solemn, resolute. "I want to come," she said. The topic had obviously been mentioned.

"Let's hope they can do it then," I said. "We're all finding this difficult. The sooner we can arrange everything the better."

"I don't mind missing school," Becky said.

"I mind you missing school," Cerys said. She shook out the towel as if jettisoning the last few grains of sand from the beach. "It's your last year. I want you to get good marks in all your assessments. I can't wait for this to be over. Are you sure you want to come to the funeral? You don't have to."

"Di said you could go round to her house instead. Lucy will be there," I said.

"Oh good, I like Lucy."

94

"It's lucky she's home from university. She'll be company for you while we're at church ... and you'll see the dolls' house," I said.

"I still want to come," she said. "Can I see Lucy anyway?"

"I'm sure we can sort something out," Cerys said.

"I need to have a chat with you downstairs," I said as I got up to go. "Don't make up your mind until you've spoken to me."

"Can I have a snack first? I'm starving."

"Let's go and find Auntie Kate," Cerys said. "Perhaps she'll let us make some toast."

Becky was the first one down the stairs. She waited for us in the hall. "Come on, Mum," she said. "Will she have a chocolate cake?"

"I don't know," Cerys said.

"She doesn't like chocolate," I said. I had never been able to get my head around Kate's aversion to something I considered to be the best treat. Becky's face fell. "Don't worry, there's bound to be something tasty hidden away. We had loads of food left over from the party."

She opened the kitchen door and Cerys and I bunched up behind her. Kate was wandering aimlessly round the room, setting pictures straight and tucking papers away into drawers. She stopped as soon as she realised Becky was standing there, watching. "Hello you; do I detect a hungry young lady?"

Becky giggled. "How did you know?"

"Wild guess," she said. She opened a nearby cupboard. "I can offer you doughnuts. Will they do? Or cheese straws? No. I know what you'd like." She walked across to the fridge and opened the door wide as she scanned the shelves. "How about chocolate éclairs?" she said, producing an unopened box.

"Wow. Yes please."

"I'd forgotten those," I said.

"You made me buy them," she said. "They're not exactly my favourites. Tuck in."

I decided to leave them to it. I felt like a not-so-young tennis ace waiting to perform on centre court. Expectations were overwhelming. Could I do it? I needed time to prepare. "I'm going to have a sit down," I said. "Come and see me when you've finished your snack."

"Ok," Becky said, mouth oozing cream from the corners. "This is yummy. Are we going to look at the photos again?"

"I left them at home."

"We brought them," Cerys said. My game plan had just improved. "They're in the car."

"Mum promised to look through them with me but she didn't have time before we came away."

"Do you want me to fetch them?" Cerys said.

"No hurry, when you're ready."

"Have a cuppa first," Kate said, bless her. She knew I needed more time to gather my thoughts.

I used my brief solitude to try and make sense of recent events. The whole process had revived forgotten memories best left forgotten. Stirring up the dregs of my life was not what I needed. I was glad when Becky opened the sitting room door some ten minutes later and I could escape from my head.

She peered into the room but seemed reluctant to enter. I sensed she didn't want to be in there with me, she must have homed in on my bitterness and regret. It made me sad and resentful all over again.

"Hi, Gran," she said in a small voice. "I've finished. Are you ready, can I come in?"

I forced a smile and tried to look cheerful. "Quite ready, come and sit down."

The smile seemed to have encouraged her. She moved across the room. "Are there more secrets?" she asked as she settled down cross-legged on the floor.

I nodded. "Lettie being alive was only the first one."

"I'm glad I saw her."

"Did it upset you?"

"No. She wasn't my Lettie, just an old lady in a bed."

"I'm sorry I didn't tell you."

"It doesn't matter, Gran."

"These secrets … well … they're not exactly secrets … not any more … they're things that happened in my life. I wasn't sure you needed to know about them. I thought you'd be too young to understand. I was wrong. You do need to know more about the past and I'm going to tell you."

I had steeled myself for this moment. I knew what had to be said. I just had to find the right words.

Chapter 13

I had trouble deciding where to begin. At the beginning was the logical answer but logic didn't come into it. I felt emotional now, anxious to do it right, nervous about her reaction to my story. "I think I'll start with the time when my father was still at home," I said. "My mother and father were not always the best of friends. Quite often when he wanted them to have an evening out she refused to go. She used Louisa and me as an excuse, but she could have gone with him. My aunt Min ..."

"His sister," she said eagerly.

"Yes, she would have sat with us. She did sometimes when we were ill and Lettie had to go shopping or something. She enjoyed spending time with us. She'd been married for years but didn't have children of her own. We loved her visits. She brought us lollipops."

"Why didn't she ... you know ... have children?"

"I have an idea, she couldn't for some medical reason. Don't forget I was only a little girl then. Grown-ups didn't discuss such things in front of children and we knew better than to ask."

"Oh."

"Lettie called her, 'Poor Min', because of that and if Papa was there he'd say, 'not as poor as if she had a house full of children.' It was one of their little jokes."

"Min's a funny name."

"It was short for Minerva."

"She was a Roman goddess."

"Fancy you knowing that."

"We went to visit a Roman Palace in year two. There was a statue of Minerva the garden."

"Nana McBain was mad about ancient Rome."

"Gran ..."

"Yes?"

"I was wondering ... what was she like? You've never told me about her."

"I didn't know her very well. Lettie didn't get on with her. We didn't go round for tea or anything like that and she only ever visited us on Papa's birthday. She was small and thin with round glasses on the end of her nose and lots of wild grey hair."

"Like Nannie MacPhee?"

"I suppose she was a bit like that. She lived miles away from us in a big house."

"Did she live there all on her own?"

"Yes ... well ... apart from Remus."

"Who was Remus?"

"He was her dog; Papa took us on the train to visit sometimes but not very often. Louisa was afraid of the dog."

"Why?"

"He was big and shaggy and he barked ... a lot. Her sitting room was full of dusty old books and Roman bits and pieces. I remember she was very proud of one particular pot a friend had dug up on his farm. She kept it on the mantelpiece with a little card beside it stating exactly where it had been found and when, it said Scragg's Hall Farm, July 1919."

"That was a long time ago."

"It was hardly cracked at all ... amazing considering how old it was and that the field must have been ploughed over and over again. There was a big easel in one corner of the room with a dust sheet thrown over it. Louisa didn't like that, either. She imagined it looked like an old man bending over to tie his shoe-laces. My grandfather, Donald McBain was an artist. He died before I was born."

"Remus isn't a Roman name."

"Yes, it is. Don't you know the story of Romulus and Remus?"

"No."

"I'll tell you about them another time." I had no intention of delving into Roman mythology on top of everything else. I suddenly remembered the weird shards of glass and other artefacts purporting to be the remnants of Roman pots in a cabinet at our home. I had never been able to see them as pots. To Louisa and me they had been the fragments of ancient eggs, stolen from some fantastical bird stalking the land in those times. It had been my job to dust the cabinet and contents every week. I had become familiar with each one.

My mother had been unimpressed by their charisma. After my father left, she emptied the cabinet and threw the whole lot in the bin accompanied by a scary tirade in French which I had tried not to hear. The words had made no sense to me but their meaning had been quite clear.

"The house smelled of dandelion and burdock," I said, trying to concentrate on the positives.

"What's that?"

"It's a drink … a bit like coke. You would have loved it. Anyway, as I was saying, to begin with Papa would give up and stay at home but in the end he wanted to go and see his friends so much that he went without her. He was still so young. They were both so young. Too young probably … I arrived not long after they married and they had very little time to get used to being together before they became parents."

"Why wouldn't she go with him?"

"She'd decided his friends weren't nice people. She didn't want to spend time with them."

"Maybe they weren't nice, Gran."

"No maybe not, at any rate she didn't go and then he started drinking too much …"

"Binge drinking," Becky said. She nodded sagely. "We had a film about that at school. It's what teenagers do. They fall about all over the place and swear a lot and then the police take them to hospital. Did Mac have to go to hospital?"

"I don't think so. I can't remember. It's all a bit of a blur what happened in the end. One day he was there and then he wasn't. We never saw him again. It was very sad. We had survived the War when life had been really difficult and Lettie never knew if he'd be injured or something worse, or if the house would be bombed and we'd lose our home and then when we had a chance to live a normal family life again, it was all over."

"That *is* sad."

"Life's not always how you want it to be, Becky."

"I know. Lots of sad things happened in the War. They sent children away from home. They had to live on farms and houses in the country … with strangers."

"How did you know about that … no, wait … I've got it, one of your 'History in Action' days?"

She nodded "It was World War II day. We had to dress up as evacuees. Mum made me a cardboard gas mask."

"We didn't have all that fun when I was at school. Anyway, another sad thing happened after that."

"He died."

"That wasn't it. It was something else, something that happened a lot later … to me. Lettie, Lou and I moved up here after the separation. Lettie wanted to be somewhere completely different. Somewhere she couldn't be reminded of Papa and their life together. She'd been told about Liverpool by our next door neighbour, John Sullivan. He was an old sailor and he knew all about it. I expect his stories fired her imagination. He'd told her about the big cruise ships that called in at the docks, the impressive buildings on the pier head ..."

"I saw those; Mum drove right past on the way here."

"Well, you know what I mean, then."

"We saw the ferry coming in. I liked the Liver birds."

"Amazing, aren't they? Lettie enjoyed travelling. She liked the idea of being near the sea. I suppose it seemed romantic to her, quite different from what she'd been used to and anyway, John had a brother who rented out property up here. He'd offered us a house until we got settled."

"Something nice happened. You got married."

"Yes, that was nice. This happened after I got married."

Becky took my left hand in hers. "Why have you got two wedding rings, Gran? Did you get married twice?"

I looked down at the rings as she turned them with gentle fingers. "No, I was only married once. It's a bit complicated. One of the rings was lost for years. I had to get a replacement and then it was found, so I had two. You see Grandad Arthur was in the navy when we met. He was quite a bit older than me. He'd been the captain of a big ship during the War ..."

"Was that the First World War?"

"He wasn't that old. I mean the Second World War, the one we were talking about before. We met in London when he was on leave."

"I thought you lived up here."

"I did. I was on holiday with Kate and Di, seeing the sights. Kate was a big fan of the designer Mary Quant. She wanted to visit The King's Road and Carnaby Street. We met by chance. He told us he came from Liverpool, that's how we got talking. It was a whirlwind romance. We wrote to each other at first and then decided to get married. I'd gone all that way and I could have passed him in the street at home one day ... only I didn't."

"Where was Great-aunt Lou?"

"She'd eloped to Gretna Green with Carter Nelson by then. They'd gone to live in America."

"How did you …"

I put up my hand. "No more questions, Becky, please. You'll make me forget what I wanted to tell you." I was finding the heart-searching difficult enough without her interruptions but I knew that now I had started I had to finish. I took a deep breath. "Where was I?"

"You were telling me about the rings."

"Oh yes. Grandad and I chose a wedding ring. It was beautiful; twenty-two carat gold with an orange blossom design engraved all round it. I didn't have an engagement ring and he wanted to buy me something special." I looked at the ring. "The engraving's worn off it now. He was going away to sea for a few weeks before he finally left the navy and the jeweller agreed to post the ring to his mother …"

"Agnes Ryder," she said.

"Yes, when the adjustment had been made, it was a little too big. That's where we were planning to live until we found a house, although we didn't in the end. We lived with Lettie instead. Anyway, the ring never arrived. I had to borrow Ness's ring for the ceremony.

I could see she was bursting with another important question. "What is it?" I said.

"Who's Ness?"

"Sorry, it was Agnes, everyone called her that."

She pulled a face. "I wouldn't want to be called Ness. They'd say I was a monster."

"Who would?"

"Gemma Stokes and the others. They're always picking on people."

"Does Gemma bully you?"

"Not really. Everyone knows what she's like."

"You should tell Miss Reid if it upsets you."

"It's ok, Gran. I tell Mia Bailey. We're best friends."

"Good for you. Well, Agnes didn't mind being called Ness. So, I borrowed her ring for the ceremony but Lettie made me hand it back straight away. She said it was bad luck to wear someone else's wedding ring on your wedding day and she was quite right."

"Did yours get lost in the post? Mia's Brownie uniform got lost in the post. Her mum had to buy her a new one."

"That's what we all thought had happened. We gave it a few weeks and when it still hadn't arrived I bought a cheap ring from a pawnbroker's shop instead. I didn't want people to think I was living with a man and not married. It doesn't matter these days, but it did then. People would have made comments."

She nodded wisely. "What's a pawnbroker?"

I sighed. An enquiring mind was all very well but not when you were trying to reveal your innermost secrets. I explained the ins and outs of pawn-broking as I saw it "... and if you don't collect it and pay back the money in time, he's allowed to sell whatever it is to someone else," I finished.

"That's not fair," Becky said.

"It is. Everyone who goes to a pawnbroker knows the rules. It's up to them whether they do a deal or not." I fingered my rings. "I got the right ring back in the end … and before you ask, the pawnbroker didn't have it … which is why I always wear two."

She was fidgeting about on the floor. "Can I ask another question now?"

"Go on then."

"Where did you find it?"

"It was hidden away in a suitcase."

"Whose suitcase was it?"

"Ness Ryder's; you see Grandad Arthur died a few years before his mother …"

"He had a brain tumour."

"… yes, and your mum and I had the job of sorting out all her belongings." For a second, I was back in Agnes Ryder's house with its sour smell of damp and neglect. I remembered the state of the kitchen cupboards and shuddered. I moved swiftly on. "The house was a mess. She hadn't been well for some time."

"Why did you have to do it?"

"There was no-one else, no other family. All her friends had died and she wouldn't let her neighbours in to help her."

"Did you find cockroaches and spiders?"

"Hundreds," I said. "And earwigs."

She giggled. "Gross," she said.

I was glad she didn't find the story distressing. Why should she? She had not had to live through it. "We found a suitcase full of baby clothes in her bedroom. Little vests, knitted hats, bootees and matinee jackets, all folded in tissue paper, preserved with love."

"I can't knit."

"I'll show you next time we have a minute. Now we come to the interesting bit … underneath everything was an envelope with Grandad's name on it. Inside the envelope was my ring, still in its little box. It had arrived after all."

Becky wrinkled her forehead. "Why didn't she give it to you?"

"I don't think she wanted me to marry Grandad. She was probably hoping that no ring would mean, no wedding."

"That's not nice. We don't like Ness Ryder, do we? I think she *was* a monster."

"I think we feel sorry for her, Becky. She couldn't bear to let him go. She wanted to keep him her little boy for ever. He was her only son … but you can't do that to a grown man." I was becoming drained by all the remembering.

"Well I think it was mean, not sad."

"That wasn't the sad part. She didn't stop us getting married, did she? I need the photographs to help me explain the sad part … and a nice cup of tea."

She jumped up and bowed. "I'll fetch the photos and order the tea your majesty," she said and ran out of the room before I could suggest fetching it myself. I did not want to be treated like royalty. I just wanted to get it over with.

Chapter 14

I needed to stretch my legs. I mooched about the room wishing I could forget all about that time in my life. Recalling it was proving more of a trial than I had expected. Telling Becky stories from the albums had been fun. I could pick and choose what I remembered.

The door opened and Kate appeared with the tea. "Cerys thinks you're taking too long," she said. "I told her to relax. I said you had to do it in your own way in your own good time. I don't think she knows what a smart kid Becky is. I reckon she's going to be a journalist or a lawyer the way she questions everything."

"That's why it's taking so long. She keeps asking me all sorts. We've even dipped into Roman mythology."

"What's that got to do with anything?"

"Don't ask."

"How are you getting on?"

"So-so ... it's not a happy story."

"You see worse on some of these children's programmes. Have you ever watched Tracey Beaker?"

"I'm surprised you have."

"I watch everything when I'm at home. Eastenders has some pretty grim story lines."

"Becky's not allowed to watch Eastenders," I said. "Did Cerys say if Kit was coming?"

"No ..."

It was an undulating 'no', more of a 'don't know' really. She looked as if she was big with news. "Has she spoken to him?" I prompted.

"She told me not to mention this ... but ... has she said anything to you about him?"

"I know he's really busy at the restaurant at the moment."

"That's what he tells her."

I took in her quizzical expression. "What do you mean?"

"She says he's always making excuses not to be with them. He's tired, he's overworked ... you know the sort of thing. He spends very little time at home and when she suggests doing things as a family, he's not keen."

"Surely you don't think he's having an affair?" The ferrets were stirring. I did not want it to be true even though the suspicion had already crossed my mind.

She shook her head. "I can't see it. Kit has always been solid. He's probably just tired and overworked. If he's busy like you say, he'll be working all hours. Anyway, for whatever reason, she's got it into her head that he is."

"What if she's right? His behaviour is worrying," I said.

"She's been through his pockets for clues."

"The little minx ... did she find anything?"

"Nothing, but that doesn't prove it one way or the other."

"Lettie's death has come at the wrong time for her; first it was Becky's appendix, then my wrist and now this. It's one thing after another."

"I told her to ask him outright," Kate said. "I bet she'll find he's just been working, like he says he has. It's silly for her to get het up about something that might be nothing. Was that the front door? She must have been to fetch the photos. Don't let on I told you."

"Of course I won't."

"I'll leave you to it."

She slipped away and I had to put Cerys and Kit on the back burner to simmer away while I concentrated on the main course. Becky marched into the room cuddling the albums like a teddy bear. "Here you are, Gran," she said. The teddy morphed into a casket of gold as she handed them over, palms upturned, like a bondsman presenting a tribute to his liege.

I accepted the offering with an imperious nod. "Why thank you," I said. "Sit down Becky. Are you all right, all these secrets not too much for you?"

"No way, this is much better than school."

I opened the first one. "Fancy you bringing these with you. It's a good job you did or I wouldn't have been able to show you this picture … it's at the back here somewhere. Ah, here it is. This is Sadie." I pulled a small black and white photograph from an envelope glued to the inside of the back cover. I glanced at it quickly before handing it over to her. I hardly recognised the smudgy little face peering out of the pram.

"You've never told me about Sadie," Becky said. "Who is she?" She scanned the tiny portrait. "Oh, it's only a baby."

"My baby," I said. I took the photograph back and drank it in. I remembered the touch of those tiny fingers; her cry, her smile. I had marvelled at her sweet breath, her sateen skin, she had been perfect in every way. What if she had lived; what then? Would things have turned out differently? I had never dared give her a career, children, an independent life. It had been too painful to contemplate. "This is the sad part. She died when she was only six months old," I said.

"Poor little baby. She must have been Mum's sister."

"That's right, her big sister." I could see she was trying to work something out. I waited.

"My auntie," the child said triumphantly. "Aunt Sadie."

"Well done. She was a dear little thing. Anyway, she caught a virus and the doctors didn't know how to make her better. Medicine wasn't as good then as it is now ... although even if she had been born now she might not have survived. Viruses can be very unpleasant for small babies."

"Why didn't Lettie make her better?"

"Lettie's medicines weren't right for babies."

"Did you take her to hospital?"

I settled my glasses into a more comfortable position. "We did take her to hospital, but it was too late." I had tried to keep her safe. I had watched her sleep, whispered endearments to her as she fed from my breast. I had sung to her, cuddled and caressed her. I had loved her so very much, yet even so, I had lost her. My eyes filled with tears. She stretched over to give me a hug.

"Never mind, Gran, when I have a little girl I'm going to call her, Sadie."

"That's nice."

"Have you told me everything, now?"

I sighed. "Not quite. There's one last big secret."

"Does Mum know it?"

"Not all of it."

"I know about Grandad Arthur, so that can't be it."

"What do you know?" I asked.

"About his brain tumour. You know I know that, Gran."

"Oh yes. That's not it," I said.

I had thought for a minute that she had been given the information by someone else and that the worst was over, but it would seem it was still down to me. I had been forced into this position. I had been confident I could deal with it but now the time had come to reveal the awful truth I was not so sure. I did not want to shatter her illusions.

Cerys had been so insistent it was the right thing to do I had allowed myself to be persuaded. I still doubted I had the courage to disclose everything but I had made up my mind to try even though every fibre of me screamed, "No don't tell her."

The trouble was that if I revealed all to Becky, it followed I would have to tell Cerys and I reckoned that would be even harder. "It all happened a very long time ago," I began. The ferrets were back and not happy at being confined. I folded my arms tight against my ribs in an effort to calm them. "Your mum was about two. I thought Grandad and I were happy. He was often away on business, but we never argued."

"Did he drink too much, like Mac?"

"No, he didn't drink. After he left the navy he worked for an engineering firm. He was often sent abroad as part of his job. He was in Hong Kong when Sadie died. He didn't come to her funeral."

"Who did?"

"There was only Auntie Kate and me there."

"Where was Lettie? Why didn't she go?" she asked, her expression changing from questioning to determined, "I'm going to her funeral."

"She was busy doing something important," I said using my well-practiced cover story. What had she been doing? I had no idea except that it had been more enticing than her granddaughter's funeral. I realised I did not have to pretend any more. "That's not true, actually. I don't think she was there because she had a guilty conscience."

Becky stared at me. "Guilty conscience, why?" she said.

"She had lots of close friends after Papa left, men who …" I began and failed. I started again. "She liked their company … it was …" the words would not form themselves into sentences. I looked into her innocent eyes and knew I could not do it.

My only option was another half truth. "I didn't know it at the time, but I discovered later that Lettie had been having an affair ..." my voice tailed off.

On the outside I was the dutiful daughter, a loving mother and grandmother; I hoped I was a reasonable person. On the inside I was a bubbling mass of resentment. What had happened was history but it still had the power to disturb me. I thought I had moved on and forgiven them both. It would seem my mother's death had ripped the scabs from those old wounds, exposed them to the iodine of re-examination and I could not bear the pain. I stood up, unable to continue. "Sorry Becky. I've got a headache. I need to have a lie-down," I said. "Go and find Mum."

The poor child must have been confused. I am sure she felt awkward. "It's all right, Gran. People do it all the time. Well, they do in Eastenders."

I tried to smile. "I thought you weren't allowed to watch that."

"I watched it at Mia's when she had a sleepover." I could tell she was trying to understand. She could see I was upset but she did not know why. There were no more questions. She must have felt instinctively that questions would have been inappropriate and not knowing what else to do, she decided to apologise. In her experience that put most things right. "I'm sorry," she said.

"What are you apologising for, Becky? You have nothing to be sorry about. Off you go and find your mum."

I went straight upstairs and indulged in a few tears. I had returned to that dark place I had tried to leave so many years before. The current circumstances were like reins, pulling me back; back to the despair and the feelings of helplessness. I seemed unable to resist them. It was not a comfortable place to be.

I lay on the bed and took several deep breaths in an effort to relax; in to the count of four and then out to the count of four, like that psycho-therapist had taught me. I intended merely to empty my mind, regain some composure and go back downstairs, refreshed; instead I fell into a deep sleep and for once there were no dreams to disturb me.

I awoke some time later to hear Kate's voice, "Genie. Wake up ... Fr. Michael's here." She knocked on the door. It opened and she stood on the threshold, a concerned expression on her face. "He needs to speak to you."

I peered at the clock on the wall and then put on my glasses and tried again. "Nearly six o'clock. I can't believe I slept for so long."

"It doesn't matter."

I sat up and dangled my legs over the mattress while I waited to wake up properly. I imagined myself on a boat in the Mediterranean dipping my toes into the warm sea. If only I *had* been there and away from the current distressing reality. I rubbed my eyes. "I'll be with you in a minute," I said.

"There's no rush, Cerys is talking to him," she said and left me to it.

When I got up and opened the door again, she was loitering by the stairs. "Sorry. I didn't mean to nod off," I said as I headed for the bathroom.

"It probably did you good. How did it go?"

"It didn't; I'll tell you when he's gone."

Chapter 15

There was no sign of Cerys or Becky when I went downstairs. Fr. Michael was sitting in Kate's rocking chair. He was a young priest with an angular face and untidy hair. It flicked up at the back skimming his long fleshy ears, toying with his collar, rasping against its starched righteousness as he turned to face me. He stood up and kicked the chair to one side, feet clumsy in the dull black shoes which hung puppet-like from his ankles. Despite his tall frame he seemed of average height with his shoulders rounded in an ingratiating stance. The chair rocked slowly to and fro behind him as if a ghostly presence had replaced his. For a moment I had the fanciful idea that my mother had joined us.

He took a few steps my way. With each one, glimpses of pallid skin appeared between sock and trouser bottom. Kate shadowed him. "You ok?" she said.

I averted my gaze from the pale flesh and twisted out a smile. "Fine thanks. Where's Cerys?"

"She's taken Becky off to Pizza Express. We thought it was getting a bit much for her." I nodded and looked up at the priest. We contemplated each other in silence. "This is Fr. Michael, Genie."

"Yes," I said.

He held out a friendly hand. "I'm pleased to meet you ... and ... very ... sorry for your loss." He spoke hesitantly in a strong northern accent. It sounded all wrong. I had been expecting cultured, confident, clipped.

My fingers brushed against his. "It was good of you to come so soon," I said and retrieved them before any proper contact could be made. "I expect you're busy. Shall we sit down?"

He returned to his seat, legs folding like deck chairs as he shuffled his feet under the rockers out of the way. "This must have come as a shock for you," he said.

"We half expected it. She'd been fading for some time."

He carried on in a chatty style, unaware of my hostility. "She seemed so well when I saw her yesterday ... she asked me to give her the last rights. I thought it was a bit previous ... but she insisted. She must have known; some people have an insight ... you know ... a premonition of the end."

"Yes. Although at ninety ..." Kate said.

"Of course," he said. He reached down to pick up a carrier bag I had failed to notice. "As I was coming to see you anyway, Mrs. Dukes asked me to give you this."

He handed over the bag with a sympathetic smile, his top lip curling to one side as if to accommodate a cigar. I glanced down at the bag ... my mother's personal effects. I tweaked my glasses. What did I want with her possessions? I had asked Mrs. Dukes to deal with her clothes. I was happy for them to be recycled in any way she saw fit. The cashmere cardigans, none of them blue of course, still had some wear in them.

Kate could see the bag had thrown me. "Your mother's life in a carrier bag," she said in a light-hearted tone.

I took a deep breath. "It's not much to show for a long life, is it?" I said. "In fact it's rather pathetic."

He scratched his nose. "I know how difficult this is for those who are left behind ... is there anything I can do to help?"

I had suffered enough banal conversation. "We can talk about the funeral," I said crisply. "I'd like to know when it can be arranged. I want to sort out everything as soon as possible."

"Sure ... well ... there shouldn't be too much of a delay. No backlog at the crematorium at the moment. Back to back funerals in the winter," he said, lip curling, again.

I knew he was trying to be conciliatory but no amount of kind words would ever make me warm to a priest after the critical ... no callous ... ones aimed at me by another priest after Sadie died.

My sin, according to Fr.O'Leary, had been to marry out of the faith and not in a catholic church which had led directly to my baby's death. He was claiming I was responsible for ending her life, hinting that it could have been avoided. I had never forgotten the man or the conversation. Sparse grey hair slicked into a side parting, the broken tooth and harsh tone causing censorious words to be lisped into my sub-conscious. His eyes, rheumy behind wire-framed glasses, had squinted down at me; the hairs that sprouted from the top of his nose like bristles on pork crackling, had mesmerised me. I could still see the frayed edge of his jacket sleeve, the wagging finger pointed in my direction with all the menace of a snake being charmed from its basket.

Kate's voice shattered the vignette. "That's a blessing," she said.

I blinked. Fr. Michael blushed. He cleared his throat. "Have you chosen the hymns for the service?"

"Lord of the Dance and All Things Bright and Beautiful," she said without hesitation. Becky had made that decision for us; no-one else had known what to choose.

"Very appropriate with her love of flowers and gardens," he said. "I enjoyed my visits to your mother, although I found it quite difficult to communicate with her ... I've never been hot on languages ... except for a bit of Latin, of course." He made a noise somewhere between a snarling dog and a braying donkey. "Now for the service … what can you tell me about her … you'll want me to do the eulogy I suppose?"

We had a brief discussion about my mother and the service. He did not stay long after that. "I'll try for Friday shall I, if not early next week?" he said to Kate as she saw him out of the door.

"The sooner the better," she said.

"Understood; I'll give you a ring."

I was relieved when the door closed behind his polite sympathy. "Thank goodness he's gone. He hasn't got a clue about the circumstances. It's such a farce. He didn't know Lettie, I mean, really know her and he doesn't know any of us either."

"He's only doing his job. We have to go through the motions, Genie. You can't blame him for something some ignorant person said to you years ago. Surely we've all moved on since then, left our old skins behind?"

"How can I move on? I don't think I'll ever be over it. It was an unforgiveable thing to say to a young mum just after her baby had died. I was in a state of shock for weeks. I couldn't even cross the road on my own."

"I know. It was cruel, but Sadie's illness wasn't your fault. You know it and I know it. It was just silly bigotry to say what he did. It doesn't matter now."

"When you're young and impressionable, it does matter," I said. "He made me suffer agonies of conscience for years." My mother's death was turning over all sorts of stones from my past. I did not know which emotion was going to crawl out next. I felt bad for making a fuss. Kate didn't need this. "Sorry," I said.

"It's fine. What's in the bag?"

I peeped into the carrier bag. "Purse, rosary, glasses," I said. I gave it a shake. "Wedding ring, watch, a bit of bling and something else," I added, pulling from it a small package about the size of a small dictionary. It was wrapped in brown paper and tied with string.

I untied the string. The wrapping fell apart to reveal the portrait of a young girl in shades of green and grey executed in a pseudo-photographic style. The light caught her cheekbones and emphasised her eyes. They were gazing upwards, a wistful expression in them, dark curls spilling down her neck to mingle with the ribbon of gauze dusting her shoulders. "This is lovely," I said. "Where on earth did it come from? It's not signed."

"Can I see? Hmm, *Electra*," Kate said as she handed it back. "That sounds Greek."

I nodded. "One of the old stories; all those Greek tragedies are the same, you know, death, destruction, sibling rivalry ..."

"... and other dysfunctional family delights," Kate said. "I get the idea. What's written on the label at the back?"

I turned it over. The print was too small for me to decipher. I took off my glasses and lifted the golden label up to the light. "It's an address. Fourteen, The Pineries," I said. "Do you know it?"

"No," she said. "It might be where the painting was framed. Artworld always stick a label like that on the back of the work they do for me. Perhaps it's your inheritance."

There was more than a touch of irony in that comment. I settled my glasses back on my nose and grimaced. "Very funny," I said.

"Let's have another look." I passed it over. She fingered the gilt frame. "It's quite well done ... strange ... she reminds me of you when we first met."

"No glasses," I said.

"No ... but there *are* some initials ... R.S," she said as she handed it back again. "Bottom left?"

I studied the painting more thoroughly. "Oh yes. I think it looks more like that girl who let us into the flats. It could be anyone."

"It might be worth something."

"I doubt it," I said. I re-wrapped the frame and put it back in the carrier bag. "It was probably a gift from one of her many admirers."

"Talking of which, did you tell Becky everything?"

"I couldn't. I chickened out. She really doesn't need to know all the ins and outs. Why Cerys was so keen for me to do it, I do not know. It was a bad idea."

"What did you tell her, then?"

"I explained about Sadie and Ness Ryder and then I said Lettie had been having an affair."

"She was separated by then. She was free to have a relationship. It was Arthur who had the affair. Becky's a smart kid. I bet she works that one out and comes back to ask you more."

"If she does, I'll have to tell her and Cerys, too."

"You still haven't said why you didn't do it before."

"Somehow I couldn't find the right words or the right time. How do you tell your daughter that your mother seduced her father?"

"It's tricky. What did you tell her?"

"I said her father ran off with a woman even younger than me, my mother had a succession of boyfriends and I didn't want to have anything to do with either of them."

I felt uncomfortable coming out and saying those things. Since my husband's death I had spent a great deal of time pretending they had never happened. I fiddled with my glasses, felt my left eye twitch and frowned, willing it to stop. It took no notice. I tried to ignore it. Kate was watching me.

"You're going to have to do it some time," she said.

"I know and I will. I've had enough of my mother's tangled life for the moment. I think I should try and speak to Louisa, explain what we've decided."

"Good idea."

"What time is it over there?"

The telephone rang and Kate went off to answer it. I tried some mental maths with the time zones. I could hear excitement in her voice. "You're not ... I don't believe it ... I wasn't expecting you until at least Friday ... of course you can stay. I'll tell Genie ... see you soon."

She came straight back into the room. "That was her. Good news. She's in London, Lou's in London, Genie."

"She can't be."

"I said she could stay here. She can have the studio. It's a good job I had that loft conversion done."

"No ... she can't possibly have got here so soon."

"She's definitely in London."

"Why didn't she want to speak to me?"

"She sounded out of breath, rushing for a train, I think. She got the message about Lettie ... sends her love. She's going to call again later. She just wanted you to know she's in this country and she'll be here tomorrow."

Chapter 16

Our meal that night was unusually sombre. I was tired. My wrist ached, being reminded of a past I had been trying to forget and thinking about Kate's cancer made it hard for me to be cheerful. "I hope we don't have to wait for ages," I said. "The end of this week would be ideal."

"The funeral's the worst thing," Kate said. "When that's over we can …who on earth is that?" she asked as the doorbell chimed.

"I'm nearest," I said. "I'll go."

"You don't have to," Kate said, already half out of her chair.

I gave her a gentle push back. "You've been running round after me all day. It's time I did something useful."

I was feeling uncharitable as I opened the door. We had been disturbed enough for one day. I was not in the mood for a cold caller or even to make polite conversation with some random visitor.

It was not a random visitor. I thought for a moment that I must be hallucinating and then I heard her voice, "Hi, Genie."

It was Louisa. There was a big smile on her face and an even bigger suitcase on the step in front of her. "Louisa," I said.

"Full title, eh? *Surprise, surprise*," she sang at me. She kissed both of my cheeks. I held her close, draping my arms round her shoulders like a pashmina, unwilling to set her free. "It's great to see you, Genie. It's been too long."

"Kate said you wouldn't be here until tomorrow," I said as my arms slackened and I retrieved my voice. "I was surprised you were even in the country. How did you get here so fast?"

"I arranged everything after I spoke to you the other day. My flight from New York was already booked. I picked up Cerys's message when the flight landed and then I ran for a train at Euston. I caught it by the skin of my teeth. I thought I might as well stay here as some dive in London."

"What made you come over?"

"A whim, I guess. So … we're orphans now." I nodded. "Are you ok?"

"Just about ... are you?"

"I'm fine … relieved, I think. It's been dragging on for so many years."

"It still feels odd."

"I know. Where's Kate?"

"She's in the kitchen." Louisa started forward but I held her back. "Wait a minute, I'd better tell you. She's been diagnosed with breast cancer."

"Oh shit," she said. "Sorry but that's awful. Is she having treatment? That can be awful, too."

"It's better than *not* having it, surely. She's due to have an op soon. It's only a small lump. She's quite upbeat about it."

The kitchen door opened and Kate appeared. "Who is it Genie?"

"It's Lou. She caught an earlier train."

"Little Louisa," she said after they had hugged. "I'm sorry about your mum."

"Thanks, but it was time."

She nodded. "How have you been?"

"Great," Louisa said, "But now I'm starving. Not much to eat on the train apart from snacks."

"We can do something about that. Genie and I were just having dinner. I'm sure we can stretch it for three."

The atmosphere round the table lightened dramatically with Louisa to entertain us. She was full of her journey and the colourful people she had encountered on the way. "You see life on a plane, believe me."

"I know," Kate said. "I don't fly so much now but when I did I used to be amazed at how many of them could nod off and stay asleep for the entire flight with everything going on around them. I always took the opportunity to catch up on whatever films were on offer."

"I watched a great Colin Firth movie. I loved Bridget Jones."

"Me too," Kate said.

Louisa hesitated for a moment. Her eyes searched mine. "Was it awful at the end?"

I glanced at Kate. "Not really, was it?"

"Not at all, it was very peaceful. Cerys and Becky were there. Becky gave her a kiss and she opened her eyes. She thought Becky was you and then she just passed away. It was as if she'd been waiting to see you before she could let herself go."

"I'm glad it wasn't traumatic. Was Becky ok? It's a bit grim for a ten year old to witness a deathbed scene."

"Becky's a wise one," Kate said. "She's perceptive. She wasn't worried. I think she'd have been upset if she hadn't been there."

"You'll be able to judge for yourself," I said. "She'll be back in a minute.

"Where is she?"

"Cerys took her off to Pizza Express," Kate said. "It was getting a bit heavy here; Genie decided to spill some of the beans."

Louisa looked at me, eyes brimming with disbelief. "Well ... *for* heaven's sake. Are you going to tell the truth, the whole truth and nothing but the truth so help you God?" I sighed and she patted my arm. "I think you should. Get it over with. You've kept quiet for far too long. Now is exactly the right time."

I found it difficult to drop off when I finally slid under the duvet. I spent a while thinking. I came to the conclusion that everyone else must be right. The truth had to come out and I was the only person qualified to report the facts accurately. There comes a time when saying nothing distorts the truth. We had reached that point.

I accepted that I would have to try again, but I would not say anything more to Cerys or Becky until after the funeral. I couldn't deal with that as well. I wanted to do it when we were all back in our own homes. It would be more relaxed there and easier for me to open up.

I decided I would tell them separately in the most appropriate way I could; for Becky it would have to be through the photographs. I could approach everything gradually, gently, so as not to alarm her. For Cerys it would have to be the unadulterated and unpalatable truth, no frills. After that I would try my hand at marriage guidance. Maybe Kit had strayed. Cerys had never been one to imagine things.

That decision made I went on to think about Kate. She hadn't said a word about her operation. It would be just like her to say nothing and put it off until after everything was over. I did not want her to do that. Louisa would be there for me and Cerys and Becky. Diana had promised to be there, too. I would not be alone and there was no need for Kate to postpone treatment just to attend my mother's funeral. I made up my mind to ask the question the next morning and having finally settled things in my head, I slept.

A glorious salmon pink sky greeted me when I opened the curtains the next morning, some parts as fiery as a volcanic eruption. I remembered the shepherd's warning. We could expect rain. "What's up?" Kate said when I finally arrived downstairs.

"Nothing really ... which day are you going in?"

"Beat around the bush, why don't you?" she said with a grin. "It's Tuesday."

"Oh good ... I thought you might have decided to put it off for now. You mustn't do that whatever happens."

"Don't worry, I won't. I want to get it over with as soon as possible."

"I've decided to stay on after the funeral. I want to be here when you go into hospital. I'll stay until you feel well enough to cope on your own again."

"There's no need."

"I remember how groggy you can be after an anaesthetic. You won't feel like doing much. I want to help. I can prepare you wholesome and nourishing meals," I said.

"That sounds ominous, but thanks. What did you have in mind, calves foot jelly?"

I chuckled. "Beef tea," I said. "That's agreed, then. Cerys is in the shower. Becky will be down soon. She was reading when I got up."

"She seems to be taking things well," she said.

"It's a shame her father's not here."

"There's still time. No point him being here until we have a firm date for the funeral."

"I know, but I've a feeling he's not coming."

"Oh? What makes you think that?"

"You know ... what we were talking about yesterday. I've had a think and there could be something in it. It's not surprising Cerys is so stressed at the moment. I hope she's enjoying this little break. She obviously needs it."

Kate shrugged. "You know what I think. *If* he's having an affair, you'll find out soon enough."

Clearly she did not agree with me. "I don't want to believe it," I said. "But I've got this feeling."

"Kit isn't Arthur, Genie."

"Anyone can be tempted."

"I know, but I don't understand when he would have had the time. He's always working at the restaurant."

"But is he? That's the point."

"Poor Cerys," she said. "Poor, poor, Cerys; I hope it's all a big misunderstanding."

"Poor little Becky," I said.

At that moment Louisa waltzed into the room wearing a pair of cream shorts and a halter-neck blouse in a startling shade of puce. "Mornin' to you both … why poor little Becky?" she said. "I could eat a horse."

"We could all have been doing that for years without knowing it," Kate said with a mischievous smile.

Louisa laughed. "I read about that. They eat horse in France. I don't know what all the fuss was about."

"It's not so much the horse meat as that we all thought it was beef," I said.

"Horse, pork, beef, kangaroo," she said. "What's the difference? You should try buffalo. It's very tasty."

"I'll pass, if you don't mind," Kate said. "I'm toying with the idea of becoming vegetarian."

"How would you survive without your bacon sarnies?" I asked in mock horror.

"Good point. Maybe it's not such a good idea. I expected you to have a lie-in, Lou. No jet-lag?" she said.

"None, I have a great constitution."

"Whatever you're eating, it certainly agrees with you," I said. "You look stunning."

Her body was toned and tanned. No-one would have believed she was in her sixties. She looked at least twenty years younger. "I try to keep in shape. It is darned hard work at my age, but Carter likes me to look good. I've told him he should take out shares in that gym. I'm in there five days a week some weeks."

"I don't think I could cope with that," I said. "Pottering in the garden and the odd bike ride keeps me fit enough."

"I'm going to have to change my top later, it's not very warm, is it?" she said. "What's on the menu? I don't know why I get so hungry when I'm travelling."

"Well, I don't have waffles and maple syrup if that's what you mean; how about eggs, sunny side up?" Kate said.

Louisa laughed. "Am I so American? I suppose I am. It's been a long time. I don't need ham and eggs. Toast with lashings of butter and oodles of marmalade, will be fine. So, I ask again; why, poor little Becky?"

Kate pulled a face. "Genie thinks Kit's having an affair."

The blue eyes goggled. "No way," she said.

"That's what I said."

"It's not just me," I said. "Cerys mentioned it to you, so there must be something in it. I sensed things weren't right between them. I don't want there to be a problem. I couldn't bear another family upheaval but I've been thinking about it. She could be right."

"Why?"

"Apparently he's been working really long hours and doesn't seem to want to spend time doing family things. It's worrying."

"It could be legit," Louisa said. "Restaurant hours are a killer. We've got friends with a restaurant. They hardly ever see each other. We always joke about how they managed to have kids. "

"Could be, but she seems to think not," Kate said. "Two rounds do you?" Louisa nodded. "Marmalade's on the table."

"Great, thanks. Well, if it *has* happened, there's not much we can do except offer our support." Louisa took the knife Kate was offering and sat down at the table.

"We could encourage them to go for counselling," I said. "But unless she mentions it to me outright I can't say anything. She's only hinted at it so far. I don't want her to think we've been discussing her private life. It will only make her cross."

Louisa nodded. "I guess people have their ups and downs and get over it."

"You might make matters worse," Kate said. "I've already told her that if she needs to talk we'll listen."

"Sure thing," Louisa said. "And your marmalade's delicious, by the way."

"Sainsbury's best," Kate said.

"When are you going to have a word with her about 'you know what'?" Louisa asked.

"Don't go on," I said. "I've decided to leave it for now. It will be easier when we get home. It's hardly a priority. She's got enough on her plate at the moment ... was that the phone?"

Kate got up. "It could be Fr. Michael."

"I hope it is. We need to get things organised."

"I don't mean to go on," Louisa said when she had left the room. "I was just thinking of you. When you've done it you'll be able to draw a line at last. It's been hanging over your head forever."

"You're probably right," I said. "I don't want to talk about it now. Cerys or Becky could come in at any minute."

"Ok."

"Was it him?" I asked as Kate re-appeared.

She nodded. "He's managed to arrange the funeral for midday Friday."

"Good," I said. "We'd better sort out the flowers."

"I need to go shopping," Louisa said. "I can't turn up at her funeral in shorts."

"Definitely not '*comme il faut*'," I said.

"I'm not bothered about that, but from what I can remember it's darned draughty in that church."

Chapter 17

Everything had been arranged. I was ready when Friday arrived. "It's raining," Becky said. She was kneeling up at the sitting room window staring at the road, waiting for her mother to get dressed.

I went over to join her and rested my arm lightly on her shoulders. It was a dismal day, the sky leaden. A gusty wind shook the oak trees lining the road and the occasional sharp shower deluged pigeons huddled under the canopy of leaves; water gushed from gutters into overflowing drains to form mini lakes across the middle of the road. Traffic splashed on regardless, windscreen wipers leaping with the joy of being liberated. "Hmm, so it is, the perfect day for a funeral," I said.

"Will Dad be there?"

"I don't think so. Your mum said he would if he could but he's very busy at the restaurant. Are you sure you still want to come?"

Becky nodded. "I told you … the Lettie in the bed wasn't the same as the one you told me about in all those stories. I'm going to my Lettie's funeral."

I dropped a kiss onto her hair. "That's sweet. I'm glad you're coming. It'll be nice for me to have you all there; my family and my two best friends."

"I am like Great-aunt Lou, aren't I," Becky said, contemplating her image in the mirror fixed to the wall above the fireplace, its arched top reminiscent of a church window. "You always say I am."

"Do you mind?"

"'Course not. It's all to do with my genes," she said. "Mr. Lopez told us about that … you know, whether you've got blue eyes or brown eyes." She pirouetted on tip-toes, stretching up to watch her performance in the glass. "Mum's got blue eyes, like me and Great-aunt Lou." She turned round to face me. "Gran …"

"Yes?"

"I was wondering ... where *is* Dad?"

"I told you. He's busy at the restaurant."

"I know but he hasn't got a close friend, has he?"

"Whatever do you mean?"

"Well, someone he likes better than us."

Swallowing my dismay at her anxiety I forced out a laugh. "Come here," I said, holding out my arms. I hugged her tight. "However many close friends your dad might have, he won't ever love any of them as much as he loves you."

The rain had stopped by the time we got to the church. The brass handles on my mother's coffin glistened in the watery sunlight as it was carried from the hearse covered in lilies. The mourners sat quietly throughout the simple ceremony presided over by Fr. Michael. There were so few of us that the organ drowned out our voices during the hymns. Louisa did not sing at all. She stared at the coffin in silence the whole time.

Efficient could best describe the brief ceremony at the crematorium. Having left the hymns behind us at the church, we were treated to some tinny music after the requisite words were spoken and then an unnerving rumble as the coffin disappeared. "The flowers were wonderful,"

Diana said as we sauntered back to the cars. "It was a good send-off."

"Yes. I was pleased with everything. I think she would have liked the lilies. It was nice of Mrs. Dukes to turn up."

"Did you manage to have a word?"

"No. I didn't feel like being introduced to anyone," I said.

"You didn't know that man with her?" I shook my head. "Becky's very grown-up for her age."

"She's a funny little thing," I said. "She comes up with such comments and the questions she asks."

"Lucy's looking forward to seeing her."

"It's good of her to help out."

"She doesn't mind. She likes Becky. Anyway it's good practice for her."

"Is she still planning to teach?"

"Yes, she's wanted to be a teacher since she was Becky's age."

"Following in her nana and grandad's footsteps," I said.

"We haven't pushed it, but I think she'll make a good one."

I agreed. I remembered having to play schools with Lucy when she was little and she had a certain presence even then. We stopped beside her car to wait for the others. "What's Chris cooking up?" I asked.

"Sausage casserole and syrup sponge I think; he thought you'd need comfort food."

"That's so thoughtful. You are lucky, Di. You've got a good one there."

"I know. Kate said you hadn't told Cerys about Lettie and Arthur."

"No but I will, when we get back home."

She put an arm around me. "It's going to be hard but I think you're right to do it."

"Am I, though? Does it really matter now they've both gone? Sometimes the truth causes more harm than good."

"I don't agree. Dark secrets have a habit of coming out eventually and at the most awkward moments. It's worse for everyone when that happens. You don't want it eating away at you forever. Once it's out in the open you'll be able to forget about it."

"I'll never be able to do that."

"No, well, I didn't mean you'd *forget* it exactly but it won't be such a big deal. Here they come. I'm off to check Chris has everything under control. See you back at the house."

"I'm glad that's over," Louisa said as she peeled off her leather jacket and draped it over a peg in Diana's hall. She fluffed up her chestnut hair and followed me into the sitting room. She had somehow managed to make the simple grey shift dress she had bought at the local boutique look like a Chanel original.

"Yes. It seems a bit weird ... you know, after all this time ... that she's not here any longer," I said.

"Come off it, Genie, she hasn't been here for years. Who was that guy with Mrs. Dukes?"

"Just one of Lettie's friends from the flats I expect. She spirited him away before I had a chance to speak to him. I'm glad. I didn't want to be introduced and have to listen to weasel words about her."

"I guess you were right. I think Kate spoke to them. Perhaps she knows. It's good of Di to feed us all."

"It's Chris who'll be feeding us, not Di."

"He's quite a character."

"He's a great cook," I said.

"Wow. Carter blanches at the thought of making popcorn never mind a meal ... unless it's burgers on the barbecue of course. He can just about manage that. Where's Becky gone?"

"I expect she's with Lucy. She's been dying to play with the dolls' house."

"Funny little thing, isn't she? Why would a child her age volunteer to go to a funeral? She didn't even know Lettie."

"She did … in a way. We've been looking through the photo albums. She told me she wanted to go to the funeral of the Lettie in the book, not the one in the bed."

Louisa smiled. "Quite *la petite philosophe*," she said.

"She's always surprising me. Sometimes she seems to understand things better than me. Actually she reminds me of you. Same colour hair …"

"Mine's out of a bottle, now."

"… same eyes, same deep thoughts ..."

"Perhaps she's going to be a shrink."

"I need a shrink," Diana said as she walked into the lounge armed with two large glasses of wine which she doled out. "Chris is such a prima donna in the kitchen. I've left him to it."

"So have I," Kate said as she arrived with another two glasses. "Here's yours, Di, Cerys will be here in a minute. She's just freshening up. Are we ready to toast the lately departed?"

"I think we should. This is her wake, after all," Diana said just as Cerys appeared in the doorway, wine in hand. "Here's to Lettie; may she rest in peace."

"I expect she will," Kate said.

"Genie and I will have some peace anyway," Louisa said.

"I hope so," I said. "Lettie."

We all raised our glasses. I took a slug and the others followed.

"No tears?" Diana said.

Louisa shook her head. "In another life, at another time," she said.

"She's right," I said. "Now we move on. I'm going to see if Becky's all right."

The door to the living room was half-open. I tiptoed over, not wanting to disturb the dolls' house fest.

"Who's this?" Lucy said. I saw her holding up a small doll in a blue knitted dress and cape, Marilyn Monroe hair tucked inside the hood which was drawn together by a narrow ribbon tied under the chin in a miniscule bow.

Becky took the doll and shook it gently, making its blue eyes blink. "Hmm ... this has to be Great-aunt Lou. She's got blue eyes."

"What about this one?" Lucy asked.

The doll in her hand was wearing a silk ball gown with a full skirt which reached to her ankles; there were tiny rosebuds sewn around the square neckline. "Lettie," Becky said without hesitation. "She's so pretty." She took the doll and traced the contours of its delicately tinted cheeks with her fingers. She tested the painted eyelashes and the rosy lips.

"This one has to be Genie, then."

The last doll Lucy had selected was made of brittle plastic, bland features painted onto the shiny face and brown curly hair moulded to the head. None of the dolls were more than ten centimetres tall but their heads, arms and legs moved. Becky seemed to enjoy parading them round the rooms in the dolls' house and making up stories about them as they sat at the table in the grand dining room or she took them off to bed. It was good to see her having fun.

"Did you play with this dolls' house?" she asked.

Lucy shook her head. "Not much. Freya was the one for dolls' houses."

"Did she have a name for it?"

"Dad called it *Tottering Towers* because he kept having to glue the roof back together she took it on and off so many times."

I was about to go back and join the others when Becky spoke again. "Did you know Lettie?" She didn't look up from re-arranging the furniture in the dolls' living room. It was an interesting question.

"No. My nana went to see her loads but she never took mum or me," Lucy said. "I think there was some mystery about her or something." That was an even more interesting answer but Becky didn't seem to like it. I saw her shut the front of the dolls' house and stand up. She adjusted her hair band. "I think I'll go and find Mum now," she said.

I did not want her to know she was under surveillance. I backed away from the door as fast as I could, nearly colliding with Cerys. "There you are, Mum. We thought you'd got lost. Are you all right?"

I slipped my arm through hers, glad not to have been rumbled. "Of course I am."

"Hi Gran," Becky said as she dawdled along behind us. "Is it lunch-time now?"

"I think it must be," I said. "I can smell delicious smells coming from the kitchen, can't you?"

"Well, I can't smell sausages. I thought we were having sausages."

"Sausage casserole," Cerys said. Becky pulled a face.

"Don't be like that, you're going to love it," I said. "Uncle Chris is almost as good with his cooking as your dad."

"You love sausages," Cerys said.

"Only with mash," she said. "I've never had them in a casserole before."

"Well, there's a first time for everything," I said. "Chris has gone to a lot of trouble for us. You're just going to have to be brave and try it."

Chapter 18

"That was a great meal," Louisa said. "Thanks Chris. Let me know when you open your first restaurant. I'll tell all my friends."

"So kind, dear lady," he said. "We aim to please. You can't beat a syrup sponge for the feel good factor." He stood up and bowed to the table. "I suppose I'd better clear up now. I can tell you girls want to chat."

"No. Leave it, Chris. I'll clear up later," Diana said.

"In that case I'm off to play snooker. Farewell one and all, parting is such sweet sorrow," he said and bowed himself out of the room.

Louisa grinned. "That man is a case," she said.

"And a great cook," Kate said.

"Well done, Becky," I said. "You've eaten it all."

Cerys looked at Becky. "You're very quiet," she said. "Do you want to go back and play with the dolls' house?"

"No thank you," she said rather primly.

"I know. Let's find a DVD," Lucy said. "Come on Becky. Race you."

"I'll win," Becky said as she ran off giggling.

"I think I'll ring Kit. Tell him when we'll be home," Cerys said.

I gave her an encouraging smile. At least they were still talking. "Send him our love."

"How long are you staying, Lou?" Kate said.

"I'm going back to London tonight. It was only ever going to be a brief trip."

"Cerys and Becky are leaving soon. I'm glad you came, even if it was only for a couple of days," I said.

"You can come and see me next time. It's not a bad flight. JFK to Heathrow is only six hours."

"She is thinking about another adventure," Kate said.

"Oh yeah, what is it this time?"

"I haven't decided yet."

"Did she tell you about Fr. Michael and the bag of goodies?"

"No?"

"Sorry, I'd forgotten all about it," I said. "He gave me a bag of Lettie's bits and bobs; personal things, you know … her watch and so on. There was a small oil painting in the bag. We don't know where it came from; I'll show you when we get back to Kate's. Remind me."

"Ok. What sort of a painting?"

"The portrait of a girl, '*Electra*'," Kate said. "I think it's quite good."

"I wonder where she got it. She can't have bought it. She didn't have a dime, only her state pension. I went into all that when we set up the payments for the flat."

"It had an address on the back," Diana said. "It's nowhere round here; we googled the street map."

"She hadn't been anywhere else for years," I said. "It's all a bit of a mystery."

Louisa laughed. "Ooh, a mystery, I doubt if it's anything interesting."

"It could have been a gift from someone," I said.

"You're probably right," she said. "And, talking of mysteries, who was that man with Mrs. Dukes, Kate? Did you speak to him?"

"Not exactly, I had a brief chat with her. She didn't introduce us. She was in a hurry to get off somewhere. I presumed he was someone from the flats."

Diana frowned. "He didn't look old enough."

"I didn't take that much notice," Kate said.

"I expect he was a professional mourner. I guess there are some old folk in there who have no family or friends left," Louisa said. "It would be pretty awful to have no-one see you off."

Kate nodded. "Or it could have been one of Lettie's young men."

"There is always that," Louisa agreed. "A leopard doesn't change its spots ... even if it is on its last legs."

"I don't want to know," I said. "I'm just relieved it's over and it all went so well."

Cerys and Becky set off for home after a brief pause back at Kate's to collect their things. "I'm sorry we have to leave but I don't want to get back too late," Cerys said. I tossed up whether I should try and persuade her to stay another night. She looked exhausted.

Kate gave her a hug. "That's fine. You go."

Louisa was next. "Look after yourself. Send my love to Kit."

"Will do," Cerys said.

I walked out to the car with them. "Drive carefully."

"I'll call when we get in."

"Will Dad be at the restaurant?" Becky asked.

"I expect so."

"Can we go and see him before we go home?"

I waited for my daughter's response. "It depends. It might be too late. You've got school tomorrow."

"I haven't," Becky said with some indignation. "It's Saturday tomorrow."

"Oh yes. So it is. I don't know."

I felt I had to speak up for the child. "She hasn't seen her dad in a while. She's been really good over the last few days. We've all been through a lot. Would it matter if she went to bed a little bit late just this once?"

Cerys smoothed down Becky's hair and tapped her nose in an affectionate manner. "Oh all right, as a special treat because you've been so good at Auntie Kate's, but it's straight to bed when we get home after that."

Becky's eyes shone. She issued a delighted, "Yessss," and jumped into the back of the car without another word.

I waved them off hoping their absence had made Kit's heart grow fonder.

I walked slowly back into the house wondering how I could have been so blinkered. How could I not have noticed Cerys was so stressed and worse, how badly affected she had been by the break-up of my marriage? I was hoping Becky would be able to avoid the same emotional damage. When I went home I would do my best to help sort things out. Until then I had to focus on Kate and Iris, but first I had to deal with Louisa and *Electra*.

I retrieved the carrier bag and took it straight into the kitchen where they were discussing the virtues of vegetarianism. "I couldn't give up bacon either," Louisa said.

"I have to find the best way to starve Iris," Kate said. "I've read all sorts of articles on food, diets; organic versus bog-standard, dairy versus non-dairy. I'm even more confused, now."

"I think a little of what you fancy, does you good," I said. "Here she is; this is *Electra*."

Louisa cast an eye over the haunting face. "Fascinating … great cheek bones but I don't have a clue where she came from."

"Nor me," I said.

"I think she looks like a very young Genie," Kate said.

"I don't," I said.

"Forget it," Louisa said. "It's just a painting. Stick it on a wall somewhere if you like it ... or take it to a junk shop. I'd better pack my bag. I'll have to make tracks soon."

"Do you want any of the other things?" I said, holding out the carrier bag like a lucky dip. Louisa did not even glance at it.

"Nope," she said.

"Do you want me to call a taxi?" Kate said. "I always use Green Line, they're very reliable."

"That would be great, thanks."

"What time do you want to be picked up?"

"Five thirty?"

About an hour after Louisa left, Cerys rang me to say they had arrived home safely. I could tell from her tone that she was annoyed. "Did you go and see Kit?" I asked.

"Yes. What a fiasco. My head was thumping before we even got there and the restaurant was really noisy. All the tables were full."

So, Kit had been telling the truth. "He said they'd been busy."

"It looked like chaos to me. Two members of staff were off with a flu bug and we had to wait ages until he had time to talk to us. We both had a coke. Becky was delighted, as you can imagine." I could imagine that. Coke was frowned on as a rule. "She was so excited to see him. She said she'd like to work in the restaurant when she's older."

It was a brave effort at light-hearted chat but her voice was strained. I wondered what else had happened to upset her. "What's wrong?"

I heard her blow her nose and then she let it all out. "He asked how the funeral went. Becky told him Lettie's box was covered in lilies. He told her it was a coffin. I told him he'd know how it went if he'd been there and he said he was staying at the restaurant again and not coming home ..." I could hear the hurt in her voice as she carried on "... I told him it felt like we were a one-parent family and he told me he was going back to work and I said I hoped that was all he was going back to and he said he wasn't going to discuss it … and then he just walked off into the kitchen. He didn't even say goodbye."

Her voice cracked and the sobs were heart-breaking. I felt useless. "Oh dear … I'm sure he didn't mean to upset you," I said, using the first platitude that came to mind.

"He did. It's over, Mum."

I tried to soothe her. "I hope not. Try and get some sleep. You're both exhausted, that's what it is. Talk to him again when you're not so tired and he's not so busy, I'm sure you can sort it out."

"I don't know if I want to." Her tears declared the lie to that; she was so distressed I reckoned she must still care.

"It sounds to me like you and Kit have a lot of thinking to do. It will take time but I'm certain if you make an effort you'll be able to patch things up. I won't be home until next week but you can ring me any time. Don't do anything silly."

"Like what?"

"Like telling him it's all over, like packing up and moving in with one of your friends, like asking Becky to take sides?" I said. "Sit on your hands for now, however much you want to retaliate." I remembered giving Becky some advice along the same lines. Paying people back only ended in tears.

"I'm going to bed," she said.

"Good idea. You must be tired after all that driving. You'll feel much better after a good night's sleep. We're all full of emotion at the moment."

I went back to join Kate. "She's not happy."

She pulled a sad face. "It's a shame everything's falling apart right now. She's upset about Lettie on top of everything else but there are two sides to every story you know. We haven't heard Kit's version of the truth."

"I can't help thinking it's partly my fault."

"Now that's stupid. How can it be?"

"I mean all that business with Arthur, us moving away. It was a pretty brutal separation. I thought she'd escaped any fall out being so young but she told me the other day that she remembered some of the things that went on. She gave me the impression she'd been left with an unsettled streak. Perhaps she's not as confident as I imagined. She's always expecting things to go wrong."

"You're not responsible for how she feels," Kate said. "She's an adult now. You did what you thought was right at the time. You couldn't have stayed here and had them in your face day after day. That would have been worse for both of you."

"I don't understand it. Kit and Cerys have always been so good together."

"I'm sure they'll sort it out."

"I hope so."

We stayed up chatting for a while. It was gone two when we finally went to bed.

We had decided to spend the rest of the weekend rubbing shoulders with the past. Kate did some frenzied ringing round on Saturday morning. She set up a series of rendezvous with old school friends; friends I hadn't met for years. One of them I had not seen since I left school and I remembered immediately, why. What she didn't know about everything was not worth knowing.

"Susie hasn't changed," I said when we left the restaurant where we had enjoyed a really good Sunday lunch.

She laughed. "Ask the Oracle," she said.

"Don't you find it a bit much?" I asked. "Why do you still see her?"

"Actually it's a smoke-screen. When you get her on her own she's ok. Her parents died in that awful plane crash in Thailand. She stayed with me for a while after that. I managed to scratch below the surface. You were busy with Cerys's wedding."

"Oh yes. I remember now … she wasn't at the party."

"She doesn't like being in a crowd ... suffers from low self-esteem, never had a long-term relationship. She's being very supportive about Iris, though. That's the one good thing about all this. It's made me see who my real friends are."

I was glad she had a network of good friends close by. My help was limited by the miles between us. "There's a lot to be said for staying put, Kate. I'm too far away to be much use to you. I wish I could do more."

She squeezed my hand. "Just knowing you're there is enough."

"I am here and anything you need, just shout."

Chapter 19

Despite the operation looming we managed to enjoy our time together but we had only postponed thinking about what was to come.

Tuesday morning arrived and we were both in reflective mood. I was concerned about what the day might hold for Kate. I speculated about what would happen if the surgeon discovered things were worse than he suspected. I could only guess at the turmoil in her mind but she must have had similar thoughts. Would it involve a major operation and reconstruction instead of a simple lumpectomy?

I did not want to tempt fate by voicing my fears; it was my role to offer encouragement and support. I took my cue from her. She always knew what to say to make me feel supported and loved. She knew when not to say anything at all. I was conscious of the many times she had buoyed me up. It was my turn to do the same for her and I welcomed the opportunity. I did not want to let her down. "The taxi will be here in a minute," I said.

"I know."

"I've got a book and a bottle of water. I'm just going to hang around the hospital until it's over."

"Ok."

"Have you got everything you need?"

She patted her legs and arms, her chest and then her head. "I think so." The doorbell rang and she jumped. "I'm scared, Genie."

"Yes, but you won't be on your own. I'll be there."

"What if they find something else?"

"Then they'll chop it out," I said. I stood up to encourage her to do the same. "Come on, Kate, you can do this. Di and I are counting on you to show us the way."

"Oh. Nice. So I'm the guinea pig, am I?"

"You were always first with everything. Don't you remember; first pair of high heels; first boyfriend; first one to leave home?"

She looked at me wild-eyed. "I really don't want to go."

The doorbell rang again. This time more persistently. I picked up her case. "I don't want *you* to go," I said. "So you'd better get down to that hospital and make sure you don't. The surgeon will deal with Iris and when you wake up it will be over, job done. You can go home and get on with your life without her."

"Life after Iris," she said. "I could write a book."

"You can do anything if you set your mind to it."

She stood up. "Ok, Genie. I'm ready."

I stayed with her until the last possible minute and sent her off to the operating theatre with a few confident words. "You'll be back before you know it," I said. "I'll be waiting."

"I'll try not to be too long," she said. I kissed her cheek. I watched as they wheeled her away and then walked down to the café.

I joined the snake of people waiting for a shot of caffeine to kick-start the morning. Slinging my bag over my shoulder with synthetic bravado I grasped the paper cup in both hands taking comfort from the warmth seeping through to my fingers.

The hospital day was just beginning but it was already alive with activity. From my seat I could see the entrance doors sliding back and forth like a comedian's grin. Groups of worried relatives were whispering in corners, new dads carrying enormous bunches of flowers and tearful children with bloodied bandages trying to be brave. Porters were pushing empty beds about as the walking wounded hobbled to and fro. I caught snippets of conversation; I sensed fear, elation; compassion, all around me but I was not part of it. I was thinking only of Kate.

I could hear a lift opening and closing in a leisurely fashion. I watched as it swallowed people with all the enthusiasm of a basking shark and then creak and groan its way upwards. I made a mental note to use the stairs. Despite all the mayhem I felt very alone.

I finished my coffee and returned to the corridor outside the ward. It was quieter there. A row of chairs lined the approach to the doors. There was no-one about. I decided to sit and wait. I felt better in the place I had last seen her. I knew she must be returning soon … well, that's what I hoped. I didn't want to be missing when she arrived. It would be a betrayal of her trust if she woke up and I was not at her bedside.

I tried to read my book but it made no sense; the same words kept re-appearing over and over again. However much I attempted a new paragraph. I seemed unable to take it in. I gave up. By the time she had been in the operating theatre for two hours my anxiety was off the top of the scale. I imagined all sorts of horrific scenarios.

I caught sight of one of the nurses who had been on duty when she was admitted, dashing off down the corridor with a kidney dish and syringe. I burst through the double doors and followed her. We met at the stairs. "I came in with my friend, Kate Grieves," I said.

"I remember."

"Will it be much longer?" I asked.

"I don't know. There's no way of telling. Sorry."

She skipped off down the stairs and I trailed back to my seat. I took a sip of water and concentrated on screwing the top down as tight as I could. I stood up and read all the posters plastered to the walls … for the third time. I wandered across to the window and looked down at the courtyard below. There was a woman, a colourful scarf wrapped ethnic-style round her head. She was sitting on the only bench I could see, reading a newspaper, white-stockinged legs stretched out in front of her like *boudins blancs*. I noticed one or two men in dressing gowns wandering about, smoking. I was glad Kate had stopped; she had been told it might have compromised her recovery. None of us smoked any more.

Diana's voice startled me. "There you are, Genie. I've been looking all over for you."

She enveloped me in a generous hug and I felt the load shift. "I'm so glad you're here. This waiting's a killer."

"She's not back yet?"

"No, not yet; they're taking their time."

"I thought it was just a small lump. A quick in and out," she said.

"That's what Kate said … oh look … the lift's coming up again. It could be her this time."

The doors clunked open. A porter wheeled out the cumbersome hospital bed with well-practiced agility and steered it towards a side ward. We craned our necks to see if we could recognise the patient lying there. Kate looked pale and vulnerable; a much smaller version of herself.

I heard Diana gasp. "What have they done to her?" she whispered. "She's got tubes coming out of everywhere."

A nurse appeared. She took Kate's notes from her bed. "It looks much worse than it is," she said reassuringly. "She'll be sleepy for a while, but that's quite normal. There's a drinks' dispenser along the corridor if you want a cup of coffee or something. You can come in when we've hooked everything up."

Diana and I exchanged glances. "I'll get us some drinks," I said. "It looks like we'll be here for a while."

An hour later and Kate was beginning to stir. The hovering nurse came over to the bed. "Miss Grieves." Kate's eyes opened. "You're back on the ward now. Are you in any pain?" She tried to say something but her throat was too dry. "Have a sip of water." She offered her a plastic cup. "If you feel the pain coming back, just press this button here and you'll get another shot of morphine." She handed her what looked like a computer mouse on a long lead.

Kate took a sip of the water. "Did they get it all out?"

"The doctor's coming to see you. He'll explain everything." She put the plastic cup back on the bedside table and left us alone.

"How do you feel?" I asked.

"I've been better," Kate said with the ghost of a smile. "A bit spaced out."

"That'll be the morphine," Diana said.

"What time is it?"

"It's gone twelve, you were down there for nearly three hours," I said.

"Does it hurt?" Diana asked.

"No." Kate felt around her chest. "I've got a big dressing but it doesn't hurt. I feel so sleepy."

"Go back to sleep," I said.

"We're not going until the doctor's been round," Diana said.

Kate closed her eyes. "Make sure you wake me when he arrives. I want to know what they found. I don't want any pussy footing around."

"What? You know us better than that," I said. "We've found the tea machine. We'll just hang about until he gets here."

148

The doctor arrived a short while later. He was a young Asian with a serious air. His glasses winked at us as he nodded a greeting. He patted Kate's hand to wake her. "Miss Grieves," he said. She opened her eyes. "Good afternoon ... Mr. Sharma. I'm your surgeon. We met in the operating theatre."

"Did you get it all out?"

"Is it all right to speak in front of your friends?"

She shuffled up the bed as best she could attached to drips. "Yes, of course," she said.

"We did get it all but it wasn't as easy as we expected."

"How do you mean?"

"The cancer was larger than anticipated. It had spread to the lymph nodes under your arm. We had to remove those too." Her eyes flickered slightly. "I'm sorry," he said.

"I'm glad you managed to take it all away. Does this mean radiotherapy as well as the chemo?" she said in a business-like tone.

"I'm afraid so, six months of treatment to start as soon as possible." He went on to explain the prognosis and side-effects of the treatment but I was too shocked to take it in.

Kate looked at me and then she looked at Diana. I gave her what I hoped was an encouraging smile. Diana burst into tears and left the room. "I'll go after her," I said.

"It's just not fair," Diana said when the tears had passed.

I was staring out of a window again; this time in the visitors' room. All I had to inspire me was the car park. I watched cars move in and out like tiles in a sliding puzzle. "I can't believe it," I said.

"Just a small lump," she said. "Only it wasn't, was it? Cancer cells in the lymph nodes, sounds so nasty. Chemotherapy, radiotherapy; either would have been bad enough. They're so threatening together."

"They mean, serious," I said turning to face her.

149

"Yes. Thank goodness she had that mammogram when she did."

"I know." I felt my own tears threatening.

"Six months of treatment, poor Kate. Only eighty-five per cent of patients survive for five years or more. That's a sobering thought. She's definitely going to need us."

"Trust you to pick up on the statistics," I said.

"It's what he told us."

"I didn't register much of what he said after the bit about it spreading. We all think we're special; it won't happen to us, any of us ..."

"Did you see the expression on her face when he told her?"

"She wasn't expecting it, was she?"

Diana shook her head in despair. "Neither were we. *Small lump* was just about acceptable. *The cancer's spread* is a whole new ball game."

We sat there thinking our own thoughts for a while. "I'm glad I don't have my mother to worry about now. I can devote more time to Kate," I said.

"What about Cerys's little problem? You know what you were like after Arthur."

I had forgotten about my daughter for the moment. Kate's shocking news had driven everything else from my mind. "Her situation will never be the same as mine. I can't believe there's a fundamental problem with Kit. I don't want to believe it. If I'm wrong, I'll have to share my time between them. Just at the moment Kate's the priority."

"We'll manage. We have to manage. She needs us to manage. Chris is very good. He won't mind if I'm not at home so much. It'll only be while she has the treatment. I wish I hadn't burst into tears. I feel such an idiot. I'll go back in a minute and apologise."

"She'll understand. We'll have to take each day as it comes and make sure she's not one of the fifteen per cent of unlucky ones," I said. "I'm staying until she's over the

150

operation and then we can sort out some sort of a rota." I could see that her tears weren't far away. I gave her a hug. "It'll be all right."

"I hope so. I'm such a coward. I was just thinking I'd been fortunate compared with you two … what if my luck's about to run out?"

"Luck didn't have anything to do with my problems. Sadie was born at the wrong time. I married the wrong man. My mother was selfish and headstrong and I was a fool. Kate said I was soft and maybe I am." I shrugged. "We make our own luck in life."

"Do you really believe that?"

"I have to or I'd go mad."

Diana sighed. "What about the law of averages? I'm not going to escape unscathed. I know it."

"Remember parabolas?" I said. "We were forever drawing the things once you showed us how and then I had the idea to thread a needle and join the dots across with cotton…"

"… and Kate decided to use different coloured threads which looked fantastic ..."

"That's it, we worked together to produce something beautiful and we're going to have to do the same thing to help her get well. We're at our best when we feed off each other. That's the way it's always worked. No statistics. If we let Iris get to us we might as well give up on Kate now."

"We'd never do that."

"Focused is what we need to be."

"Of course; you're right," Diana said. "You're so good at all this. I'm absolutely useless."

I nudged my glasses upwards. "You're not. You've been there for her as much as I have, probably more. Anyway, I've had years of practice. I had to learn the hard way. All I can say is that just when you think you can't take any more, you get the strength from somewhere to carry on. We mustn't go down the 'what if' route."

She gave me a wintry smile. "Ok. We'd better get back in there and see if she wants anything."

"I must phone Cerys first. I said I'd let her know how it went."

"More stress for her to deal with."

"She doesn't need it, but I promised."

"I'll stay with Kate for now."

When I returned to the room, Kate had dropped off to sleep. Diana turned as I opened the door. She walked over and ushered me outside again. "She's not good," she said. "I told her I'd stay until you came back."

"What's happening with the treatment?"

"She'll be in here a couple of days and then there's only a three week wait until the chemotherapy starts."

"That's quick. It hardly gives her time to get over the op."

"She said she's pleased about it. She's keen to get on with the chemo. She's determined not to let Iris win."

"Good. I'm glad she's thinking positive."

"I said it was the beginning of the fight-back and we'd be there every step of the way." I nodded. "And then she said she appreciated it but she wished we didn't have to be."

"That's typical. She doesn't like to lean on anyone," I said.

"She's been fortunate so far. She hasn't had to."

"Well she'll have to, now; whether she likes it or not," I said.

"Sorry, Genie, I have to go. I feel mean leaving you to it but Chris asked all the kids round for a meal tonight. I ought to be there."

"There's no need for you to stay. Get off home."

"Are you sure?"

"Definitely; I've got my book," I said patting the neglected paperback. "See you tomorrow."

"I'll be here as soon as I can."

Chapter 20

The rest of Kate's stay in hospital was uneventful. It was a healing time when we could both reflect on our recent life-changing experiences and listen to each other's hopes and fears.

"I'm grateful to Iris in a way," she said on the morning of her discharge.

"Why?" I said. I was feeling tetchy. The taxi was late and I didn't think standing around waiting for it to arrive was what she needed. There had been a subtle change in her since the operation, a fragility that had not been there before.

"She's made me see things more clearly. Work out what's important in my life. I refuse to waste any more time worrying if I've eaten enough fibre or put on a few extra pounds. In future I'm going to concentrate on doing the things I want to; seeing the friends who mean a lot to me, trying to put something back into society. I might do some volunteering; meals on wheels or whatever. Try and make a difference … make my life worth something."

"That's great," I said. "It's always good to have a plan. Ahaa … here it is at last."

The driver was chewing gum. He looked bored. "Where to?" he asked as if it was the last piece of information he needed.

"Chestnut Close," I said swallowing my indignation at his casual attitude. "Just off The Southern Road." He grunted and revved the engine, taking a run at all the speed humps along the way.

It was hardly more than a fifteen minute journey to Kate's; she winced at every jolt and jerk. "I'm not giving him a tip," I said. "He was late and I didn't like his attitude or his driving skills."

"Ok," she said in a very un-Kate-like way.

I helped her out of the car. "I'll sort him out, you go ahead."

"I'm glad that's over," she said as she let us into the house.

"How are you feeling now you're out and about?"

"Not too bad; a bit weak. My arm's uncomfortable where they took out the lymph nodes but that's all."

"I think we need a night in with a pizza and Johnnie Depp," I said.

"That sounds good to me."

I could see she was exhausted. "Go and sit in the lounge. I'll come and join you when I've put your bag upstairs."

She stayed in bed until late the next day. It was warm. We had lunch outside in the garden. I had made us double-decker sandwiches; the sort that are bursting with vitamins and flavour. Calories and mayonnaise seeped out at the first bite. Kate nibbled at one and left the rest. "Not hungry?" I said.

"Not really."

"Never mind; perhaps you'll be hungry later."

She took several calls from well-wishers after that and then had a rest in her room. I couldn't rest. I felt the need to be doing something practical. I had been sitting around for far too long. I checked the fridge and then headed for the shops.

When I returned there was no sign of her. I presumed she was still asleep. I put the shopping away and reached for the kettle. She came downstairs shortly afterwards. "You don't have to stay, Genie. I'm feeling much better," she said.

I poured us both a cup of tea. "Let's see how you are tomorrow. I should really get back to the garden but I'm not going until I'm sure you're all right."

"Stop clucking," she said. "I'll be fine."

I knew she hated people fussing over her but I felt the need to feed her up before the chemo kicked in and left her feeling sick and too tired to eat. "I did some shopping while you had your rest. You should be all right for a few days if you don't feel like going out. I'm cooking your favourite meal tonight."

"Aw that's kind. I haven't had a carbonara in ages."

"We're having pudding, too."

"You're really spoiling me. I hope it's one of your crumbles."

"You'll have to wait and see. What time did you say we'd go round to Di's?"

"Eight thirty."

"I'd better get on with it then."

Some twenty minutes later I was doing my impression of a contestant in The Great British Bake Off, up to my neck in flour, bowls all around me, whisking eggs and milk by hand, when the doorbell rang. I left Kate to answer it. I could hear muffled voices and when she appeared in the doorway there was a puzzled expression on her face. "It's Mrs. Dukes," she said.

"Mrs. Dukes? What does she want?"

"To see you, she's in the lounge."

"She's probably found another loose end," I said, brushing flour from my top with a hasty hand.

"She's being very cagey. She wouldn't say."

As we entered the room Mrs. Dukes attempted to get out of the chair into which she had squeezed herself; there was a lot of huffing and puffing before Kate urged her to sit down again. She eased herself back with a sigh. "I'm sorry to disturb you, Ms McBain, but I had to come."

"That's all right. What's the problem?"

"It's just … oh dear, how can I put this … to tell you the truth I've ... um ... been struggling with my conscience."

"I'm sorry to hear that."

"Your mother told me not to say anything, but I feel I have to."

"Go on," I said, wondering what little trick my mother had left up her sleeve.

"Well, as you know she didn't have many visitors apart from you and Miss Grieves and sometimes Mrs. Spires. I didn't meet all of them, I can't be on duty twenty-four seven, but earlier this year I noticed that someone else was visiting on a regular basis."

"You mean a man?" Kate said. Mrs. Dukes nodded. "Now there's a surprise."

"I didn't think anything of it at first but he kept coming every so often and then about two months ago a younger man turned up."

I tweaked my glasses. I was beginning to feel uncomfortable; I thought my mother's peccadillos had been dealt with. I didn't want to hear it … whatever it was. I interrupted Mrs. Dukes rather more sharply than I intended. "I don't see why I need to know about this. It's over. She's gone."

She smiled indulgently. "I'm not explaining it very well. It was Frankie, that's the girl who answered the door to you the other day. She noticed they were chattering away in French when she took coffee in to them. I thought that was a bit odd and then Frankie told me he wanted to paint your mother's portrait."

"Uh oh, a weirdo," Kate said.

"No he wasn't, not at all. He was quite charming actually. Your mother had started to get muddled and I decided I'd better find out what was going on in case he'd been asking her for money or something. I do have a duty of care to my residents. Alarm bells were ringing at that stage."

"Hang on," Kate said. "Was this the man who came to the funeral?"

"Yes it was. When I asked her about him your mother said he was ... there's no other word for it ... family."

I could not believe what I was hearing. "Family, what do you mean, family?" I asked indignantly, "I know all the family."

"Her nephew, apparently; she said you didn't know about him. She made me promise not to tell you. She said you'd be upset."

That statement did not ring true. My mother had never been bothered whether something would upset me or not. "This is ridiculous, I'm not upset. Why would I be? There are no nephews. My mother only had a sister and she died years ago. She didn't have any children. She never married."

"That doesn't mean she didn't have children," Kate said.

"I know but I went to her funeral in France and there were no sons in evidence then. My father had a sister but she couldn't have children. I know that for a fact."

Mrs. Dukes shrugged her shoulders. "Oh well, I don't know. My thinking was that if he was your cousin you might want to get to know him now your mother's gone."

"Perhaps he was the black sheep of the family," Kate said. "Packed off to Australia and forgotten by the rest of the McBains ..."

"Or the *Marot*s if he was on my mother's side; no, I just don't see it." The whole idea of an unknown nephew, cousin or whatever seemed completely implausible. "Perhaps he was just a con man."

"He seemed perfectly respectable to me," Mrs. Dukes said.

She seemed put-out that I should question her judgment. I decided to give her the benefit of the doubt. "So this 'nephew' was an artist. What was his name?" I asked.

"Robbie Snow."

"I've never heard of him," I said. "And Snow's not a family name."

"I think I've heard of him," Kate said. "I'm sure I read something about a Robbie Snow recently."

"How did he find her?"

"He didn't say but he did make a point of introducing himself to me the next time he came. Frankie must have told him I'd been asking questions. He kept going on about Frankie's cheekbones and then he asked me if it was all right for *her* to pose for him as well."

"What a busy little artist," Kate said. "I hope you told her not to do it."

Her colour rose. She examined her hands and then massaged invisible hand cream into the palms. "I said it would be all right. She sat for him a couple of times in my office, that's all," she said shifting uncomfortably in her seat. "It wasn't anything iffy. He didn't ask her to take off her clothes or anything. He was just fascinated by her cheek bones. He was so pleasant I couldn't see any harm in it."

"R.S. ... Robbie Snow. Could Frankie have been *Electra*?" Kate said.

"She could have been. I said it looked like her, but why did my mother have the picture? Why didn't he take it away or just give it to Frankie?" I noticed Mrs. Dukes' confusion. "We're talking about the picture in that bag you left with Fr. Michael."

"Oh ... I didn't check through it. I asked one of the girls to pack up her things."

"It must have been the one he painted. It was called *Electra*."

"Perhaps he gave it to her as a keepsake," Mrs. Dukes said. "That would have made sense if he was her nephew."

"Did he give you his contact details?" I asked.

"No. I didn't feel I should take them. He wasn't her next of kin or anything like that and he always rang before he visited to make sure it was convenient. That's how he knew about the funeral. I'm sorry I can't tell you more."

I found the whole scenario unbelievable. I did not want to let myself be taken in by some elaborate fairy story made up by my mother. I decided it was all a fabrication of her failing mind. "There are no nephews," I said again, more firmly this time. "I never heard of any scandals; I'm sure my aunt would have told me if there had been. We were quite close."

"I'd like to meet this Robbie Snow," Kate said. "I know where I've seen the name. It was in the local paper; something about an exhibition, I think."

"He might not even be Robbie Snow, famous artist. He could have plucked the name off the internet and used it to make himself look better than he is," I said.

"He obviously has some skill, whatever his name," Kate said. "That portrait's good. Are you sure you don't want to meet him?"

"I could go with you, dear," Mrs. Dukes offered.

"I am, quite sure ..." I said, but I was beginning to waver "... although ... why should it have been a con? She was practically penniless."

"He might not have known that," Kate said.

I shook my head. "We're just going round and round in circles here."

"We know she made stuff up," Kate said.

"It was probably just another of her little games," I concluded wearily.

"Well, he's certainly an artist, whether he's part of your family or not and I'm thinking of having a portrait done," Kate said.

I stared at her. "What?"

"I think a portrait of Iris might be amusing."

Mrs. Dukes looked bewildered. "Iris?" she said. "Is that your daughter?"

"No," Kate said.

"Your sister?" she asked.

"No. I was quite attached to her once. She taught me a lot. I don't want to forget her."

"Oh, I see," she said with an understanding smile. "It's always difficult when a relationship breaks down. Do you still see her?"

I thought she might not get Kate's bizarre sense of humour. I decided to intervene before the joke went too far. "Not exactly," I said. "Tell her the truth, Kate."

There was laughter that evening when she narrated the story for Diana's benefit. "You are naughty, Kate; poor Mrs. Dukes."

"I explained afterwards. She didn't mind."

"I wonder why he suddenly turned up like that … out of the blue," Diana said.

"I wish I'd made an effort to speak to him at the funeral, now," Kate said.

"This is all very boring," I said. "I can't imagine why you're both so interested. I don't care who he is."

Kate was not prepared to leave it. "I'm going to my art class next week, if I feel up to it. I might find out something then. They're bound to know where Robbie Snow hangs out; they're a cliquey bunch these artists and then at least we'll find out if he's pukka or not."

"Chris is home," Diana said. "I heard the car. Let's ask him if he knows about Robbie Snow. Someone in the art department may have mentioned him."

The door opened and Christian's head popped round it and then the rest of his bulk. "Ah," he said, "Is there space for a little one?"

"There's always space for you," Kate said. She patted the cushion beside her.

He meandered into the room and sat down in the middle of the settee, squashing her into the corner. "How are you, my darling?" he asked after he had kissed both of her hands.

She laughed. "All the better for seeing you. Now move over we need you to be sensible. Do you know someone called Robbie Snow?"

He shuffled away from her. "Snow, Snow, quick quick Snow. I don't think so ... why?" He frowned at her. "Is this a trick question?"

"He's an artist," Diana said.

"He painted *Electra*," I said. "Di and Kate seem to be obsessed with him."

"Ah Electra," he said. "Now you're talking. What a girl, what a play, the passion and fire ... those Greeks and their tortured souls; evil mothers, wicked stepfathers, wronged daughters, all thrown into the mix for good measure, great stuff."

"Be serious, Chris," Diana said. "Has anyone at school ever mentioned a Robbie Snow? He's a local artist."

"His name rings absolutely no bells, beloved, unlike yours," he said throwing her a beaming smile.

"Hmm evil mothers and wronged daughters," Kate said. "That could be significant. I wonder if *Electra* was meant to tell you something, Genie."

"Like what?" I said. I was beginning to dislike *Electra* despite her charms.

"Did you bring the painting with you?" Diana said.

"No I packed it in my case ready to take home with me."

Kate reached for her bag. "One of your senior moments," she said as she rummaged about in it. "You only *think* you did. You left it on the hall table. I've got it here. I had an idea Chris might be able to help solve the mystery," she added as she produced it with a flourish.

161

She made me smile. She still had all her marbles, despite Iris; in fact she was more with it than me. "It's a good job someone knows what they're doing," I said.

Christian considered the painting. "V-e–r-y good," he said. "I like it." He turned it over to examine the back, "Fourteen The Pineries. That's the new gallery behind Carluccios. I walked passed it last week when I took a bunch of kids to the theatre."

Kate's eyes gleamed. "So it is. I remember now. That article I mentioned? It wasn't an exhibition; it was all about a new gallery opening in town. Well done, Chris."

"Do I win a prize?" he asked.

"You can have one of my chocolates," Diana said. "They're those Belgian ones you like."

"Where did these come from?" he asked eyeing the box greedily.

"Genie gave them to me."

"I'll have the caramel one, thanks," he said and passed the box back to her.

"I wonder why he didn't make himself known to us at the funeral," she said. "Mrs. Dukes must have explained who we were."

"That proves he's not family or he would have done," I said. "My mother was making it up so that he seemed more respectable and he just went along with it to please her."

"This puzzle is exactly what I need," Kate said. "It's a gift … an antidote to Iris, if you like; something else for me to think about."

"I want you to leave it," I said.

Christian scratched his head. "I haven't a clue what you're on about. I need a beer," he said and ambled out of the room.

"I'm planning to do a lot of walking in the next few months," Kate went on. "I want to keep fit. I'm not going to let Iris get the upper hand."

"You don't want to do too much too soon," Diana said.

"You sound like Cerys," I said. "She's always telling *me* not to do too much."

"The Pineries is as good a place to start as any. It can't be more than a mile from the house and it's a pleasant walk past the war memorial. It won't be too tiring."

I sighed. "Do you have to? I'm trying to draw a line here."

"It'll be fun playing Miss Marple," she said.

"What harm could it do, Genie? You know she's not going to let it go," Diana said.

"I fail to understand how some mysterious painting by an unknown artist could be germane to my life," I said.

"It might be," Kate said. "You just don't know."

"It will take her mind off things," Diana said.

I was obviously wasting my breath. They were ganging up on me. I didn't stand a chance even though the whole idea was laughable. "All right, all right, I give in," I said. "But don't blame me if it all goes wrong."

Chapter 21

I left for home the following afternoon satisfied that Kate was well enough to manage on her own. It was too late to check on the garden when I got back, but I was straight outside after breakfast the next morning.

It was early, too early for the traffic hum; just me, the birds and the bees out there, my favourite part of the day. Everything fresh, hours stretching ahead waiting to be filled with, well, you could never be quite sure what.

It was not long before Becky discovered me out there, dead-heading the fuchsias. I had always had success with them. They provided effortless colour in even the shadiest spot and they were easy to propagate. I loved their exotic blooms, delicate and yet so hardy; I called them my botanical ballerinas. I stroked the tutu of a particularly pretty example, bright lilac with veined cerise towards the centre, the giant stamens dangling delicately downwards like the legs of a prima in pumps. I was brought down to earth with a bump.

"Gran, Gran; you're back."

I turned to see the child hurtling towards me. I welcomed her into my arms. She clutched at me fiercely, her face hidden in my fleece. "How are you Becky? Did you miss me?"

Her voice was muffled. "Yes."

She seemed reluctant to let me go which was both unusual and alarming. "Let's go in and get a drink," I said as we walked towards the house hand in hand. "What's been happening while I've been away? I want to know about school, home, everything."

"Nothing much," she said and then clammed up.

"I don't believe that. How are all your friends?" No information was volunteered. She had nothing to tell me about school. There were no questions about my trip. Something was very wrong. What had happened in my absence?

I opened the back door and kicked off my crocs, heading for the fridge. "Would you like some apple juice?" I asked. The child nodded. "How's your mum?"

"You saw her last night."

"Yes, but only for a few minutes. She was going out somewhere."

"Aerobics," Becky said. "Dad came round to keep me company."

"He came round?" Now I was even more worried. Was the rift more serious than I had imagined?

"He's moved into the flat over the restaurant."

The ferrets were back. I tried to breathe deeply and then faked a cough to oust them. How could things have gone so wrong while I had been away? "I see," I said.

"They had a big row," she said. "I hid in my bedroom."

"Oh Becky, I'm so sorry." I felt desperately sad for her. I of all people knew how she felt. I knew the situation from both sides. I could not figure out why Cerys had not mentioned such a fundamental change in their circumstances to me.

"Can we look at the photos?" she said in a small voice. I understood. She needed the comfort of the familiar. "We'll go and sit in the lounge," I said. "Bring your drink with you. Here, I've found you something nice." I produced a small chocolate bar I had been intending for my elevenses. "It's a 'welcome home' treat."

"Thanks, Gran."

When she left, I was free to consider my options. I could intervene in some way to help mend the marriage or leave Cerys and Kit to sort it out between them. At the moment that seemed unlikely. I really wanted to help rekindle their affection for each other. I found it hard to accept that this was the end of everything. They had always been so happy together. It was simply not possible to fake affection like theirs.

There had been a gang of them at school, girls and boys always in each other's pockets. Some had paired off early but Kit and Cerys had remained friends until, as so often happens, their friendship blossomed into romance some years later. There had been a fairytale wedding and a seamless move into parenthood. I did not believe such a strong bond could be broken but before I did anything, I had to speak to my daughter. That would have to wait. I knew she was busy with a conference at work until later. What was the worst that could happen? She could tell me to mind my own business.

I avoided her the next day while I mulled it all over and then telephoned her that evening. "Sorry to call you so late," I said. "I wondered if you were free for a coffee some time tomorrow."

"Becky told you, didn't she?"

"She said Kit had moved out, if that's what you mean; how about lunch instead?"

There was a pause while she considered my offer. "All right, I finish at twelve tomorrow. I'll come round then."

At least she was prepared to talk. It was a start.

I didn't sleep well that night. My head was full of sorrows past and fears for the future but I had lunch ready in good time, sandwiches and a couple of filter coffees. Kate rang to give me an update just before Cerys was due. "Well, I've been," she said.

"Where have you been?"

"The Pineries of course; the square looks amazing. Not a cigarette end in sight and no paper cups rolling about the place, either. It made me think of one of those little squares in France."

"It won't stay like that for long."

"I hope it does. There don't seem to be any take-aways."

"Did you visit the gallery?"

"I did indeed. I took one of my watercolours. I finished it last year but I'd never bothered to get it framed. They had some fantastic pieces of art in there ... put my feeble efforts to shame."

"What sort of things?"

"Landscapes, giant portraits of pop stars; one-off sculptures, misty water colours. There was a lot of gorgeous glass too. Next time you're here you'll have to come and see for yourself."

"It sounds good."

"You'll love it. The girl behind the counter said they hadn't been open long."

"That's why it wasn't on the Google map."

"It must be. They had a place out of town before. I told her I was looking for a painting by Robbie Snow and, guess what? He owns the gallery. They had a few of his pieces on display. Most of his best ones are up in London apparently. He's exhibiting in Islington for the next two weeks."

"Sounds like he's doing all right ... does he take commissions?"

"That's the best bit. He does," she said. "She gave me one of his cards and some brochures. There was a photo of him on the front of one of them."

"Does it look like the nephew?"

"I'm not sure. If it is him, he was much younger when the photo was taken. I'm going to see Mrs. Dukes and ask her if she recognises him."

We chattered on for a bit until I heard the door. "I'll have to go, now," I said. "Cerys has just arrived."

"Is everything all right?"

"There have been ... um ... developments. I'll call you later," I said and hastily returned to my seat by the window.

"Mum."

"I'm in the lounge," I called.

She looked harassed and a little apprehensive. I tried a reassuring smile. "I've got ham or cheese and pickle," I said. I had spent a long time deciding on the best way to say what I wanted to say. I was only going to mention Kit in passing. I hoped she would open up without too much probing.

"Ham, please," she said. She sat down and I passed a plate over to her. "Thanks. I haven't got long. I promised to help Dale this afternoon."

"How is she? I haven't seen her for ages."

"Still as chaotic as ever, that's why she needs help with her filing. I was going to ask you to pick up Becky so I can get on with the invoices." I had a vision of a teenage Dale walking to school with Cerys, one sock up, one sock down, books spilling out of her bag, her drinks flask dripping down the road behind her like Hansel and Gretel's bread trail. She may have been disorganised but she was also a successful businesswoman and a good friend to Cerys. I wondered if she knew what was going on.

"I'll do that, no problem. It was Becky I wanted to talk to you about ... amongst other things." Cerys nodded and munched away at her sandwich. "She was quite upset yesterday."

"I know. It's all this business with Kit and me."

"Exactly ... so ... do you want to talk about it?"

"Not really."

That was not very encouraging but I wasn't prepared to be put off. "Has he been having an affair?"

"I don't know for sure but things aren't good between us."

"Can't you work things out, for Becky's sake?"

"If we're not happy, she won't be, and besides, we managed without Dad. Becky will manage fine without Kit," she said treating me to a flinty glare.

I tweaked my glasses. "It wasn't quite the same for us. I had no choice and your father *was* having an affair."

"I know all about that."

This was it. The moment I had been dreading. "No, you don't," I said.

She put the empty plate back on the tray and looked at me as if I had gone mad. "What do you mean? I've heard the story a million times. I know it off by heart."

"You don't know all of it."

"What else is there?"

"I didn't tell you about the other woman …"

"You said it was his secretary, someone much younger than you."

"Well, I didn't tell you the truth." I felt like an Olympic swimmer about to dive. Once the words were out of my mouth it would be for Cerys to decide if I would sink or swim. I had to do it, whatever the consequences. It might just make a difference. Kit's misdemeanours could never be as bad as her father's and were therefore possibly forgivable. I filled my lungs with air and jumped. "It was Lettie."

I watched the colour drain from her cheeks. She opened her mouth to speak but no sound came out. I waited for what seemed like forever as she continued to gape at me. "Lettie … your mother?" she said eventually, or rather squeaked, her voice rising in disbelief.

I sighed. "Yes, my wonderful, glamorous, exotic, un-motherly, mother."

"I don't believe you."

"She was very young when she had me. I don't think her maternal instincts had kicked in." I was still making excuses for her. I had to get out of that habit. "She saw me as a rival not a daughter. Now can you see why I didn't want to tell Becky everything?" She looked stunned. "I didn't want to tell you either, but as you're having this trouble with Kit I thought you should know." I could see distaste and shock in her face. "However unsavoury it is, it's true."

"How could she have done that to you?"

"It takes two, you know."

"Yes, but honestly, it's awful. You can't tell Becky, you really can't. Does Kate know?"

"Di and Kate both know. They had to pick up the pieces after he left. Even then I was prepared to have him back for your sake … and mine. It never happened. He died before I had a chance to ask him to re-consider."

"How can you be so reasonable about it?"

"He was the love of my life. I was prepared to forgive him even after what he'd done. My mother was everything I wasn't. He was dazzled by her. She seemed to be irresistible to men. They were round her like bees round a honey pot after Papa left. I couldn't compete with that. My only chance was to wait until she got fed up with him but it wasn't to be. Kit isn't like your father. Your relationship with him has always been good."

"It was once, not any longer."

I let that pass. "Looking back, I'm not sure now that ours ever was. It was a bit one-sided. There was the age difference for a start and then it was tainted by his mother and ruined by mine. You can't just give up on Kit because of suspicions. You have to get to the truth and then you have to talk about it, see if you can salvage your relationship."

"I don't understand how it happened," she said. "How could he? How could *she*?"

I did not know what else to say. I had felt exactly the same at the time. That was not important now. My major concern was Becky and how her parents' relationship problems were affecting her. I wanted to move the discussion on. "I'm worried about Becky. You must understand how she feels. I know how she feels. Don't you remember how hard it was for us? You can't let her suffer like we did, please. What can I do to help?"

She shook her head. "Nothing, Mum, you can't do anything."

"There must be something … I know, I'll give Becky her tea tonight. You can go and see Kit straight from Dale's. Spend some time with him. Try and find a way back."

"I don't know; there have been so many hurtful things said."

I felt as if I was turning into an agony aunt but it had to be done. "You've got a lot to lose if you don't even attempt to mend things. Becky doesn't understand. She needs both her parents. Do it for her."

"How do you get over something like that?" she said ignoring my plea.

"When you have a child to consider you have to. It was hard. I don't know what I'd have done without Kate and Diana. I've drawn a line under all the heartache. That was then and this is now," I said firmly. "Shall I give Becky her tea? Will you talk to Kit?"

"It won't do any good."

"You don't know that. It has to be worth a try."

"I'll think about it." The thinking was short-lived. I could tell she really wanted to. "Ok then, but don't expect miracles."

Becky greeted me with a smile and a kiss when I went to collect her after school. It was a poignant moment. I realised it might not be much longer before she would be too embarrassed to acknowledge me in such a way in public. "Where's Mum?"

"She's helping Dale this afternoon. She asked if I could pick you up. I thought it would be fun for us to have tea together. We haven't done that in ages."

"Can we have fish fingers?"

"If you like," I said.

"And chips?"

I frowned. "Can you have fish fingers without chips?" She giggled and tucked her hand into mine. "I've found a DVD for us to watch later."

"What is it?"

"It's one of the *Worst Witches*. You still like those, don't you?" Her eyes lit up and she nodded. "And I've bought munchies," I said lifting up my shopping bag as we walked along so that she could catch a glimpse of the goodies inside.

"Ooh … popcorn and coke, thanks, Gran."

"How was school?"

"Okaaay," she said.

"Is there a problem? I hope it's not that Gemma Stokes again."

"Mia Bailey's off sick. I've got no-one to play with at break-time." I was surprised. I had the impression she had lots of friends at school. "Well, not no-one exactly," she went on, "But they're not Mia."

I was glad then that I had decided to treat her. Without Mia's listening ear she had lost her safety valve. "Never mind, I expect she'll be back soon. In you go. Wash your hands and then you can lay the table."

The evening passed quickly. We did not talk about her parents splitting up and anyway I was hoping that would be some way to being sorted by the time she went home. My hopes were dashed the minute I saw Cerys's face when she arrived to pick her up.

"Did you manage to have a chat?" I asked.

"No. He knew I was waiting for him but he didn't show up."

"Were they busy again?"

"Yes, but he could have spared five minutes, couldn't he? It's useless, Mum. He doesn't want to know."

I was disappointed. What on earth was Kit playing at? "You can't just give up. Do you want me to talk to him?"

"No, I do not. Shh … Becky's coming."

Becky emerged from the lounge dragging her feet. "Hi Mum. Do we *have* to go now?" she asked.

"Yes we do, it's already late. Have you got everything?"

"Your school bag's in the kitchen," I said turning the child round by her shoulders and giving her a gentle push. I wanted to have one more try at making Cerys see sense. "Try again, please," I whispered. "Give him one more chance. You just need to sit down and talk."

"Got it," Becky called from the kitchen.

"Why are you so keen for us to stay together?" Cerys whispered back. "Surely if things aren't good between us it's better to have a clean break."

"No. Becky needs her Dad, just like you needed yours … and I needed mine."

Cerys left with Becky and I was left with my thoughts. I was determined not to give up on their marriage until the divorce papers dropped through the letter box. It was all so depressing. I needed a lift. I went to call Kate to give her the promised update. "Sorry I couldn't chat this morning," I said. "How are you feeling?"

"Not too bad, it's healing nicely. I'm just gearing up for the first dose of chemo, now."

"Do you have to stay in hospital for that?"

"Only for a couple of hours ... I hope it doesn't make me sick."

"Are you going to have one of those ice caps to stop your hair falling out? There was a big article about them in the Mail."

"I can't be bothered. It's really short as it is. I'm keen to get on with it now and come out the other side."

"That's good. We don't want any negativity."

"I've got something else to tell you. I've been to see Mrs. Dukes."

"What did she say?"

"He is the real thing."

"I'm not sure where this is going. He might be Robbie Snow, artist, but it doesn't mean he's my cousin."

"No, but you know that portrait I was talking about, I wasn't joking, I am going to have me painted in the altogether."

"Kate, really," I said.

"I don't expect you to understand how I feel ..."

"Try me."

"I'm clean now Iris has gone; fresh and more interesting. I've lost a few pounds. I like my shape better and it's such a great scar. I'm quite proud of it. My body's looking good. I want to celebrate that."

"Of course you do."

"I'll be able to quiz him about *Electra* without him suspecting a thing."

"That's going a bit far don't you think?"

"Not at all, it's a project, a goal. It'll give me a reason to keep going and get to the end of this wretched chemo."

"Well, if you think it will help ... have you told Di?"

"She just laughed. I don't think she believed me."

"Is she going to the hospital with you?"

"She is. How's the Cerys situation? You said there had been developments. Is that good or bad?"

"I'm not sure. It might help in the short term. He's moved out."

"Oh no; that's such a shame."

"Exactly, so I decided to tell her about Lettie and Arthur."

"I get it … kill or cure. How did she take it?"

"She was shocked," I said.

"As you would be; it was a bizarre situation."

"I was hoping it might put things into perspective for her. What could be worse than what her father did? Kit hasn't done that. He might not be guilty of anything except overwork. He needs to be given a chance."

"I see where you're coming from ..."

"Is there a 'but' in there?"

"Well you can't compare the two," Kate said. "You don't know what else has been going on."

"Probably nothing. Anyway, I hope it works. Poor Becky is really suffering."

"I knew she would be. Her whole life's been turned inside out. Why don't you bring her here when the holidays start? I'll be between treatments and more or less ok according to those in the know."

"I suppose it might cheer her up to spend quality time with us. Cerys and Kit could definitely use some time together without her."

"That's what I'm thinking."

"I'll have a word with Cerys, see what she says. Thanks, Kate."

I told Cerys about Kate's idea the next night while Becky was at Brownies. Her reaction was lukewarm to say the least. "I've got the weeks mapped out, Mum, nothing too stressful; swimming, cinema, meeting up with friends; the odd day out."

"We won't be away long. You'll have plenty of time to do all that with her. If Becky's not here you can discuss things with Kit without interruptions. He must be able to take some time off, surely."

She frowned. "You'd think so, wouldn't you?"

"You could both do with a break. You look worn out."

"It's all this worry. It doesn't seem to matter how long I sleep I'm still tired when I wake up."

"Take the initiative; suggest it. I'm sure he'll agree."

"I get the impression he doesn't want to spend any time with me or discuss anything. It's like he's deliberately pushing me away."

"Why would he do that?"

"So that I finally tell him where to go maybe … and then it wouldn't be his fault if our marriage fails?"

"That doesn't sound like Kit. He's not manipulative. Why are you so convinced he's having an affair?"

"Because he's always finding excuses for us not to be together; because he doesn't care when I tell him how upset I am; because I make plans to include him and he lets me down at the last minute. Becky's noticed. She asked me if he had a 'special friend' he liked better than us." I remembered her asking me the same question. Unshed tears glittered in my daughter's eyes and I wondered if I could be wrong. Could there be something to her suspicions after all? Was their relationship irreparable? She stood up clutching her cardigan to her chest. "I've got to fetch Becky. I know you think I should try, Mum but I doubt if anything I do is going to change the situation."

"I'm sorry. I didn't realise it was so bad. I'd still like to take her away. She needs to be able to relax and forget her parents' problems for a few days. All this pressure isn't good for her or for you for that matter."

"No, you're right. It will do her good. I'll tell her this evening."

I was so distressed at what she had said that I found it difficult to sleep that night. I made up my mind to pay Kit a visit without telling her; I wanted to see if he would talk to me, explain how he felt about everything. Perhaps I could make him see things from a different angle.

I knew Cerys would be cross if I told her what I had in mind. She would probably try and stop me but I'd decided that what she didn't know wouldn't hurt her. I remembered her saying she was due at work early in the morning. If I called at the restaurant before the lunch-time rush, I stood more chance of a private chat with him without her finding out.

Chapter 22

The next day I cycled to the restaurant and sauntered in through the door, helmet slung over my arm like a rifle, remembering Clint Eastwood in one of my favourite films. I was ready to exact my '*Fistful of Dollars.*' It was not difficult to find an isolated table. There were not many customers about. The breakfast rush was over and it was too early for the ladies who lunched. I ordered a cappuccino and asked the waitress to tell Kit I was there.

He arrived with the coffee and despite what Cerys had told me the previous evening, seemed pleased to see me. His hair had been recently cut and he was clean-shaven, no designer stubble in sight. His white chef's tunic was crisp and spotless. He looked in charge of his life and his restaurant. Only his eyes gave away the strain of the previous few weeks to anyone who knew him well. "Hi Genie, how are you?" He bent down to kiss my cheek. "What can I do for you?"

I wasn't sure how to begin. I did not want to waste my one chance to influence things by alienating him. I started with a smile. "I haven't seen you for weeks," I said. "I wanted to check how everything was coming on. You don't mind, do you?"

"No, of course not." He glanced around. "We're doing all right. Most of the wrinkles have been ironed out but that restaurant round the corner is hot competition. It means hours of hard graft for us to keep ahead."

"Are you living in?"

He avoided my eyes. "I am at the moment. Some nights I'm not finished until one."

"We missed you at the funeral."

"Yes. I'm sorry about that. There was a major glitch with one of the ovens. I couldn't leave everything to Bob. That's sorted now. Cerys said it went well."

"It was fine," I said. "Although it dragged up all sorts of unpleasant memories; we had a difficult relationship as you know."

"Yes."

He looked uneasy. I thought the small talk had gone on for long enough. I did not want him called away before I'd been able to say my piece. "Cards on the table time," I said, shifting uneasily in my seat.

"What do you mean?"

I tweaked my glasses and swept some stray curls away from my forehead, heart hammering in my chest. I felt very uncomfortable interfering in their lives but this was a gamble I had to take for my daughter's sake. "I'm worried about Cerys … and Becky. Neither of them is very happy at the moment. Cerys thinks you might be having an affair." The words were out. I covered my embarrassment with more words. "I realise mothers in law are supposed to keep their distance but I hate to see them unhappy, so I'm asking you now, are you or aren't you?"

He picked up a menu from the table and flicked a corner with his forefinger and thumb, mouth set, eyes fixed. "I know that's what Cerys thinks ... it doesn't seem to matter how many times I tell her I'm not, she won't believe me. I'm doing all this for us but that's not good enough apparently. She's testing me all the time. It's like she wants to push me to breaking point. It's always about Cerys. I moved out to get time to think. I'm sorry Becky's suffering. It's not her fault."

I could feel myself getting irritated. It did not seem to bother him that his wife felt hurt and sidelined; and how could he not have noticed his daughter's distress? "No, it's not Becky's fault but she's beginning to think you don't care; I'm worried it didn't occur to you that she *might* be upset. She's a sensitive child. She understands more than you think."

"I'm sorry she's upset, of course I am, but to be honest I haven't had time to consider her feelings. I knew she had her mother and you. I thought that would be enough. I needed a bit of space, that's all. Cerys has got a blind spot where the restaurant's concerned. She won't accept that there's a mountain of work to do to get it running smoothly."

"Have you tried talking to her?"

"She won't listen. What can I do?"

"Try again." He was the one with the blind spot. He could not see that Cerys needed his affection and reassurance. It was then that I realised I was also at fault. I had not noticed that my daughter was so insecure. "Cerys remembers her father leaving. She doesn't want Becky to lose her father in the same way. I hoped she'd come through all that unscathed but it seems she hasn't. It's all so complicated, more complicated than you can imagine. You should ask her about it, ask her what went on. You have to get together and sort this out before it goes too far."

"I don't know. What good will it do; why go over all that again, hurting each other? She'll only accuse me of not caring. I've had enough, Genie."

I heard sadness in his voice. I sensed his hopelessness and realised that he was as upset as she was. My help was vital to them both. My heart went out to him. "You won't know unless you try. I think it will be different this time. She needs you, Kit. They both do."

Arthur had given no-one a chance to talk him out of his decision to leave; if only his father had not died so suddenly. He might have spoken up. If only my father had not left my mother. None of this would have happened if he had stayed at home. He had been the beginning of it all. I wanted to be the end.

"I'm very fond of you, Kit. You're like the son I never had. I want you both to be happy. You were made for each other. It might not feel like that at the moment but you have to work at a relationship. It's never plain sailing. Look, I'm taking Becky up to Liverpool to see Kate when school breaks up. I'd like you to find time while we're away to sort out your marriage. You can't just give up on your family. I know you. I don't believe that's what you want. They mean too much to you."

The words were spilling out of me. I couldn't judge how they were being received but I carried on regardless. "Forget about the restaurant for a few days. Take Cerys away somewhere. It'll all still be here when you come back." I was surprised at my forceful delivery but my daughter's troubles had always brought out the tiger in me.

"Has she agreed to this?"

"She doesn't know anything about it. I didn't tell her I was coming to see you. She doesn't need to know," I said. "This idea has to come from you. If you don't do something soon it might be way past doing anything to mend your marriage and that would be tragic for everyone."

"Why are you doing this, Genie?"

I heard Clint's voice. I knew what to say. "Why? Because I knew someone like you once and there was no-one there to help."

I had to wait a while to see if my little stratagem had worked. I thought it best not to broach the subject with Cerys again and much as I wanted to find out what was going on, I resisted the urge to ask. I concentrated on keeping Kate's spirits up instead. I called her every other day to check on her progress. She had good days and bad days, which was only to be expected. She seemed to be getting weaker. I was counting the days until the chemo would be over and she could recover her strength.

After the third treatment her mood was low. So low it was much harder for me to cheer her. "I'm sorry you're not feeling too good," I said.

"Come on now, what did you expect? I'm being poisoned. My body's protesting."

"But you're poisoning the cancer cells at the same time."

"Tell my stomach that. It doesn't help, Genie."

"Sorry."

"I'm thinking of giving the radiotherapy a miss."

"Is that wise?"

"It could do more harm than good. I'm still researching it." I didn't know what to make of that. It was her choice of course and I knew it would be an informed one when she made it. It wasn't for me to influence her either way. "At my age, I think I'd rather take my chances with what I've done so far. I'll finish the chemo."

"Ok," I said. I trusted her judgment. It was her body after all. "Becky's getting excited about our trip," I said.

"I hope I'll be up to it."

"Do you want to cancel? We could come some other time."

"No way, she needs a holiday and anyway I want to see you. I'm going to make sure I feel all right. Feed me some more positive vibes."

"Right, well, the worst's over. You only have three more sessions of chemo, two by the time we come … and I'm bringing peppermint creams."

"I can't wait. I've made an appointment to see Robbie Snow while you're here. You could come with me if you like."

"I don't know."

"You don't have to decide now. I'm too tired to chat any more. I need a lie-down."

"Speak to you soon." I put the phone down with a sigh. I'd been doing a lot of sighing since I found out about Iris. It was a timely reminder that none of us goes on forever.

Why would I want to meet Robbie Snow? I walked out into the garden to mull it over and heard Cerys calling from the house. "Mum, mum, I've got something to tell you."

I tweaked out a nettle and turned to face her as she joined me. "What is it? You look as if you've lost a penny and found a pound."

"Kit's asked me to go to Cornwall with him while you're away. He wants to try out the Rick Stein place, see if he can adapt some of the menus."

"That's wonderful," I said feeling smug. "Are you going with him?"

"Do you think I should? It's a long way from Liverpool if there's a problem."

"There won't be a problem; it's up to you."

"I can't decide. What if we just argue the whole time?"

"There's a simple answer to that. Don't argue. Bite your tongue if you have to … 'save your breath to cool your, porridge', as Nana McBain would have said; that was one of her favourites." I wanted her to decide for herself. If she suspected I was attempting to influence her in any way, it might have the opposite effect to the one I wanted.

"We do need to talk," she said.

"So … you'll be going, then?"

She nodded. "I think I will. Thanks Mum." She gave me a hug.

I was pleased my plan had worked. "Make the most of it," I said. "But I'm not sure why you're thanking me."

"For helping me to make up my mind; can I tell him about Dad and Lettie?"

"I think you should. I'm tired of all the secrets. Talking of which, you know I told you about Robbie Snow, well, Kate's going to meet him. It *was* him and not a conman."

"That could be interesting."

"I've never met an artist before; I might go with her. It will be a new experience. I'm always telling Becky to be brave and try out new things."

"Perhaps he'll want to paint your portrait."

We linked arms as we strolled back to the house. "Well he'll be out of luck," I said. "Who'd want to look at me?"

"I noticed *Electra* on the wall in the lounge."

"I thought I might as well put her up. Louisa didn't want her. She looks good in there, doesn't she?"

"It's like she's always been there."

"Right, well if that's all, I have to go and find the peppermint cream recipe. I told Kate we'd be taking some with us."

"Save some for me," she said.

"I'll make sure there's plenty for everyone," I said as I watched her walk off home; there was a spring in her step. I had done all I could. Now it was up to them.

Chapter 23

Becky and I boarded the train for Liverpool just over a week later. Kate had had her fourth dose of chemo a few days earlier. Diana had reported that the side effects were worse than ever. Hopefully she should be recovering a little by the time we got there. We would have to tailor our activities to suit her energy levels.

Becky could not sit still. "I've never been on a long train journey before," she said as we got under way. Her eyes were shining as she looked this way and that. It was almost as if she wanted to soak up everything she could in the least possible time.

"Take off your coat. I'll fold it up next to mine," I said. "Let's swap places. You sit by the window. We're going to travel through some lovely countryside but we go so fast you'll miss most of it unless you keep your eyes peeled. Did Mum give you a drink for the journey?"

She climbed over my legs and heaved her rucksack onto her knees. "Yes and snacks for us, too." She unscrewed the lid of her drink flask. "Do you want some, Gran?"

"No thanks, I've got my water."

"Mia Bailey's jealous I'm going on an adventure," she said as she tucked into a mini box of raisins.

"It is a bit of an adventure. Auntie Kate's got all sorts planned for us."

"Are we going to see Di and Chris?"

"I expect so."

"And …" the child hesitated.

"And … what …?" I asked.

"Aunt Sadie," she said in a small voice.

My smile ebbed away. "If you like," I said. She had surprised me again. I thought Sadie had been a passing fancy; who knew what went on in that head of hers?

"I'm going to read for a bit," I said.

Becky pulled a book from her bag and we sat in silence for a while until she became restless again. "Can you see the cows?" she said.

We were travelling past empty fields enclosed by scrubby hedges coated in dust from the track. In the distance, standing aloof, remote, withdrawn like spent cotton reels, were the power station cooling towers that had dominated the horizon for as long as I could remember. I scanned the hillside between. It was dotted with cows, mud-spattered, ruminant, tails flicking from side to side. "Yes, over there."

"And on the other side, see? Big black ones," she said pointing them out to me.

"Oh yes. Some of them are lying down," I said. "It must be going to rain. Let's play, I spy. I spy with my little eye something beginning with 'T'."

"I know," she said straight away, "Tree."

I shook my head. She glanced around the carriage for a while and then contemplated the landscape outside the window. She gave me a beaming smile. "I know, I know, tractor."

"Well done ... it's your turn."

"I spy with my little eye … something beginning with 'C'." She leant her shoulders against the back of the seat with a self-satisfied smile.

"Cat," I said without looking.

"No."

"It has to be caravan, then."

"No. Where's the caravan?" she asked, staring out of the window.

I laughed. "Nowhere, I was just guessing."

"Concentrate, Gran," she said.

"This is my last go," I said. "Cloud, it has to be cloud."

"No. Shall I tell you?" I nodded. "Carriage," she said.

"That's very good."

"Now it's you," she said.

We played on until neither of us could think of another suitable word. "Let's do a crossword, instead," I said.

We finished the puzzle as we were crossing the Runcorn Bridge and not long after that we pulled into Lime Street station. I did not experience the sense of apprehension which usually overwhelmed me at the end of this journey. There was no longer the duty visit to my mother to be endured. I was excited; looking forward to spending time with my friends and showing Becky some of our favourite places. Diana was there to meet us. She was alone. "Where's Kate, is she all right?" I asked.

"She's a bit tired, that's all. She'll be feeling better tomorrow. She can't wait to see you both."

"How's everything going?"

"Not too bad. We're two thirds of the way through now. All her hair's gone. We bought her some little hats to keep her head warm. I told her she looked like a rabbi. It gave us a laugh choosing them."

"We've bought Auntie Kate some ginger tea. Mum said it was good for nausea," Becky said. "That means feeling sick," she added.

"Good," Di said. "She has been feeling a bit sick."

"I hate feeling sick," Becky said.

"I think everyone does," Diana said. "Auntie Kate hasn't been too bad considering, but I'm sure she'll like the tea."

"How's she been managing?" I asked.

"So-so. She's not up to cooking. I've made a casserole. I put it in the oven before I came to fetch you. You're all eating at Windgather tomorrow. Chris has been planning the menu for days."

"Yum," Becky said. "Will Lucy be there?"

"She's away, I'm afraid, travelling."

"Oh … where's she gone?"

"All sorts of places; when you come round we'll get the atlas out and I'll show you."

"Can't we use Google Maps?" Becky asked.

"There speaks a true child of the millennium," I said. "Books are boring."

Becky looked peeved. "No they're not."

"We could, but I thought I'd get some crayons out and you could trace the route to and from Australia," Diana said. "We can flip backwards and forwards and count the miles." Diana had not changed. She always knew how to make learning fun for a child.

Becky's face was a picture. "You'll let me draw on your book?"

"Of course I will. You won't be spoiling it you'll be making it come alive. When Lucy comes home I'll be able to show her what you've done. She'll see how far she's travelled and when I look at the atlas in the future I'll remember all your hard work and Lucy's trip … and you."

Becky positively glowed.

Kate was asleep when we arrived. Her room was in darkness. I tiptoed away from the door without disturbing her.

"Can I go up and see her?" Becky asked.

"No, she's asleep. You'll see her tomorrow. Aren't you hungry?" She nodded. "Let's get the casserole on the table and then you can watch some telly before you go to bed."

We made short work of Diana's casserole and after I had sorted Becky out and tidied up downstairs, I went back to check on Kate.

A bedside light cast a gentle glow in the room. I was shocked at the change in her. She was lying under the patchwork quilt, eyes dull and cheeks gaunt as she stared up at me. This defeated shadow was not our Kate. The little skull cap she was wearing, like Di had said, gave her the appearance of someone in holy orders.

I walked over to the bed and kissed her pale cheek. I noticed her eyelashes were missing and the skin was smooth and bare where her eyebrows should have been. "Hello." I was saddened to see a solitary tear roll down her cheek. I tried not to show it. "How's it going? You look like Cardinal Richelieu."

She grimaced. "Thanks," she said. "It's hard. I didn't realise how awful I'd feel and then there's this tiredness … the tiredness is a killer. I hardly do anything most days until the chemo wears off and then just when I'm feeling more or less like me, it's time for the next dose."

"It must be worse being on your own."

"I feel so isolated. I used to go out such a lot. People phone of course but being stuck here not being able to do anything … it's just not me."

I squeezed her hand. "You're two thirds of the way through according to our mathematician; that's nearly there. You can do this."

"Sometimes it's hard to put a positive spin on things," she said.

"You're allowed to get fed up once in a while. You can't be positive all the time."

"Where's your lamp, Genie? I need some of your magic."

I smiled. She must have perked up a bit if she remembered our old joke. "Sadly I didn't bring my lamp but I have brought Becky."

"Dear little Becky. How is she?"

"She's desperate to see you. I told her she'd have to wait until the morning. She's reading in bed; she feels very grown up to be away from her parents and so excited about everything."

"Did Cerys go with Kit in the end?"

"We saw them off yesterday. Fingers crossed they'll come back better friends."

"Amen to that."

"Do you want me to get you something to eat?" I asked. She shook her head. "How about some ginger tea, then, it might help."

"I don't have any."

"We brought some with us."

"In that case, yes please. Di's been a saint. She brings me little tit bits to tempt me and on the days I'm feeling ok she's there to take me out for a coffee or something. Have you both got what you need?"

"Don't worry about us. Cerys made me pack everything *and* the kitchen sink. Anyone would think I'd never taken a child on holiday before."

She managed a smile. "It's good to have you here, Genie. Tell Becky I'll see her tomorrow and then the fun will begin."

The following morning I was up early. I checked on Becky. She was still fast asleep. I left her and went downstairs letting myself out into the garden to wander about for a while. I explored Kate's borders, enjoying the early morning air. It held the promise of a perfect summer's day. There was a trace of dew on the grass, not a breath of wind and the sun had started to climb in the sky. Her geranium pots were looking good. I swung round like a weathervane to take it all in. The lawn, the bushes, everything was looking good. I had brought my gardening gloves with me expecting to have to offer a helping hand but it would seem someone else had also had the same idea. I was glad. She couldn't cope with the gardening. She barely had enough strength to get dressed.

Stooping to admire the primula sheltering under the overhang of a glossy japonica bush, I spied a slug crawling back to its lair. I searched feverishly for a substantial twig and flicked it away from the flowers. Slugs were not my favourite garden companion but they had their place, hopefully as breakfast for a hungry thrush.

It was time to drag myself away from nature. I walked back indoors untangling the spiders' webs clinging to my head like Ena Sharples' hairnet. I reckoned I must have picked them up from under the trees. I didn't mind spiders in the garden. I dreaded them coming into the house. They seemed more sinister inside especially the ones with wafer thin legs and tiny bodies … and then there were the evil-looking brown ones that dashed off so quickly there was no chance of catching them.

Kate had always been my hero as far as catching spiders was concerned. She dealt with them efficiently by means of a glass and a sheet of paper unmoved by their scuttling, but there would be no spider hunting this time. If necessary, I would have to steel myself to do the job. I wondered how she would be. She wanted to get out and about with us, but I didn't want to force her or make her feel bad if she didn't have the energy. I opened her door as quietly as possible, trying not to spill the tea I had brought with me. "Are you awake?" I whispered.

"Only just," she murmured extending her arms, rotating them like a rotary dryer in a gusty wind. "Oh ... thanks for the tea. Did you sleep well?"

"Very well, thanks." I pulled back the curtains and perched on the end of the bed. "I've just been outside. I was going to offer to tidy up the garden for you but there's no need. It looks great."

"That's Michael. He comes round once a week and does the basics. I'm lucky with my neighbours. What do you want to do today?"

"Anything you like. Are you up to gallivanting? "

"You bet," she said gamely as she wriggled herself into a sitting position. "That'll be the park then … and an ice cream at the kiosk for Becky."

"We'll have ice creams too. It looks as if it's going to be hot."

"I have to keep out of the sun now. I've been told to wear a hat and cover up."

"Oh dear," I said rather lamely. This would have been another big blow for her. She was a seasoned sun worshiper.

"Yes, sod's law with all the sunny weather forecast. Why couldn't we have had a normal summer this year, rain followed by more rain?"

"Never mind, we'll both stay out of the sun. You know I'm more at home with cloudy skies and a sea fret."

"I guess I'll get used to it. It's a good job I like hats."

"Cerys gave me orders to make sure Becky wears hers every day … unless it's raining of course. We've brought her cagoule for the rain and she made me pack an umbrella. She's such a fuss-pot. We'll all have hats."

"We'll be like The Three Musketeers."

"All for one and one for all," I said. "I'm going to wake Becky now. What do you fancy for breakfast?"

"I'm getting up. I'll see you downstairs."

She only managed a mouthful of porridge. "No toast," she said.

"Orange juice?"

She shook her head. "Just tea, thanks."

Our progress to the park was slow. Kate needed to sit down as soon as we got there. We sat licking ice cream cornets on a bench under a big chestnut tree and watched Becky flying round on the roundabout with some other children. "She looks happy enough," she said.

"Yes, it's good to see her enjoying herself. I've got a new DVD in my case so we'll get a bit of peace later on."

"I like to hear her chatter."

"When are we going to see Robbie Snow?"

"We ... you said you didn't want to come."

"Can't a girl change her mind? I've decided it might be quite fun and Becky should get to see more art."

"She'll love the gallery."

"That's what I thought."

"Tomorrow afternoon at three; we'll go into town in the morning. I want to buy her something nice."

"What did you have in mind?"

"Something Cerys wouldn't buy her. I haven't done much grand-godmothering to date, so I'm going to start ... from tomorrow."

I laughed and gave her a hug. "I'm glad you're feeling better. There's something else we have to do tomorrow if we have the time. Becky wants to visit Sadie."

"We'll make time. It'll be nice and cool under all those trees."

She had a rest after lunch and we were couch potatoes until it was time to go round to Windgather for our meal. There was no sign of Christian. "He sends his apologies," Diana said. "He's playing in a snooker tournament but he's done all the donkey work."

He had prepared *coq au vin*, one of my favourites. Kate could only manage a few mouthfuls. "I'm really sorry," she said.

"Don't worry about it," Diana said. "Is your tongue sore?" Kate nodded and gritted her teeth angrily. "The ulcers?" she nodded again. "They did warn you."

"I know. I thought I could deal with it," she said, her lips barely moving. "I felt fine before they decided to give me that awful stuff. It makes you wonder if it's worth it."

"I have jelly babies," Becky said. We all looked at her and she blushed. "I mean after I've taken my medicine.

Mum says medicine doesn't do you any good unless it tastes nasty."

Kate smiled. "Thanks, Becky. I'll have to give jelly babies a try."

Diana showed Becky the atlas after we had cleared up and they followed Lucy's route as promised. We chatted happily for a while until I noticed that Kate had gone quiet. Diana had noticed, too. "Have you had enough?" she said.

"I'm sorry to be so boring," Kate said.

I stood up. "It's time Becky was in bed anyway."

Diana came to the door to see us off. She gave the child a kiss. "Have fun tomorrow. Where are you going?"

"Auntie Kate's taking me shopping."

"I am indeed," Kate said. "But first I have to catch up on some sleep. You don't want me nodding off in the changing rooms. Thanks for a lovely evening, Di."

"Tell Chris we enjoyed all his hard work," I said.

"Thanks for showing me the atlas," Becky said.

"You're all very welcome."

"She's nice, isn't she?" Becky said as we piled into Kate's car. "I wish she was my teacher."

Kate was fumbling with her seatbelt, shifting this way and that as if she couldn't get comfortable. Maybe it was pressing on her scar. She didn't complain and not wanting to make an issue of it, I turned the key in the ignition and craned round to face Becky while she sorted herself out. "What's the matter with your teacher?" I asked.

"Oh … nothing … it's just that she never notices when I put up my hand in class."

"That's disappointing if you know the right answer. Are we all ready, now?"

"I'm ready," Kate said. "Becky?"

"Yes," Becky said.

"Off we go, then."

"Don't worry about your teacher," Kate said. "She probably needs new glasses."

"She doesn't wear glasses, Auntie Kate."

"Well, there you are then. She obviously needs some." Becky giggled. "Teachers are a law unto themselves. The secret is not to take them too seriously. Do as you're told, keep your head down and your homework up to date. That's the best plan."

"Auntie Kate's full of good ideas," I said.

"It worked for me; school's like an assault course, obstacles everywhere. Unstylish uniform, who's your friend, who's not; those awful dinners ..."

"I take a packed lunch."

"Good. If you let things get to you, you'll go mad. Teachers are just one of the hurdles you have to jump over ... not literally of course." She scratched her chin. "I don't quite know where I'm going with this."

"I think I know what you mean," Becky said. "Listen and learn and don't be upset if the teacher ignores you."

"Exactly," Kate said. "If you understand that you'll be fine."

"It sounds like you should have a go at counselling," I said.

"I could ... I might," Kate said enigmatically. "I'm ready for anything, now. The future is an open field, a blank sheet of paper ... a ... whatever," she said having run out of inspiration. "Who knows how I might choose to fill my time. Iris has given me a second chance. I don't plan to waste it."

Chapter 24

"Can we go into Top Shop?" Becky said as we drove into town the following morning. "Mrs. Bailey goes to Top Shop."

"Who's Mrs. Bailey when she's at home?" Kate said.

"Mia's mum."

"Mia?"

"Mia's my best friend."

"Oh right. I don't see why not."

"I'll park in here," I said selecting a car park as near to the centre as I could.

"There's a space over there, right by the meter," Kate said. "That's handy. I usually have to drive round this one a few times before I find a space. Let's try H&M first," she went on, eyeing up the tempting windows on the pavement opposite. I fed the machine and she grabbed Becky's arm. "Come on, no dawdling," she said. She marched her in through the doors and I followed on behind like a lady's maid.

We visited a succession of shops and she sat down in each of the changing rooms to hold court while Becky paraded in front of her in all sorts of unsuitable outfits. There were tiny skirts and tight shorts, dresses that left nothing to the imagination and items that were only suitable for a fancy dress party. "You're not thinking of buying her that one," I protested as Becky twirled about in a shiny shift dress which barely covered her bottom and seemed to be fashioned from tin foil, leaving nothing to the imagination.

"Of course not," Kate said. "We're just having fun." Eventually they settled for a pair of tight jeans with sparkly cat motifs on the pockets and a dear little canvas bag covered in flowers.

"Lunch now," I said. I could see Kate was flagging. She obviously needed to do things in short bursts, "How about The Sandwich Box?"

"That will do nicely," she said. "They do the best cakes."

We had a leisurely lunch and then I was back in the driving seat to take us to St. Saviours.

"Here we are. This is it," I said as we parked the car and approached the graveyard on foot.

"It doesn't look spooky," Becky said. "I thought all graveyards were spooky."

"Not this one," Kate said. "It's lovely here."

"I've always liked graveyards," I said. "They're such peaceful places, especially this one. It's perfect on a hot summer's day, cool and green; perfect on a windy day with the shelter from the trees and perfect in the winter with the headstones and branches crinkling with frost."

"You can learn a lot of history from headstones," Kate said. "I often come over here to sketch. I love the trees. Look at this one, Becky." She stretched her arms around a gnarled pine with toothbrush leaves and giant pine cones attached in twos and threes half way down the spindly branches. "You have to love them." Becky giggled.

"Less of the tree hugging," I said. "No-one hugs trees nowadays. You're showing your age."

"I'm not just *anyone* ..." Kate said "... and trees are our oxygen. We need to show them we appreciate their place in the eco-system."

"Oh, I do," I said taking the lead. "I'm just not going to hug one to prove it. It's down here, Becky." We walked in single file between the plots until we came to Sadie's little slab. "The flowers are here again," I said. "I wish I knew who kept leaving them." We looked around.

"There's no-one about," Kate said.

I couldn't remember having seen anyone else in the graveyard on previous visits. "No ... I can't say I'm surprised. It's always deserted. I ought to find out who's doing it, though. Some poor soul is missing out on a floral tribute."

"Sadie," Becky said as she knelt down by the stone. "That's all it says."

"You sound disappointed," Kate said. "What did you expect?"

"Well, they usually say something like, *Beloved daughter only sleeping* or, *Safe with the angels* and a date ... or something."

"You are a funny little thing," I said. "Since when have you been an expert on gravestones?"

"Sometimes when I'm with Dad and we go to the cash and carry, I have to sit in the car while he collects boxes of things. It's right opposite St. Mark's church; I can read some of the headstones from the car window." She stood up and took my hand. "Thanks for bringing me, Gran. Now I know where she is I can think about her here, safe under the trees. I don't ever want to forget her."

There was a lump in my throat. I tried to cough it away. No-one else had ever shown such an interest in my Sadie. I felt a sense of continuity. Becky would keep her memory alive when I was no longer there to do it myself. "We won't ever forget her, I promise."

"Right ladies," Kate said. "It's the gallery next and the mysterious Robbie Snow."

In complete contrast to the graveyard, the square behind Carluccio's was buzzing with life. It was pristine, as Kate had explained, blanketed in off-white paving stones which had not yet fallen prey to chewing gum or autumn leaves.

The sun-shaded tables dotted at relaxed intervals outside the open doors of the restaurant added to the Mediterranean feel of the place along with several young plane trees neatly distributed between the paving, their roots protected by shawls of gravel.

Becky ran slender fingers down one of the slender trunks. "These are cool," she said. "They look like wine bottles on coasters."

"So they do," I said appreciating her individual take on the trees. I cast my eyes upwards. The square was surrounded by blocks of flats and town houses standing in clusters like debutantes at a ball, their double glazing shimmering in the sun. "What do you think of the buildings?"

She put a hand to her eyes and squinted upwards. "They're very tall. The windows look like diamond tiaras," she said.

"It's my turn," Kate said. I'm going for the window boxes. What do you think about those? The colours are stunning. They wouldn't last a minute in my garden. I'm no good with plants."

"Like jewelled necklaces," Becky said dreamily.

"Your geraniums are doing all right," I said.

"That's because I've got Michael. It doesn't matter if I forget to water them. We just have time for a drink before my appointment, would you like a milk shake, Becky?"

The child's eyes glowed. "Yes please."

"I'll get them," I said. "Tea for two and a milk shake?"

Kate nodded. "We'll bag a table in the shade, over there. What would you like to do tomorrow?" she asked as they sat down. I knew Becky was safe with Kate. It would be good for her to bend someone else's ear for a change.

"It's my last day," I heard her say. I turned to watch them as I joined the queue. It stretched all the way from the counter, out of the shop, the tail-end touching the edge of the paving. Becky's shoulders sagged as she spoke and her face fell. "I don't want to go home."

"I know. Never mind, we've got the rest of today first. We'll have to do something bigger and better than we've already done," Kate said in bracing tones. I moved a few steps nearer the till and saw the child shrug. She seemed unusually sulky. "What's the matter?" Kate asked her, gently.

Her eyes were moist as she answered. "I want to stay here. It's not nice at home. Mum's always shouting."

It was as I had feared. Becky's home life was not as relaxed as it should have been. I did not blame my daughter. She was under enormous pressure; too much to be contained. Some of it would inevitably bubble over and affect a child as perceptive as Becky.

"Sometimes mums have a lot to shout about," Kate said. "Perhaps when you get back things will be different."

Becky did not seem convinced. I saw her shake her head. "It's since Dad's been staying at the restaurant."

"How good are you at writing letters?" Kate asked.

"I don't know. I never write letters."

"I tell you what, we'll write to each other. Forget about emailing, anyone can do that. Putting pen to paper is more satisfying. It's exciting waiting for the post, wondering what's inside the envelope. You can report on your moody mum and I'll tell you how I'm getting on with Iris." Becky giggled. "When we've been to the gallery we'll go and buy some writing paper and stamps to start you off. This is going to be so much fun."

"What's going to be fun?" I asked as I returned with our drinks on a tray.

"Becky and I are going to be pen friends," Kate said.

"I haven't got your address."

"That's easily sorted. Have you got an address book?" I asked.

She wrinkled her nose. "No," she said with an inflection which implied that this was a foolish question.

"I'll buy you one later and after tea we'll write in as many addresses as we can remember."

"I know Mia's address."

"You know mine and I'll write Kate's down for you … that's a good start. Drink up now. We don't want to be late for Robbie Snow."

Kate kept her hat on as we walked into the cool interior of the gallery. "I'll go and find out where his studio is," she said.

She made a bee-line for the young girl standing behind the counter as I guided Becky round the various portraits and seascapes on display.

"Look at this one, Gran, a cat like *Bijou*," she said.

"So it is." I contemplated the blue-grey cat, fur fluffed up to perfection, a haughty expression on the feline features. It bore a striking resemblance to the real thing. "It's very like him, even the superior expression."

"He's sitting on his cushion," she said.

"*Bijou's* cushion was red, not blue," I said. I saw Kate beckoning us over. "Come on, Auntie Kate wants us."

"His studio's up here," she said standing beside a half-open door at the back of the shop. "He's expecting us."

The landing at the top of the stairs was small and square. It connected with a passageway filled with light; a succession of windows let into the roof led us towards a set of double doors, waxed pine like the skirting boards and skylights. "It smells funny up here," Becky said. She wrinkled her nose. "A bit like the taste of ice cream cornets."

"I expect it's all the new wood," I said. "It's odd there aren't any of his paintings out here."

Kate leaned forward to peer through the glass panel above the vertical handles of the closed doors. I joined her. "I like his beard," she said.

"Beards seem to be in fashion these days."

"Yes, very on trend," she said with a wry smile.

"Can I see, Gran?" I heaved Becky up by the armpits so that she could get a sneak preview of Robbie Snow. "He doesn't look at all mysterious," she said.

"What does mysterious look like?" Kate said as I set Becky down on the floor.

Her smooth forehead buckled, she scrunched her lips like tissue paper and then pronounced, "Tall; thin; dark clothes … and steely grey eyes."

"Bravo," Kate said. "I think you're going to be a writer; those letters will be good practice for you."

"It's a mystery where she gets it from," I said. "I could never persuade her mother to read a book let alone write a decent essay."

She gave me a knowing glance. "I seem to remember you were always scribbling away. Are we ready, ladies? Let's go in."

Robbie Snow turned as the door opened. "Miss Grieves … and friends?" he said.

"That's right," Kate said. She did not offer to introduce us.

"Come and sit down." He indicated a leather couch pushed up against the wall.

Becky was staring at a lacquered screen beside it, folded like an accordion. The panels were covered in exotic flowers and nacre birds with cascading plumage. She inched towards me as we obeyed his instruction. "Look at those flowers, Gran," she whispered, wide-eyed. "They look almost real." She put out an exploratory hand to caress the leaves.

I nodded and admired the petals, iridescent, glossed by the bright light streaming through the French doors which opened out onto one of the balconies on the front of the building. They offered spectacular views over the town, past the park to the sea beyond.

Kate was obviously taking in the panorama. "Great outlook," she said. On the balcony, to the left of the window, stood a wrought iron table and two chairs and on the other side, sprouting from an aluminium planter like a lollipop on a stick was a healthy-looking olive tree. Robbie Snow was obviously not a fan of window boxes, or maybe like Kate, his fingers were far from green. "You get a birds-eye view of everything from up here. It's very smart."

"We haven't been here long, still settling in. The stock room's full of canvasses we haven't had the time to hang yet."

"We wondered why there isn't any of your artwork in the corridor," I said.

"My wife's coming over to deal with that, today" he said.

"All the units seem to be occupied," Kate said. "The developer must have been laughing all the way to the bank."

"They were snapped up in no time. We were lucky to get this one. I'd had my eye on it for a while."

"How did the exhibition go?" she asked.

"You mean Islington ... very well, thanks. It's always a nightmare getting everything in the right place at the right time but we managed to pull it off."

"It must have been a lot of hard work," she said.

"My wife does the displays. I leave it all to her. It's more than my life's worth to interfere. I'm just the artist." He grinned and I felt myself warm to him. "I understand you have a commission for me."

"If you're prepared to take it on," she said. "I'd like a portrait of me."

"No problem."

"There's a slight twist."

"Do you want us to wait outside while you discuss the details?" I said.

"No, it's fine. You can stay. I'm not going to beat around the bush Mr. Snow ... "

"Robbie, please."

" ... Robbie ... I'm having treatment for breast cancer. I want a portrait of my ravaged body."

He did not flinch. "A brave move; I think I can manage that. When do you want me to start?"

"I have two more doses of chemo and three weeks of radiotherapy to get through first, so let's say October, November some time?"

"That ties in nicely. We're spending the summer in France with my uncle. I'll be back at the end of August. I have one or two things I need to do then. November should be ok, will you contact me nearer the time, let me know how you're doing?"

"Yes, of course."

Becky was fidgeting in her seat. "Excuse me," she said suddenly. "Does your cat live here?"

He smiled. "How did you know I have a cat?" he said.

"I saw the painting downstairs."

"Ah, I see. No, he lives at my house, not here."

"Is he a Blue Persian?" she asked.

"He is. That's very clever of you. Have you got a cat?"

She shook her head. "What's his name?" she asked.

"Blue," he said.

"Does he eat fish?"

"Becky, that's enough" I said sharply. I smiled an apology. "I'm sorry, Mr. Snow. She's always asking questions. I think it's time we went." I stood up and hauled Becky to her feet. "Come on. Are you ready, Kate?"

She stayed where she was. "I'll be right with you I just want to ask Robbie a few more questions."

"We'll wait for you downstairs," I said and we left her to it.

"I've … um … seen some of your work before," she said.

"Have you?"

204

"That's what made me pick you to do the portrait. It was the face of a girl, '*Electra*'."

"*Electra* … I remember. She had fantastic cheekbones."

"Is she a regular model?"

"No, I met her by chance when I was visiting one of my uncle's friends in some sheltered flats here. He can't get about much at the moment, knee job. I went instead. As soon as I saw the girl I knew I had to try and capture her face."

"Is she local? She looked foreign."

"Romanian, she's a Care Assistant at the sheltered flats. It's not often you find such a good subject. Portraits are my thing."

"I'm glad I picked an expert to do mine."

"I'll give it my best shot."

"I wondered about the name, *Electra*. It's so unusual."

"It was my uncle's suggestion. It seemed to work. He said she reminded him of someone he knew years back."

"It must be difficult to find an appropriate title each time."

"Not really. As the painting develops something always springs to mind."

"I'd better go," Kate said. "They'll be wondering what's keeping me. I'll be in touch."

"Good luck with the treatment."

"Thanks."

"All sorted now?" I asked when she reappeared in the shop.

"I think so."

"He seems like a nice chap. Did you tell him we'd seen him at the funeral?"

"No ... right, Becky, operation pen friend is about to commence. There's a stationers down the road from here. We'll try there first."

The rest of the afternoon and evening was filled with making chocolate chip cookies, writing out addresses and playing card games. Kate's grand-godmothering went down a treat. When Becky was in bed I sat down next to her on the sofa and kicked off my shoes. "These few days have passed too fast," I said. "Have we worn you out?"

"No more than Iris," she said. "It's been lovely having Becky here. I haven't been bored once. Thanks for bringing her."

"She's really into this pen friend idea. I've a feeling you're going to be inundated with post."

"Good, I'm looking forward to it. Genie ..."

"What is it?"

"You know I said I didn't mention seeing Robbie Snow at the funeral?"

"Yes ... why?"

"I mentioned *Electra* to him instead."

"You didn't ... what did he say?"

"He said she works in a sheltered housing place. He met her when he was doing his uncle a favour, visiting an 'old friend'."

"That would be my mother."

"It has to be, doesn't it and *Electra* has to be Frankie. You were right."

"Robbie Snow wasn't her nephew at all; he was this friend's nephew."

Kate nodded. "She was half right. You don't have to worry about long lost relatives any more or Lettie keeping secrets from you. She wasn't."

"I wasn't worried. I knew there weren't any stray nephews. She was so manipulative, wasn't she?"

"She always knew how to jerk your strings," Kate said.

"Of course, she could have just been confused when she described him as *her* nephew."

"That's possible."

"I'm annoyed she upset Mrs. Dukes. That poor woman had to put up with a lot of nonsense from her."

"Well, you don't have to worry about that any more either. It's finished, Genie; game over for Lettie."

"I suppose you're right."

"What do you mean? Of course I'm right."

"Yes ... I don't know ... I can't seem to get used to it. Do you think she'll always be in my head?"

"It's early days, yet. The memories will fade. They'll end up under a pile of new memories and then you'll lose your marbles and you won't be able to remember anything at all."

I laughed. "I don't know if that's reassuring or not," I said.

"That's just how it goes, Genie. We'll spend our twilight years sitting side by side asking each other the same questions over and over again and driving Cerys mad."

I put up my hands as if to fend her off. "Enough already. You'll be giving me nightmares again."

Chapter 25

At Becky's request we spent the last few hours before our departure, painting. Having seen all the works of art in the gallery the day before, she wanted to produce one of her own to take home for her mother.

"You can do one, too, Gran."

"I don't know about that. I'm not much good at painting."

"Oh, give it a go, Genie. I'm doing one," Kate said. "Wasn't your Grandad an artist?"

"Yes, but I'm not him. You're good at art," I said. "You know how hopeless I am." My protests had been ignored and being bowled along by their enthusiasm I took up a brush. My efforts gave us all a laugh and ended up in the bin.

Becky's picture was an interesting one. With Kate's help she had drawn a sleeping cat, painted it all the colours of the rainbow and had then surrounded it with trees. "There," she said as she returned her brush to the pot of water for the last time. "What do you think, Gran?"

"Hmmm ... very good," I said. "I've never seen a cat like that before; why all the stripes?"

"It's like Joseph's coat," she said. "It's called '*Joseph's Amazing Cat*'."

"It shows great imagination," Kate said. "Well done, Becky."

"Yes," I said. "Well done."

There were tears that afternoon when it was time for us to leave. Becky hugged Kate as if she were the last mast standing in a shipwreck. "Come on now Becky. We can't start being pen friends until you get home. I'm expecting you to write first," she said, prising the child's arms from around her waist. "Have you got your Mum's painting?"

"It's in my bag," I said leading Becky towards the door.

She sniffed and wiped her eyes with the back of her hand. "Can I come again soon?"

"Perhaps you could come and see me when I've finished all the treatment. I'm planning a celebration."

Becky glanced up at me. "Can I?" she asked.

"We'll have to ask your Mum. She'll probably want to come too."

"Have you heard from her?" Kate said.

"Not a peep. I'm taking it as a good sign."

"Here's the taxi, right on time."

I gave her a hasty peck on the cheek. "Good luck with the rest of it," I said.

"Ring me," she called from the door and with a brief wave she retreated indoors.

The countryside whizzed by as we hurtled towards the south and home. Becky had been staring out of the window for most of the journey which had allowed me to get into my book. Her legs moved restlessly. I checked my watch. "We've made good time," I said. "I can't believe we're nearly there."

"I hope Mum and Dad have had a good time," Becky said.

I thought she seemed rather subdued. "You're very quiet. Questions all dried up, have they?"

"I keep thinking about Auntie Kate," she said.

"How do you mean?"

209

"Will she be all right," the child asked raising troubled eyes to mine. I fiddled with my glasses. I didn't want to tell a lie but I did not want to frighten her either. "She's having all her treatment and she'll feel much better when it's over," I said.

The eyes did not waver. "Yes, but will she be all right?"

I sighed. "I'm sure she will. Nothing's ever certain but we have to think positive and knowing Auntie Kate she'll sail through everything. She's relying on you to write to her and stop her from getting bored. That's the worst bit about the chemo. Apart from making her feel ill and tired, she doesn't like having to stay in all the time. She misses going out with her friends."

Becky looked determined. "I've decided I'm going to write something down every day and then send her a long letter each week."

"It's a good job she bought you so many stamps; it sounds like you're going to need them."

My telephone buzzed and saved me from further interrogation. "I expect that's your mum, I texted her the train times last night," I said. I checked the screen. "Yes … she's back ... they've had a good time ... she'll be waiting for us at my house. Your dad had to go to the restaurant with some fish they brought back with them."

Becky frowned. "I don't like fish."

"You like my fish fingers."

"Yes but they're not the same."

"They're full of fish."

"There aren't any bones and I like the crunchy bits on the top."

"Ah the secret to that is a spoonful of mustard and some cheese in with the breadcrumbs. Fish is very good for you. Brain food, Papa used to say. If you're going to do a lot of writing you'll need some fish to keep the ideas coming."

She hesitated for a moment. "Can you give Dad your recipe?"

"I can but I don't think he needs a recipe for fish fingers."

"I'm going to ask him to put them on the menu at the restaurant."

I tried not to smile. "I shouldn't think he'll want my fish fingers on the menu. Grown-ups don't eat them as a rule."

"You do, Gran."

There was no answer to that. "You'd better pack all your things away," I said. "Not long now."

I could see Cerys hovering by the door as the taxi drew up. "I can't wait to tell Mum everything," Becky said as she scrambled out onto the pavement.

"Off you go then, I'll bring your bag."

She skipped up the path and into her mother's arms. "Here we are all safe and sound," I said, bringing up the rear and feeling a bit like a donkey with panniers. I deposited the luggage on the floor in the hall and followed them in to the kitchen.

Cerys held Becky at arm's length. "I'm sure you've grown," she said.

"I've bought you a present," Becky said. "It's in my bag."

"I've got one for you, too. The kettle's on and there's a can of coke for you in the fridge."

"She'll be your friend for ever," I said.

Becky danced about in delight. "I love coke," she said. "Where's my bag, Gran?"

"I left it in the hall with mine."

"I want to give Mum her present."

"You'd better fetch it then."

"Wait," Cerys said. "Open that can in here. We don't want to spill it on Gran's floor." Becky did as she was told and then skipped off into the hall.

"So," I said. "How did it go?"

"I'm so glad I went," she said. "We talked about everything. Kit's agreed to look for a manager to help run the restaurant and he's going to have one weekend off every month."

I beamed. "So it was just over-work. All you needed was a bit of quality time together."

"I've got something else to tell you …"

I had to wait for that revelation as Becky burst back into the room with her gift. "Here it is, Mum."

"Ooh this is exciting," Cerys said.

Becky gave her the mug-shaped parcel wrapped in some foil Kate had recycled from Christmas. "It's a mug," she said, unable to keep the secret any longer.

"Becky," I protested. "It was supposed to be a surprise."

"It's beautiful." Cerys held the mug up in the air. "I love all the butterflies." She took a small package which had been tucked out of sight in a corner by the breadbin and handed it over. "And here's yours," she said. "A gift all the way from Cornwall, Dad and I are going to take you down there as soon as we can. The beaches are beautiful and …"

Becky had already torn off the paper. "This is excellent," she interrupted leaping up and down like a puppy at a letter-box, "Thanks, Mum."

I smiled at her mother's astonishment. "It's only a pen," she said.

"Yes but I can use it to write Auntie Kate's letters. I'm going to be her pen friend," she said importantly. "She helped me paint you a picture as well. Where is it, Gran?"

"Right here," I said as I produced the scroll-like painting from my handbag.

Cerys unrolled the picture. "This is lovely, it's very colourful. I like the cat. You've painted a lot of trees."

"Auntie Kate loves trees. She says they're our oxygen. I'm going to write to her every week."

"Well, I've got some news for you to tell her. You're going to be a sister."

Becky stopped bouncing about and I sat down in a hurry. She was pregnant. I had not been expecting that. My sixth sense must have deserted me. "This is great news. You're going to have a baby, when?" I said.

"November, sometime, I haven't got the exact date yet. I haven't even been to the doctor. We only found out yesterday. I hadn't got a clue I was pregnant. I thought I was past all that. I'd decided I felt odd because of my age or because I was stressed out about everything. Kit suggested I take the test. I only went along with it to please him. Seeing the blue line was the last thing I expected." Becky ran out of the room. "Oh dear, do you think she's upset? Perhaps I shouldn't have said anything until later."

"I'll go." I followed the child into the hall. She was busy putting everything she had removed from her bag to find her mother's gift, back into the rucksack, a strange expression on her face ... almost fear. "What are you doing?"

"I'm getting my stuff so I can go home and start a letter to Auntie Kate. She'll want to know about the baby won't she?"

"Don't you want a baby brother or sister?"

"I do, but ..."

"What is it, Becky?"

"I was thinking about Sadie. It made me sad. What if our baby dies?"

I held her close. "Sadie wasn't born under a lucky star like your baby will be," I said. "She was born at the wrong time. Now is exactly the right time for your little one to arrive. Don't be sad. We'll all be there to watch over the baby ... keep it safe."

"Ok," Becky said. She managed half a smile. "That's what I'm going to tell Auntie Kate."

Chapter 26

When Cerys went for her first hospital appointment she was nearly five months pregnant. It was not going to be easy at her age. She had a history of high blood pressure. I knew I would have to help out.

Fortunately Kate was bearing up well. Each time I rang she was a little more up-beat. When we spoke a couple of weeks later she was relieved and triumphant. "I've had it," she said. "That was the last one."

"Hooray … when do you want me to come up?"

"Next week?"

"Do you mind if I bring Becky again? Cerys is exhausted. This pregnancy is taking it out of her. She's been told to rest."

"Of course you can bring her. She's written to me every week you know."

"I thought she might."

"They're not just short notes either. I know all about your snails, the dinner ladies at her school, how many times her mum's thrown a wobbly, everything. It's a problem knowing what to write back I'm leading such a boring life at the moment but it's great to get her letters. They cheer me up no end."

"Yes, that was one of your better ideas. It's too easy to sit at the computer all day."

"It's doing us both good."

"I told Louisa I'd be coming up again soon. She said she might fly over for a few days. Carter has some air miles she can use. You could end up with a full house."

"That'll be brill … as long as you don't mind me sneaking off for a nap every now and then; I've been trying to persuade Di and Chris to go away. They've put everything on hold for me this summer. If you're all here perhaps they'll finally do it."

"They should just have time before school starts," I said.

"I can't understand why Chris doesn't retire. He's plenty old enough."

"I can," I said. "He'd lose his ready-made audience. It's going to be a wrench for him. I don't suppose he'll go until he's pushed."

"He's been an inspirational teacher. Perhaps they'll let him carry on with some drama workshops or something. Anyway, listen to this. I had an email from Robbie Snow. He wants to take some photos before he starts the painting. I was hoping you'd come with me. Do you think Louisa would look after Becky?"

"Considering that she's always banging on about how much she'd like a granddaughter, I expect she'll jump at the chance."

"I'm all fired up now. I know the next few days will be difficult and then that's it. I'm not going to put myself through the radiotherapy, not at my age."

"Is the oncologist ok with that?"

"It's up to me. The left breast's dicey. I don't want to risk the side effects. You can get heart problems and dreadful lymph oedema ... oh I don't know ... one minute I will and then I won't. Iris keeps tipping the scales."

That wasn't Kate. She didn't do indecisive. I knew I would have had all the treatments going and then some, but I was not her; it was her choice, not mine. I decided to talk about something else, something I understood. "Cerys is going for another scan soon," I said.

"Don't tell me there's a problem with the baby."

"No, just routine; they seem to scan them at the drop of a hat these days."

"Does she know if it's a girl or a boy?"

"Not yet. I told them not to tell me when they find out ... if they find out. I don't want to know until he or she has arrived."

"Is Becky all right with everything now?"

"She's over the moon. She's asked me to teach her to knit so that she can make something for the baby."

"I don't remember you being into knitting."

"I'm not, Louisa was the knitter but I can manage the basics. That's all she needs at the moment. She's doing quite well. It stops her asking to see those photo albums all the time. We went through them over and over again after Lettie died."

"You can understand that."

"Yes, but I'm looking to the future now; seeing you well again, meeting my new grandchild and going on another adventure. How do you fancy the land of the midnight sun?"

I heard her groan. "I don't fancy anything right now. I have no energy at all. I need to recover a bit before I even think about travelling."

"There's no deadline. We can go when you're well enough. I'm not in a hurry to make plans and book tickets."

"It could be a while."

"That's fine. I don't want to leave until Cerys has had the baby anyway. By then you'll be raring to go."

"Maybe. I'm not making any promises."

"When I'm ready I'll let you know. See how you feel then."

Diana rang when I was contemplating suitcases again. We didn't often speak on the phone. Kate had always been our conduit. I experienced a frisson of unease. Had Kate suffered a set-back? I went through the side-effects of chemotherapy in my mind. There couldn't be many left she had not already experienced. "Is everything all right?"

"All good," she said.

I felt my shoulders relax. "That's a relief," I said. "I thought you might be calling with bad news from Kate."

"No. She's doing well. The difference in her since she had the last one is amazing; still tired but so much happier."

"It's been a hard slog. I'm glad it's over."

"So am I. I just wanted you to know I won't be there to pick you up from Lime Street this time. We're going away for a few days."

"She said you might. That's fine. I'm sure we'll find a taxi. The station's usually heaving with them. Where are you off to?"

"Spain; it's a last minute deal. I didn't want to go but Kate is adamant she'll be ok. I can't make up my mind if she's right not to have the radiotherapy."

"Me too ... it's up to her, though, isn't it? She's worried about the side effects," I said.

"She says she's going to watch her diet and keep on with all the exercise; I hope it will be enough."

"She told me she might try some complementary therapies. She's already bought a load of vitamin pills."

"They can't do much harm, can they?" she said.

"I expect she'll talk to her GP about them."

"Will you still be here when we get back?"

"Probably not; Cerys doesn't want Becky missing school right at the beginning of term, it's her last year at primary."

"That's flown by. How is Cerys ... is the baby all right?"

"Yes, no traumas there, thank goodness. She's getting bigger by the minute. She's been told to rest but she's finding that difficult; it's hard for her to let things go."

"What about Kit?"

"He can't wait to be a dad again. He's really spoiling her."

"Ahh … it's nice to hear some good news for a change. I'm glad it all worked out, Genie. See you when I see you, then."

"Have a great holiday," I said. I reckoned she deserved it after all the hours she had dedicated to Kate over the summer.

The sun was shining when we disembarked from the train at Lime Street. "There *are* loads of taxis, Gran," Becky said, swinging the rucksack from its padded straps.

"I told you so. Take your pick."

"That one over there," she said.

"I don't know which one you mean, Becky. Point it out to me."

"I mean the one with the super smiley driver," she said waving her hands about excitedly and swiping me with her bag. "Sorry." I smiled. It was good to see her excited. "I'm really looking forward to seeing Auntie Kate."

"I don't think we'll be doing much this time. She's still a bit under the weather."

"I don't mind. I've brought my knitting."

"Great Aunt Louisa might be there when we arrive."

"I like her, she's funny."

I wheeled my suitcase over to the waiting taxis trying to identify the driver with the super smiley face. It was easier than I thought. Sitting in the driving seat of the second taxi in line, listening to his radio and chortling away to himself, was a middle-aged man, clean-shaven and with a comb-over. I could hear classical music coming from the cab and then the warbling of an opera singer. He started humming along, tapping his fingers on the steering wheel in time to the beat. "Is this the one?" I asked, stopping beside the cab. He heard me and grinned at us, jumping out to reveal an open-necked shirt, baggy jeans and worn leather sandals. "I'll take your bags," he said as he relieved me of my suitcase and grabbed Becky's rucksack. He stowed them neatly in the cab. "Are you ladies on holiday?"

"Visiting friends," I said.

"Not the Albert Dock, then."

"Been there, done that."

"Where to?" he asked.

"Crosston ... Chestnut Close."

"Jump in."

Becky pulled at my sleeve. "What's the Albert Dock?" she whispered.

"You know what a dock is."

"A parking place for ships."

"Well, this was a dock for big ships years ago. Now all the buildings have been turned into a tourist attraction with shops, restaurants a museum, a tribute exhibition to the Beatles ..."

"The beetles? I don't like beetles."

"The Beatles were a famous pop group from the sixties."

"Can we go?"

"Not this time."

"When, then ..."

"Soon, I promise."

Louisa had already arrived at Kate's when we got there. She threw open the door before we had time to get out of the taxi and ran down the path to greet us. "Mwah mwah," she said, treating Becky and then me to several over the top kisses. "Kate's resting. I've ordered take-away for supper. I hope you like pizza, Becky."

"It's her favourite," I said.

"I like Hawaiian and Margarita," Becky said.

"That's lucky," Louisa said, "That's exactly what I've ordered and a hot chilli one in case anyone's feeling adventurous," she added looking straight at me.

"I hope someone's going to help me out," I said staring back at her. "I couldn't possibly eat a whole one on my own. I'm going to see Kate."

Kate sat with us while we ate but she did not eat much herself. Becky yawned through most of the meal and there were no complaints when we suggested she should go up to bed.

"I won't be far behind her," Kate said. "I want to look my best for Robbie Snow. What are you going to do with Becky while Genie and I are at the gallery, Lou?"

"I've got a plan."

"Which is?"

"Yawn, yawn, jet lag," she said with a mischievous grin. "I'll tell you guys tomorrow. I'm off to bed now; nightie, night."

"She loves to tease," I said. "I'm not sure I like the sound of her plan. Her plans have a habit of turning into disasters. What do you think she's up to?"

"It can't be anything too awful if she's taking Becky with her."

"Don't count on it. Louisa's famous for pushing the boundaries," I said. "She *is* Lettie's daughter."

"So are you."

"I've got more of Papa's genes. We'll have to persuade her to tell us what's what before she mentions anything to Becky," I went on, being very aware of being *in loco parentis*. "It might not be appropriate for a child her age."

"What are you suggesting … what would Louisa say to you, Genie … take a chill pill, sis?" Kate said with an attempt at an American accent.

"I am chilled," I said indignantly.

She laughed. "It's so good to have you all here again."

My opportunity to vet Louisa's plan came a few hours later when we were alone in the kitchen. "Right, while Becky's thinking about getting dressed, what's the plan?"

"We're going to stake out the churchyard. We have to solve the mystery of the flowers and who keeps putting them on Sadie's grave."

"Good luck. The place is always deserted," Kate said as she sauntered through to join us.

"Silent as the grave," Louisa said in a dismal voice, "Just as it should be."

"What happens if you do see someone in there?" I asked, determined to risk assess the whole outing.

She thought for a moment. "We'll make a citizen's arrest."

Kate could hardly contain herself. "It's not a crime," she said.

"I don't want you upsetting people; I'm just concerned that someone else is missing out," I said.

"All right, we'll ask who they are and explain they've made a big mistake," Louisa said.

I couldn't find any flaws in that. "As long as you promise to do it politely," I said. "Don't forget you'll have a young, impressionable child with you." I could not help thinking that Becky was probably more sensible than Louisa.

"Sure. I'm going to tell Becky we're off on a ghost hunt. Ok?" I nodded. I guessed she would probably love that idea.

"I hope you've remembered we promised her a McDonalds for lunch," Kate said.

"We'll meet you there. What time?"

"We should be finished by twelve, make it, twelve thirty. I've just had a thought ... I've got something Becky might like to take with her; a ghost hunting must-have," she said and she wandered out of the room again.

When Becky appeared and Louisa explained where they were going, she bombarded her with questions. "What do I need to take with me? What should I wear? Do you think we'll see anything? I didn't know ghosts came out during the day. Doesn't it have to be dark? I thought they walked about at midnight."

"You're thinking of vampires," Louisa said. "I'm not making any promises but the chances are good. They're always hanging around graveyards." She considered Becky's t-shirt and shorts. "You're fine as you are. You just need your hat."

"What if we can't remember where Sadie is?"

"We'll find her between us."

"Are we still going to McDonalds?"

"Sure we are."

"It's a lovely day for ghost hunting," I said.

"Ghosts don't leave flowers," Becky said prosaically.

"I've found these." Kate had re-appeared dangling a pair of binoculars from their strap. "My dad used them for bird-watching but they'll be just as good for ghosts ... do you want to borrow them?"

Becky beamed. "Thanks Auntie Kate. I'll put them in my bag."

"Have you got your hat? It looks as if it's going to be hot again," I said.

Becky sighed. "I've got *everything*," she said.

Kate and I watched as Louisa guided the child out of the house and down the road. "I hope the gates to the churchyard are open this early," Kate said.

"I didn't know they locked it up."

"They've had to. There's been a bit of trouble with teenagers drinking in there and leaving beer cans and other rubbish behind. Dancing on the graves at midnight," she said with a ghoulish grin.

"I don't know if I like the sound of that," I said. I had a sudden vision of the drunken revellers using Sadie's stone in a game of hopscotch.

"It's been dealt with now. Sadie's safe," she said, reading my mind.

"I hope they find her all right."

"It's only a small churchyard."

"I expect Louisa will be topping up her tan ... she loves the sun almost as much as you do."

"I don't, not now."

"Sorry, I forgot."

"I don't mind. I've caught enough rays over the years to last me a life-time."

"I bet Becky tells Louisa about the tree-hugging."

"I hope they have fun."

"So do I. Louisa talked it up into such an exciting adventure it might be a bit of a let-down."

"They'll be fine," Kate said.

"I wish I could sneak up on them and keep an eye on things."

"Whatever for?" she said. "Now who's the fuss-pot? Come and help me choose a hat."

My mind was still on the ghost-hunting expedition but it was much later before I found out what happened when Becky gave me a blow by blow account.

"Can you see anything?" Louisa asked as Becky squinted into the binoculars.

"Well, there aren't any flowers on the grave today."

"Excellent. That means we stand a chance of seeing who leaves them there. Let me know if there's any action. I'll just lie over here and rest my eyes for a minute." Louisa settled herself down on the grass in the sun and closed her eyes.

The child scanned the area. She followed a butterfly flitting past some daisies. She picked out several insects and then she concentrated on a blackbird hopping about in the clipped grass near Sadie's grave, stopping every so often to turn its head this way and that as if checking for danger. It suddenly flew off with a warning cackle and she homed in on a spectral form with long white hair and flowing robes. "Great-aunt Lou," she said breathlessly.

Louisa gave a gentle snore. Becky raised the binoculars and saw forget-me-knots and violets. She stood up and watched the flowers move towards Sadie's plot. She looked higher. There were no eyes in the haunted face, just mirror like orbs glinting in the sun.

She dropped the binoculars on Louisa's foot, waking her with a start. "Ow," she said. "What's happening? Becky what is it? You look as if you've seen a ghost."

"They *do* bring flowers," the child said as she sank down onto the grass.

Louisa picked up the binoculars. She focused them in the direction of Sadie's plot. "Oh shit," she said. "And don't tell your gran I said that."

"It *is* a ghost," Becky said.

Louisa's eyes narrowed. "That's the first ghost I've ever seen wearing Jimmy Choos."

"What do we do now?"

"We follow her. Don't look so scared, honey, you're with me. She's heading off. Get your bag. Let's go."

Kate took more than the usual amount of care with her appearance before we left for the gallery. She was standing in the hall, a hat in either hand. "Which one?" she said expecting me to choose between a pink crocheted skull cap and a gold satin beret.

"The gold one I think."

"Me, too, the other one reminds me of that science teacher we had in the third form. What was her name? You absolutely loved her."

"Mildred Wylde. My first crush," I said.

"I liked Mr. Ben."

"That wasn't his name."

"I know. Fancy calling your son Benedict Benedict," Kate said. "Ah … *those were the days, my friend. We thought they'd never end, we'd sing and dance for ever and a day* ..." she sang at me "... long hot summers, wild parties, never a cross word ..."

"There might not have been in your house. Are we taking the car?"

"Taxi, it'll be here in about ten minutes."

She was smiling as it deposited us by the square. I reckoned she must be keen to get the project started. "Do you remember Daniel Murray?" she said.

"No, I don't think so."

"You must remember him ... Fern's boy friend. He took photos of her in some choice poses."

"Oh ... yes ... I do now. He plastered them all round the school one night after she chucked him," I said.

"What a palaver, as my mother would have said. It was a good job the cleaners took them down before school started."

"Not before we saw them, though. He was expelled wasn't he?"

"Yes. Do you remember Mrs. Tring ticking off Fern about her immodesty? How times have changed," she said. "She only revealed a bit of cleavage ..."

"... and rather a lot of leg," I said.

"I'll be revealing a tad more than that," she said with a chuckle as we walked into the shop. "Well, here we are and up we go."

"I don't need to come up, do I?"

"No chickening out, Genie, you have to come with me. I need a chaperone."

"He's the one most likely to need a chaperone ... oh, all right, but I refuse to look while he's taking the shots. I wonder what's happening at St. Saviour's. Do you think Becky and Lou have met anyone?"

"Not a chance."

"It was nice of you to lend her your dad's binoculars."

225

"I never use them. I hope she finds something interesting to study. The flora and fauna of a graveyard," she said grandly.

"Discuss," I added. "That sounds like the sort of homework topic Miss Wylde might have set."

"Well at the very least she might see a few worms. It is a graveyard after all."

"Kate, really," I said. I frowned at her but I was secretly pleased; Iris was beginning to lose her grip. Kate was on the way back.

Chapter 27

Robbie Snow was thorough with his photo shoot. As Kate lay on the leather couch, head resting on a silk cushion, the lower half of her body swathed in a silk sheet, he asked her to turn her head this way and then that. He suggested that one arm would look better draped along the back of the couch as if it were a chaise longue. She bent her knees and then straightened them out but at no stage did she object to his suggestions. She seemed to be enjoying herself.

"Nearly finished," he said. "Just one with you looking this way, slight tilt of the chin ... perfect ... right, that's enough for now. These will be a great help when I get started."

She pulled on the towelling robe he had given her at the start of the session and moved behind the screen to get dressed. The extension phone on his desk buzzed. He leant over to pick it up and threw me an apologetic smile. "Excuse me ... yes, we've finished. Tell her to come up." He glanced my way again. "It's my wife," he said.

He turned to face the door as Kate emerged from behind the screen and a tall willowy blonde in a white sundress and very high heels walked in. Hair cascaded over her shoulders like a lace mantilla as she pushed her sunglasses to the top of her head in a casual fashion. She rested her hands lightly on his shoulders and knighted him with airy kisses. "Mission accomplished," she said.

He took her arm and turned her to face us. "Isabella, this is Miss Grieves and ..."

Louisa and Becky suddenly burst into the room, flushed and out of breath. Robbie and Isabella started in surprise. I wanted to disappear through the floor. Trust my sister to make a scene. "I thought we were meeting at McDonalds," Kate said.

"Just a minute," Louisa said. "Who *is* she?" she asked pointing an accusing finger at Isabella.

"Isabella Snow," I said. "What's the matter, Lou?"

"She's been leaving the flowers," Becky said. "We followed her. It was her, she's the ... ghost." She gasped the last word out, her face now white as a ricecake.

"We'd like an explanation," Louisa said hands on hips, a combative look in her eye.

"Louisa, really," I said. "There's no need for this. It was obviously a mistake, that's all."

Robbie appeared to be amused rather than put out at this turn of events. "Ah the young lady who likes cats," he said. He turned to Louisa. "You seem to have a problem with my wife."

"I'm sorry," Isabella said. Her voice was soft, her posture relaxed. "Have I done something wrong?"

"Too right you have," Louisa said.

I could not understand her attitude. Why was she being so belligerent? I wanted to calm things down. "This is my sister, Louisa. She lives in Connecticut," I said. I can only blame my embarrassment at their precipitate arrival for that silly comment. "I think there's been a misunderstanding. Someone's been leaving flowers on my daughter's grave. Louisa seems to think it's you."

"It *was* her," Louisa said with some annoyance.

"There's no mistake," Isabella said. "It's Sadie's grave."

Becky burst into tears. "She's our Sadie, not yours." I could not understand why she was so distressed. I put an arm round her sobbing frame and let her cry into my shoulder. "Of course she's our Sadie," I said soothingly. "Don't get upset about it. I'm sure Mr. Snow will explain everything."

"It's quite simple," Robbie said. "My uncle had a friend who lived in a flat near here. She died and he likes to leave flowers on her granddaughter's grave in her memory whenever he's in the country. He's just had a knee replacement and he's not very mobile at the moment. As I was busy this morning he asked Isabella to do it for him, that's all."

"This friend of his was Lettie," Kate said. "I told you."

"Violette McBain was my mother," I said. "Sadie was my baby daughter."

"Oh … I'm so sorry," Isabella said. She looked baffled, embarrassed, bewildered. "He thought there were no relatives living nearby. Would you rather he didn't carry on?"

Becky tugged at my sleeve. "Tell her she's ours, Gran. She doesn't need his flowers," she said in a loud stage whisper.

"I think that might be better," I said. I tweaked my glasses and smoothed down my hair. It was a kind gesture but, like Becky, I did not want strangers taking liberties with my daughter's memory.

"I'll tell him," Robbie said. "He'll understand"

Kate stood up. "We'd better go," she said. "I'll be in touch."

We left the gallery with as much dignity as we could muster. I wanted to be alone to think, but the McDonald's promise had been made and so that was where we went.

It seemed as if all the pre and school-age children from miles around had descended on the restaurant. It was noisy and uncomfortably warm. Over-excited children hurtled about, falling over each other and squabbling as they waited for their food to be prepared; the smell of chips, burgers and sickly sweet desserts left me cold. "What are you going to have, Becky?" Kate asked.

"I'm not hungry thank you," the child said politely. She was preoccupied and unsmiling. I took in her pale face and then I noticed Louisa's agitated manner. I decided to concentrate on Becky. Louisa would have to wait. "What's the matter?" I asked.

"Nothing," she said and stared down at her feet.

"Have you gone off nuggets?" Kate said.

"No," she said.

"It was so embarrassing," Louisa said. "I'm really uptight about all this. I'd like to meet this friend of hers who wants someone else to put flowers on the grave of a baby he's never met and she practically ignored all her life. What a cheek. When is she going to let go?"

Kate's was the voice of reason. "Let's get on with lunch. I'm just having chips," she said, "And a coffee."

"I'll get them," Louisa said. "I can't sit here. I need to be doing something. Are you having a drink, Genie?"

"No thanks."

"I'm not either. It would choke me the way I feel at the moment."

I looked at Becky. She was shuffling uncomfortably in her seat. "Do you need the toilet?" I asked. She shook her head; it drooped down over her chest like a parched sunflower. "Well how about a coke, if you don't want anything to eat?"

"All right," she said in a small voice.

It did not take long for us to finish the meagre lunch which had been anticipated with so much pleasure. It was no treat for me or for Becky either, from what I could tell. Kate ate her chips. We attempted some small talk but no-one really wanted to engage. We waited for Becky to finish her coke and left as soon as we could.

"What do you want to do this afternoon," I said as we made our way outside. She had been silent for at least ten minutes. The whole day was turning into a disaster. She shrugged her shoulders and said nothing. This was not how it was supposed to be. We were supposed to be making her holiday fun.

"I'm heading back to the gallery," Louisa said. "I'm going to tell Robbie Snow to ask this uncle of his to stop dishonouring Sadie's memory. You go home with Kate. It will only take me five minutes."

"We've already made that point," I said. "I'd rather you didn't."

"You don't have to come with me."

"I think we should all go back to my house and think about this," Kate said equably.

"Good idea," I said. I could see Louisa was unhappy about her suggestion.

"This needs sorting now," she said.

"Perhaps we should consider our options first," I said. "Becky's tired. I'm sure Kate could do with a rest; come back with us and we'll talk about it."

"Ok," she said grudgingly. "But I am going to have this out with him and soon."

I failed to understand why she was so edgy. Becky was still tight-lipped. It was a dispirited bunch of souls who hailed a taxi to return to Kate's. She ran up to her room the minute we got in. I made a pot of tea. Kate looked worn out.

"I'm not going to quit," Louisa said. "I've got to find out what's going on." I had seldom seen her so fired up about anything.

"He was only trying to do something nice in memory of a friend," Kate said.

"I don't know why you're so up in arms," I said. "Sadie was my daughter. If anyone's upset it should be me and I'm not. We don't know anything about his uncle. He might be a really nice man. He was obviously close to Lettie or he

231

wouldn't have known about Sadie's grave. I agree with Kate. He was just trying to do something kind. The pansies were lovely."

Louisa shrugged. "It doesn't feel right, I'm not happy about any of this."

"What if Lettie asked him to do it?" Kate said.

Louisa frowned. "She didn't even go to the funeral. When was she ever bothered?"

"When you get older and you're ill, you start thinking about things differently, believe me," Kate said. "Iris has made me think about a lot of stuff … she may have done."

"It's possible," I said. I liked that idea. It would have made my mother a little more motherly.

"I don't buy it. It's not like her at all. She was as hard as nails. She never cared zip for Genie. You're not telling me she was going to change," Louisa said.

I heard a door close upstairs and wondered if Becky had overheard our conversation. "I think we should let it go. I'm going to see if Becky's all right. She might be coming down with something."

I found her sitting cross-legged on the bed scribbling in a little notebook. She looked up when I opened the door and slipped it under the pillow. I pretended not to notice. "Hello Gran," she said with an attempt at a smile.

"What is it, Becky?" I said. "Have you got a headache?" I felt her forehead. It was cool.

"I'm all right ... Gran …"

"Yes?"

"Can I ask you something?"

"You can ask me anything," I said warily, wondering what was coming next.

"I've been thinking about Sadie and Lettie and everything ... and …would she have liked me?" she said.

I flinched, upset she had been made to question her lovability, something all children should be able to take for granted. I knew revealing Lettie's true character would be unsettling for her. I was cross with myself for having been persuaded to tell her about my mother and for allowing Louisa to be so forthright with Becky in the house. I refused to allow my mother to cause trouble from beyond the grave. I decided to prevaricate a little. I gave the child a hug. "Of course she would. She would have thought you were *charmante* and *jolie* and she would have taught you how to cook and sew and all sorts of things. She might even have let you brush Bijou," I said. It was an Oscar-winning performance.

She smiled. "Gran …"

"Yes," I said, smiling, now myself.

"Can I have some toast? I'm starving."

We all played Scrabble that evening and when Becky had gone to bed, Louisa carried on with her campaign.

"I'm determined to have this out with Robbie Snow," she said.

"Leave it," I said. "Least said soonest mended."

"That's dumb," Louisa said. "I've made up my mind. I'm going to see him tomorrow, whatever you say."

Kate sighed. "What good will it do?" she asked.

"I want to ask him how we can find this uncle of his and then I'll get in touch and warn him off, that's what."

"Robbie said he'd do that."

"I want to do it. It's important."

"I suppose you'll go whatever we say," I said. "Just don't tell Becky what you're doing. You'll only worry her."

"I won't say anything. You can tell her I'm going shopping. I want to get Carter a sweater before I go back. They're much better quality over here … and some marmalade."

"What about the boys?"

"I promised them the left-over air miles. Clive's never been to the UK."

"It'll be great to see them … when they finally get here," I said. "We'll put out the red carpet."

I expected her to smile, make some crack or other but she simply said, "Goodnight," and went up to bed.

"What *is* her problem?" I asked.

"Let her sleep on it," Kate said. "She'll have calmed down by tomorrow."

I wished I had Kate's optimism. Something was bugging Louisa. I had a feeling it would not be so easily resolved. "She'll only make herself look foolish if she goes in there, all guns blazing," I said.

"She'll have come to that conclusion herself by then."

"I hope so," I said but my knowledge of my sister told me otherwise.

Chapter 28

Kate and I were enjoying a quiet five minutes with a bacon sandwich while Becky had a lie-in when Louisa appeared downstairs the next day. Her youthful bloom had faded and although her make-up was perfect, it could not hide the bags under her eyes. "Are you all right?" I said.

"I didn't get much sleep last night," she said. "I was trying to work out the best plan."

I sighed. "Not another plan."

"I'm determined to get that information from Robbie Snow. I'm going to tell the girl at the gallery that my friend's lost a scarf ..."

"Meaning me?" Kate said.

"Of course; she's bound to remember us after yesterday's debacle ... a very expensive Liberty scarf of sentimental value and she thinks it might be in his studio somewhere."

"What if he's not there?" Kate said.

"I'll offer to wait for him."

"And if he's out for a while?" I said.

"Easy ... I'll call back later."

"What if she suggests you go up there and have a look round for the scarf without him?" Kate said. "You won't find it."

"I've thought of that. I'll say he must have put it away somewhere for safe-keeping."

"You seem to have thought of everything," I said. "I'm not surprised you couldn't sleep with all that going round in your head."

"How about a bacon sandwich before you go?" Kate said.

"Just a coffee," she said. "I'm not hungry."

It was a relief when she finally left the house. I did not share her determination to hound Robbie Snow. I felt sure that now he understood the situation he would explain it to his uncle and there would be no more flowers on Sadie's grave unless we put them there ourselves.

With Louisa's restlessness dealt with and after the emotional turbulence of the day before, Kate and I decided on a lazy morning.

"Shall we sit outside this afternoon?" I asked after lunch had been cleared away. "It seems a shame to waste all this lovely weather."

"I've got some lemonade in the fridge," she said, "And I think there may be some mini Battenberg cakes left; we could take them outside and have a picnic."

"I'll get on with my knitting," Becky said. "Have you seen my hat?"

"It's on the hook behind your door," I said. "Mine's on my bed. Would you bring it down for me?" She skipped off and I went to find the garden umbrella so that Kate could sit in the shade, while she searched for glasses and a tray.

The pots of geraniums on the decking were in full bloom. They gave off their distinctive metallic scent as I brushed past on my way to the summer house and I wondered how my garden was doing without me. I could not resist the urge to nip off a few dead flower heads on the way.

The garden was laid out in a simple style; decking and lawn with borders down each side. The summer house was at the far end under the middle-aged mimosa which had been a mass of yellow flowers on my last visit. The feathery, fan-like leaves stood still in the heat of the day, flirting with the broad hands of the horse chestnut a few feet away in a neighbour's garden. Despite Kate's claim of being a plant terminator everything looked remarkably healthy. Honeysuckle cascaded down from the fence in profusion; only the jasmine was past its best. A mass of brownish-white flowers littered the ground beneath the bulk of its glossy leaves.

By the time I had sorted out the umbrella Becky had perched herself on the edge of the decking between the geraniums, back hunched, sunhat pulled down and legs dangling like a flower-pot man, as she concentrated on her knitting. She glanced up as I passed her a glass of lemonade. "Thanks, Gran. I left your hat in the kitchen. Will Great-aunt Lou be back soon? I want to show her how far I've got."

"I don't know," I said. "I think she's searching for gifts to take back to the States."

Kate joined us, suitably protected from the sun in a fine lawn shirt, baggy linen trousers and a straw hat. "I expect she'll be ages," she said. "I saw her shopping list."

I had no idea how long she would be or even what she was doing. I was glad I did not know. I wanted to leave well enough alone. "This heat is almost unbearable," I said.

"There's thunder forecast."

Becky beamed. "I love thunderstorms," she said.

"Well I don't," I said.

"It's only the angels moving their furniture," Kate said with a grin.

"It's not," Becky said. "It's all to do with unstable air and cumulonimbus clouds. We've got a weather station at school. There's a big book in Miss Morgan's office. Now I'm in year six, I'm on the rota to note down the outside temperature every day and the air pressure."

Kate gave me a startled look. "Right, well, that's me told. I think it will be science for you, not journalism."

"I don't care how a thunderstorm forms," I said. "I still don't like them."

I found out later that as we were discussing meteorology, Louisa was on her way back to the gallery weighed down with carrier bags, having been unsuccessful in tracking down Robbie Snow at her first attempt.

It was nearly two o'clock and the rush had passed when she arrived at the gallery. The girl noticed her at once. "He's just come in. If he's not in the studio, he'll be in the stock room."

"Could I leave my shopping here? I don't want to have to lug it all the way upstairs and down again."

"I'll put it behind my desk."

"I didn't mean to buy this much, it just sort of happened. There were so many bargains about."

"I know. All the shops are getting ready for their winter stock to come in. I hope you don't end up with an excess baggage charge."

"Fingers crossed."

"I told him you'd be coming back, go on up."

Louisa ran up the stairs and walked along the corridor as before. Robbie was nowhere to be seen. There was a man sitting on one of the wrought iron chairs on the balcony. He had a picture frame on his knees, glass gleaming as he buffed it with a yellow cloth. He had not heard her. She moved closer to the balcony and then stopped, undecided as to whether she should engage him in conversation or not; she was aware of the murmur of a voice behind her and turned to see Robbie Snow on his way back from the stock room, mobile held up to his ear.

She sat down on the couch to wait for him and as her eyes veered towards the balcony again she saw the man place the frame carefully on the table beside him. He turned to face her, silvery hair brushed back from his forehead in crinkling waves. Their eyes met. "Hello," he said.

She felt the colour drain from her face. "Oh shit," she cried and jumped up. "And I mean that. It *is* you. I knew it. What the heck are you doing here?"

Robbie flipped his phone shut just then and walked into the studio to join them. "I see you've met my Uncle Jamie," he said affably. "Sorry to have kept you waiting. You've had a wasted trip, I'm afraid. I don't have the scarf."

The old man got up and grabbed the walking stick suspended from the back of his chair to steady himself. "Robbie, would you mind if we had a few minutes alone?"

Robbie looked startled. "What is it? What's going on?"

"I'll explain later ... please, Robbie," he said and watched as Robbie shrugged and turned tail.

He started to walk towards her but Louisa didn't want him anywhere near her. "Don't you dare come any closer," she said.

Her words stopped him in his tracks. He sighed. "I knew this wasn't going to be easy."

"It had to be you. I didn't say anything to Genie, but I just knew it."

"Let me explain."

"I won't hear another word without her. We're staying with her friend, Kate; come round to the house tonight. You can explain then."

"I don't know Kate. Why should she be involved in our affairs?"

"*Our* affairs, that's a good one," she said sarcastically. "Robbie's got her address." Without another word, she left the room, ignoring Robbie's puzzled, "Is everything alright?" as she passed him on the stairs.

When she returned to the house Kate was resting in the lounge. I was outside with Becky. "It's a shame it's clouded over," I said. "I hope it's not going to rain." I heard Kate calling me. "I'm just going to see what Auntie Kate wants." Becky was concentrating on her knitting. She nodded but did not look up from her needles.

As I approached the back door, I met Kate coming out. "Louisa's in a state," she said quietly. "I'll stay with Becky. You go and sort her out."

"What now?" I said.

She shook her head. I found Louisa pacing up and down the kitchen like a train traveller in search of the buffet car. I could see something was very wrong. She looked pale despite her tan and she was visibly upset, not her usual frivolous self at all. "You look awful. What's up?" I guessed Robbie Snow had not liked her attitude. "Did Robbie get angry with you?"

"No. I've got something to tell you. Come and sit down."

She was acting so strangely that I felt uneasy. "What is it?" I said. "You haven't been shoplifting have you?" She shook her head. "Has something happened to Carter?"

"No, Carter's fine."

"Is it the boys? It's not Cerys," I said. She seemed to be struggling. Now she had put the fear of God into me. My knees gave way and I sank down onto a chair. "It's the baby, isn't it? She's lost the baby. I knew this would happen. She hasn't been resting like she should. How on earth am I going to tell Becky?"

She shook her head. "It's not Cerys or the baby."

"Well, what else can it be?"

"I saw Robbie Snow and I met his uncle."

"Right … so far so good. What did he say to get you in this state?"

"He didn't say anything. It was his uncle. He was also someone we know."

Now I felt sick. I suddenly knew what she was about to say but I had to ask the question. "Who was it, Lou?"

"It was Papa."

Chapter 29

Those three words caused the bridge I had built to cross the incongruities in my life to crumble. I could feel myself losing control; falling into the turbulent waters below. There was no safe place for me. I was drowning in emotion.

My stomach heaved as I bolted upstairs to the bathroom ignoring the lightning which lit up the landing and the crack of thunder making the house reverberate around me. I locked myself in. When the nausea passed, the storm broke. I had not sobbed like that since Arthur left. It was a while before I could stop. As the window repelled the cascading rain, water streamed from my eyes. I gave in to the outpouring of grief until my ribs ached and my throat felt raw and then I grabbed a handful of tissues and tried to calm down; I licked the saltiness from my lips and tried to attempt a smile; it was too soon, but I had to go back downstairs before Becky noticed I had gone and began to ask questions.

I heard Louisa knocking. I was not ready to talk. I needed to be on my own a little longer to come to terms with what she had just told me. It seemed impossible and yet it must be true. She had seen him, spoken with him ... how was I supposed to feel? He had been long gone, only a brief part of my childhood, never a part of my adult life and to preserve my sanity, only remembered fleetingly. For all practical purposes I did not have a father. The knocking stopped and she went away.

I splashed cold water on my face and glanced at my reflection in Kate's make-up mirror. I saw a hurt child; a young woman betrayed and then, me; older, without a doubt, but no wiser. I tried to smooth out the lines on my forehead. I could do nothing with the pain in my heart and the sour taste in my mouth.

What had he been doing for all those years? Why had he not made contact? How could he have allowed all those bad things to happen and not lifted a finger to help? Had he cared if we had been safe? Had he thought of us on our birthdays? Had he ever wondered what sort of people we had grown up to be? I much preferred the convenient death I had inflicted on him; dead and helpless to help, that was how I liked him. At least then he would have had an excuse.

How could I find serenity knowing he was alive and close by? I tugged at my curls, wanting to tear them from my scalp. I needed that physical pain, I knew there would be relief when I stopped. I could not deal with the emotional pain; I had learned that it did not respond so readily.

My eyes watered. My scalp burned. I let go of my hair and started on my teeth. Squeezing out a generous portion of toothpaste onto my toothbrush I scrubbed each one with vigour. Over the years I had managed to push him far from my life. Now I felt betrayed, deserted; hurt all over again.

As I performed the requisite two minutes I tried not to look at my face. I could not let Becky see the swollen eyes and tell-tale blotchy cheeks. I turned on the tap to wash away the remains of white froth that clung to the plug-hole, watching as it curled slowly away. I lay the toothbrush on the window-sill and then sat on the edge of the bath, waiting to feel more in control.

Eventually I unlocked the bathroom door and peeped out. The coast was clear. I made a dash for my room and repaired my make-up and changed my glasses. With shades protecting my eyes I felt better able to face the world.

I suppose I had half guessed it could have been him. As far as we knew he had passed away years before but with no proof of that, there had always been a question mark at the back of my mind.

What I did not understand was how he could be Robbie Snow's uncle as well as our father. Perhaps Louisa knew. The questions would have to wait. I didn't want Becky upset any more than she had been already. The whole situation needed careful handling.

When I got downstairs everything was calm. Becky had been rained off the decking. She was watching a DVD in the lounge. Louisa and Kate were in the kitchen. There was an uneasy silence as I entered the room.

"Why are you wearing sunglasses?" Kate said. "It's pouring out there."

"My eyes are tired. I think I've got a migraine coming."

She stared at me. "Something's happened."

I turned to Louisa. "You tell her," I said.

"Ok. Something unexpected *has* happened," she said. She got up and closed the door. "I don't want Becky to hear us. You're not going to believe this ... but ... it would seem that Robbie Snow's uncle is also our father."

There was utter amazement in Kate's face. "What? No," she said. "I don't believe it. How can he be?"

"That's a very good question," I said. "You're the one with all the answers, Lou, you tell us."

"I don't know."

"I thought he was dead," Kate said.

"Apparently not," Louisa said. "I asked him to come round later and explain."

"He can't," I said, horrified at the idea.

"I didn't want to hear the story of his miraculous resurrection without you and I was scared I might say or do something I'd regret if I stayed in that room with him a moment longer."

I frowned at her. "I don't know if I'm ready to see him."

"You'll have to be. I want to find out where he's been, what excuses he has."

"I can't imagine how shocked you are," Kate said. "It is shocking news. I don't know what to say."

"I don't know what to *think*," I said. "I don't know what Cerys will think and what about Becky? Can't you put him off?"

She shook her head. "I need those answers."

"We should keep Becky away from all this." Kate said. "It wouldn't be right for her to witness what might be an awkward scene. Shall I take her to the cinema?"

"This is awful," I said. "You shouldn't have to patch up our lives. You've got enough to deal with."

"I don't mind ... really I don't. I haven't done much today."

"I suppose it would be better if she wasn't here, so long as you're not too tired."

"We'll have to tell her later," she said. "We can't keep this a secret."

"For sure," Louisa said. "But she doesn't need any more raw emotion at the moment. What a cheek, suddenly appearing like that. Where's your wine, Kate?"

"I don't know. I haven't been drinking since the chemo; there might be a bottle left. I'll go and have a look."

Kate went off to find the wine and I had a moment of inspiration. "Perhaps it's not as sudden as you think."

"How do you mean?"

"I think he's been giving us a helping hand. The flowers, *Electra*, Robbie Snow ..."

"That's what I thought."

"Why didn't you say something?"

"I didn't want to upset you. I may have been wrong. You didn't think it was strange that someone unrelated wanted to leave flowers on Sadie's grave. I did. That's why I got so uptight about it. I would have looked a complete dumbo if it had been legit ... I had to be absolutely sure before I said anything to you."

"I'm the dumbo," I said. "What are we going to do?"

"We're going to hear what he has to say and then make up our minds," she said.

I did not recognise this side of my little sister. She did not do serious and stubborn. I felt a sneaking admiration for her focus and determination. "I'll go and tell Becky about the cinema," I said.

She saved me the trouble; the door opened and in she strolled, yawning like a lion. "Is it tea-time yet?"

"We'll have to eat soon. Kate was thinking of taking you to the cinema but if you're too tired ..."

She perked up straight away. "I'm all right. I'm not tired at all... what are we going to see?"

Kate walked in behind her. "I don't know what's on. We'll just have to take pot luck. Here's your wine," she said, handing the bottle to Louisa. "Don't go mad, it's the last one."

"You're a life saver. I know where the glasses are. Does anyone else want some?"

"Maybe later," I said.

"Are we going to the little theatre?" Becky asked. She had remembered that there was a small independent cinema in the town. It showed art films mainly but in the school holidays there was always a programme of children's films on offer and a massive confectionery bar.

"We are," Kate said.

"Goodie," Becky said. "We'll be able to have sweets before we go in."

"You'll be having your tea first," I said.

"I've got one of Christian's shepherd's pies in the freezer, it won't take long," Kate said. She held out her hand to Becky. "Come on let's get it in the oven."

As they busied themselves with the preparations I had time for a quick word with Louisa. "What did he look like? Are you quite sure it was him?"

"Just like he did before, except older. His hair's lost its colour but it was definitely him."

"I'm surprised he recognised you. You were very young when he left."

"Good point."

"Where's he been all this time?"

Louisa shrugged her shoulders. "I didn't ask and I didn't give him a chance to say much either. I couldn't. I was too shocked. We'll find out tonight."

How we got through that meal without revealing what was on our minds, I will never know. Becky chattered about food and films and we made appropriate comments as and when necessary. I was relieved when they left for the cinema and then apprehensive. "I wish he'd hurry up," I said. I pushed my glasses up my nose. "What time is it?"

"Five minutes later than the last time you asked," she said. "Are you ok now? You worried me earlier."

"It was the suddenness of it. I wasn't expecting anything like that. I'm going to find this so hard. We struggled for years after he left. He can't just walk back into our lives like nothing's happened."

"I don't think he expects to. I'm not going to make it easy for him but he's an old man now. We don't want to give him a heart attack."

"No," I said, remembering my conversation with Kate all those weeks before. I didn't want his death on my conscience for the rest of my life.

The doorbell rang. I started shaking. "I'll go," Louisa said her expression grim. "Don't run away. I need you here with me."

I could not have run anywhere. The ferrets in my stomach were more energetic than ever, bouncing this way and that like balloons on a stick. My legs were like bendy straws, the sort that lean over the edge of a glass, float about and fail to stay in your mouth however hard you grip them with your teeth. I unclenched my jaw. I clutched at my stomach and tried to cross my legs. They refused to flex at first and so I crossed my ankles instead and then grabbed my knees forcing them back so that my feet slid under the chair. I kept them under such strict control that my wrist ached and my knuckles blanched.

"We're in here," I heard Louisa say. The door opened wide and I sat up straight as Robbie appeared and then my father ... it was him. He walked slowly with the aid of a stick. His face was like parchment and his hair sterling silver but the eyes were the same; dark and full of emotion. I would have recognised him anywhere.

"I'm pleased to see you, Genevieve," he said a slight waver in his voice. "How have you been keeping?"

I could not speak. My tongue was stuck to the roof of my mouth, my throat constricted. Robbie helped me out. "I hope you don't mind me being a part of this. I'm due an explanation too. I had no idea we were cousins."

"Robbie's my nephew," Papa said, "Min's boy."

"We were never told about him," Louisa said. "I thought she couldn't have children."

"That's what we all thought. Your mother didn't want you to know anything about me or my family after I left."

All of a sudden my resentment boiled over and I found my voice. "Have you any idea what you put us through? Why did you leave so suddenly? Why did you just disappear? Where have you been for all these years?"

He licked his lips. "I'll answer the last one first, France. Could I have a drink of water please?"

"Does anyone else want a drink? I'm having a glass of wine," Louisa said waving the bottle about like a station-master's flag.

"Yes please," I said. "A large one."

"I'm fine," Robbie said as she re-filled my glass.

No-one spoke while she was out of the room. I was aware of Papa's scrutiny but refused to meet his eyes. I took a few mouthfuls of wine. "Here we are," she said, breezing back in with a pint glass filled to the brim.

Papa accepted her offering. "Most kind," he said.

His reply jarred on my ears. It had been years since I had heard anyone use that expression. It took me back. I did not want to go there. The past must stay where it was. I was struggling enough with the present. Louisa took charge. "Now, let's start with the whys. Why did you disappear? Why didn't you keep in touch? Why didn't you let us know you were still alive?"

"And why did you leave her to ruin my life?" I added quietly.

Chapter 30

"Before I say anything else," Papa said, "I want you both to know that I'm sorry, really truly sorry … for everything." I stared at him and saw sincerity in those dark eyes. "I know you won't believe me but I thought of you both every day. I never, ever stopped loving you."

"You had a funny way of showing it," Louisa said. "You just waltzed off and let us think you were dead. That was nice; a very loving way of going on."

He sighed. "You must remember that what happened … happened a very long time ago."

There was a bitter quality to Louisa's words as she answered him. "If that's your excuse it won't wash."

"No excuses, only facts," he said. "Your mother and I married far too young, too young to know ourselves properly, never mind each other. I loved her and she loved me but for the people we really were, that wasn't enough."

"It was enough for you to make two children with her and then abandon them," she said sharply.

"We know you had an affair," I said. "Surely you could have kept in touch. Did you marry again, have more children?"

"It was complicated," he said. "There are no other children."

"People have been having affairs for ever. It's always complicated," I said.

"You were no different from any other cheating husband," Louisa said. "I know fathers who've managed to keep in touch with their children after a marriage break-up despite moving miles away. Don't try and make your situation something special or your life more complicated than anyone else's. If you're going for the sympathy vote, you're knocking on the wrong door."

He shook his head. "It was the circumstances of my time that made it so difficult; it led me to do a very … foolish … thing. Your mother found out. She made me leave. I wasn't going to; I didn't want to, I hoped we could get over it."

"Who was she?" I asked. "Did you stay with her?"

He sighed again ... a deep shuddering sigh that seemed to come from the depths of his being. His head fell and his shoulders collapsed like a domino run. "He was someone I met at work. His name doesn't matter."

"Oh shit," Louisa said. She poured herself some more wine and gulped it down.

I could not move. I could not think. I could barely breathe. I glanced at Robbie. His face said it all; disbelief, shock, pity ... acceptance.

"After she threw me out I took a post abroad. I never saw him again. I wrote to your mother from time to time; sometimes I got a letter in return …"

Now I wanted to scream or tell him to shut up. She knew he was still alive. She had known it all along. He must have known about Arthur. How could he have let her get away with it? How could he not have come to my aid? Did she do it to turn the screw, hurt him, make him jealous and punish him through his daughter? Had it all been my fault? That was a thought that had haunted me for years. "I can't believe what you're telling us," I said. "I don't *want* to believe it."

Louisa was equally incensed. "You kept in touch?" she almost shrieked at him. "She never breathed a word."

He winced; his hand shook as he sipped from his glass. "I thought she had a right to call the shots after the way I'd behaved."

"You were so wrong."

His eyes glistened as he sat there shoulders bowed, staring at the glass, turning it slowly between his fingers like a child with a snow globe, trying to see through the swirling flakes of our lives. "Maybe I was. She told me a little of what had been happening with you. I didn't find out about Arthur until just recently when I went to visit her. She wouldn't agree for us to meet before then. I was heartbroken. I felt so sad for you, Genevieve. She refused to discuss it. I don't know what possessed her to behave like that. When I met Frankie at the flats and she reminded me of you so much ... of the way you were when I left ... I realised I had to work out a way for you to find me. I had no right to intrude on your life, either of your lives. I'd let you both down. I didn't want to force myself on you but I wanted you to find me, if that's what *you* wanted. It was little enough."

"Very noble," Louisa said sarcastically. "Why were you suddenly so bothered?"

"I could see your mother was fading. I knew that if I didn't make overtures soon it would be too late. I didn't know where you were. Your mother wouldn't tell me. She was the link between us and once she'd gone, you would both be lost to me. She did at least show me some recent photographs. That's how I recognised you, Louisa. I couldn't believe my luck when you appeared in Robbie's studio. The photographs, seeing Frankie's likeness to you, Genevieve and hearing about what happened with Arthur gave me the jolt I needed. I had to do something. I had already asked Robbie to paint a miniature of your mother for me to keep. I hoped when he visited the flats and saw

251

Frankie he'd want to paint her portrait. It might seem silly now but I thought I could leave it as a clue. It had to be worth a try."

"I'd rather paint portraits than anything else," Robbie said. "Those cheekbones were amazing."

"I suggested the name, *Electra*. I'd seen the play years ago. The plot had some echoes of what happened to us. When he'd done it I asked if he'd mind me giving it to my friend ... your mother ... as a parting gift, a keepsake ..."

"That's what Mrs. Dukes said," I blurted out. "She said it was a keepsake."

He gave me a benign smile and inclined his head slightly. "He very kindly agreed. I knew you'd be bound to find it after she died ..."

"I really wanted to put her in my exhibition," Robbie said. "I think she's one of my best efforts."

"It's a great picture," Louisa said. "Everyone's said so."

"... and so, I gave it to her and explained who Robbie was and that the painting was my way of making contact with you as she wouldn't tell me where you were. It was a hint ... a trail to follow if you will; a portal through which you'd be able to reach me. I hoped you'd like *Electra*. I thought you'd want to know where she came from, be intrigued enough to find out more about the artist and then through Robbie find me. I told her it was time you both heard the whole story and she agreed. After all, there would be no recriminations; by the time you found *Electra*, she would be gone."

"And she agreed. She knew about this?" Louisa said. "I can't believe she said nothing."

"That was up to her. It was all a terrible muddle. I'd caused so much trouble already I didn't want to make matters worse by insisting she told you and anyway I couldn't actually make her do it. Not only that, I had no way of knowing what sort of a reaction I'd get from you girls after all this time, but Robbie is blameless and your cousin.

I wanted you to have the opportunity to meet, at least. It was possible you'd like each other, perhaps even become friends. Robbie isn't me."

"It's a shame we weren't given the opportunity before," I said.

"Ok," Louisa said. "What you're saying makes sense but I don't understand all the cloak and dagger stuff."

"I didn't have a way to get in touch with you."

"I get that," Louisa said impatiently. "But why *Electra,* Why didn't you just leave your details with Mrs. Dukes?"

"I didn't know if she'd been told about me. It might have put you in an awkward position if you didn't want to make contact. I thought the painting was a better, more personal way of making contact without involving anyone else. I hoped the title would strike a chord, especially with you, Genevieve. I remembered how much you loved reading. Especially all those gory tales of the Greek gods. I hoped it would make you want to find out about her story if you didn't know it already. I thought you might see the parallels in our lives. I suppose I was hoping you'd guess I must have had a hand in it. Who else would have known what went on?"

"It was a bit of a long shot," Louisa said.

"I didn't know what else to do. I wasn't thinking straight. It made sense to me at the time. I know it sounds a bit hit and miss now, but it was my best option then; Frankie and Robbie made the whole scheme possible."

I wanted to be cynical, but what he said rang true and he was right in a way. Kate had noticed the resemblance. She was the one who had been keen to solve the mystery and she had made the connection with Robbie, but it had been the flowers, not *Electra* that had finally led us to him.

I was touched he had recalled my love of gruesome tales. I had a flash back of memory; a hard-back book, a picture of a flying horse on its cover, nostrils flared, white wings spread like an eagle about to land. The idea of sharing such stories with Becky had never occurred to me and yet I had been fascinated by them as a child. "Myths and Legends," I said.

He nodded. "We read them together."

"You must remember that book, Lou. We were given it for Christmas one year. It had a picture of Pegasus on the front."

Louisa shook her head. "Wasn't I a bit young? Milly Molly Mandy was more my sort of thing."

I turned to face him. "It worked," I said. "But it was Kate who noticed the resemblance, not me. She wanted to follow the clues."

"Did she? *Electra* said it all. I agonised for years over what had happened although I didn't know the worst then. I needed you to understand that I realised how much pain I'd caused you without you feeling obliged to give me anything back. I didn't deserve it. It wasn't for me to ask anything of you, either of you."

"Well, you got that right, at least," Louisa said.

"It was my fault, I know that. I was trapped by fear of exposure. You have no idea what it was like back then. I wanted a chance to explain, to make amends before it was too late. Time and tide," he said.

His hair glinted like foil. Dark shadows bathed his eyes; his pallor emphasised the pronounced creases in his forehead and cheeks. All the heart-searching had left its mark.

"Sadie's flowers," I said.

"Yes. Your mother told me. I wish I had been there for you."

"Kate was there."

He smiled ruefully. "I'm glad. I'd like your forgiveness. I don't deserve it but I'd like it all the same."

Robbie had his own questions. "I don't understand why my mother never mentioned Genevieve and Louisa. She didn't even say anything when I moved up to Liverpool. I had no idea you'd been married. I didn't know you had a family until you told me earlier."

"Min didn't like Violette, that's why she never mentioned her. Violette was beautiful, exotic; unusual. All the characteristics I loved in her, my sister shied away from. She wasn't one to make waves. She was scared of what other people might think. What I'd done was scandalous in her eyes. I suppose it was, then. She felt it reflected badly on the family and I suppose it did. She was delighted when they moved north. She had a good excuse not to keep in touch and she didn't have to worry that her friends would find out about me."

"You make her sound awful, uncaring. She wasn't," Robbie said.

Papa shrugged. "That's just how it was. She wanted to play by society's rules and who can blame her. It was to be kept a secret in the family. We'd all taken an unspoken vow of silence. I didn't want to talk about it. I was terrified the truth would emerge and I'd have to take the consequences. The sad thing is of course, had it happened a few years later there wouldn't have been any and Violette and I might have had a second chance."

"Mum was over forty when I was born," Robbie explained. "She lost her first husband in a road accident. She'd only been married to my father for a couple of years when I turned up. I was quite a surprise by all accounts."

"That's why 'Snow' didn't ring any bells," I said.

"You were both much older than me. I suppose it didn't occur to her that I might like to meet my cousins. You remind me of her, Louisa."

"I always wondered where I got my baby blue eyes from," Louisa said. I could tell she liked him. "Where is she now?"

"No longer with us I'm afraid. She died last year. My dad's still alive. He lives down in Bristol."

Suddenly I heard my mother's voice again, *"Toujours là"*, she had said. "She tried to tell me, Lou. I didn't get it. Still there, that's what she said to me. Tell Louisa he's still there, but I didn't understand. If only I'd realised at the time what those words signified."

"One swallow does not a summer make," she quoted. "And I have no idea where that came from ... it was too little too late." She looked at Papa. "You could have just called," she said. "You must have known Mrs. Dukes would have our numbers."

He put his glass down and shook his head. "No, I couldn't." She looked daggers at him. "I've said my piece. You know everything there is to know. I'm tired. It's been a long day. I can tell you'd rather I wasn't here. It's up to you two now." He stood up and leant heavily on his stick. "If you want to keep in touch, Robbie knows where I am."

We heard the front door open. I had forgotten about Becky. We couldn't hide who she was. We could not pretend he was someone different. She might recognise him from the photograph the minute she saw him. "Becky's back," I said. I looked to Louisa for guidance.

She understood. "Don't say anything else," she said menacingly. "It's Genie's granddaughter."

"I'm back, Gran," she called from the hall. "It was really good, all about a rat that can cook and he was French. It had a really funny name ... the film I mean, not the rat, *Ratatouille* and ..." she came running into the lounge, bringing a blast of fresh air with her. She stopped dead the minute she saw Robbie and then Papa. She gasped. "Gran," she said again and seemed to melt into my side.

I knew at once how to play it. She would never know her grandfather, how could I deny her a great grandfather? "It's all right, Becky," I said. You know Robbie, don't you and this is ..."

"I know who it is," she whispered. "Is he real?"

256

He laughed. "Indeed I am." He held out a hand to Becky and smiled at her in that charming way he had. Her eyes were rounder than usual and as blue as the bluebells my mother had so despised as she stretched hers out to him with a shy smile, wary of losing contact with me. He shook it briefly. "Nice to meet you, Becky," he said. "And this must be, friend Kate," he went on, treating Kate to another of his smiles. "I was just leaving but I hope we'll meet again soon."

"Just a minute," I said. "Do you have to leave right now?"

He looked at Louisa. "Do I?" he asked. You could have heard the beating of all our hearts as she made up her mind.

"Yes, I think you do," she said.

I detected the distress in her eyes and then the disappointment in his. "That's fine," he said. "I'll go, but don't make Robbie pay for my mistakes, please."

Chapter 31

"What a charming man," Kate said when they had gone. "Why didn't you want him to stay? I wouldn't have minded."

Louisa glowered at her. "I don't believe we're having this conversation," she said. "It's weird ... he's weird. How come he's all sweetness and light now when it suits him? I still say he could have called."

"He explained about that," I said.

"Well I don't buy it."

Becky's eyes were like saucers. "He is quite old," she said.

Louisa opened her mouth to say something else. I gave her a meaningful glance. Becky did not need to hear her opprobrium. "He's ninety," I said. "That is quite old."

"Where has he come from?" she asked.

"He was in France, all this time."

"Why was Robbie Snow here?"

"Papa's his uncle. Do you remember me telling you about my aunt Min?"

"You mean Minerva," Becky said.

"That's right. Robbie's her son."

"He's our cousin," Louisa said.

"You said she didn't have any children."

"She didn't. Robbie turned up much later after her first husband died and she married again. He was a surprise baby."

"Just like ours. Does Mum know?"

"Not yet. We'll tell her when we get back home. You were right about *Electra*, Kate," I said. "He was trying to make contact, tell us in a round-a-bout way that he was still alive."

"I thought it must mean something."

"Who was *Electra,* Gran?"

"You've seen the picture in my lounge."

"Yes, but who *was* Electra?" she asked.

"She was a character from Greek mythology. There was a play about her. Some awful things happened to her and her family," I said.

"Like what?"

"Well, she plotted with her brother to kill her mother."

"Why?"

"I'll tell you upstairs, it's past your bed-time."

There were a few more questions along the same lines and by the time she was finally in bed it was well after eleven. I tucked her in and went back to join the others.

"Look at the time," I said. "Her mother would be horrified if she knew she'd been up so late."

"What the eye doesn't see ..." Kate said. She yawned.

"You must be exhausted. I feel really guilty about all this."

"You have to stop feeling guilty about things, Genie, there's no need. Everything is fine, I'm enjoying the drama; Di's going to be sorry she missed it. Do you mind if I text her?"

"Text away ... I wonder what Cerys will say."

"Are you sure you shouldn't phone her?" Kate said. "She needs to know what's been going on."

"She will but it's not the sort of thing you can explain in five minutes over the phone. I'll tell her when I get back.

It's really strange; it makes me feel quite young to know my father's still alive."

Louisa glared at me. "It makes me feel quite sick."

"What he told us, well, it explains a lot. Why she didn't want to talk about him, why she destroyed all the photographs…"

"And why she felt the need to have so many other men," Louisa said. "I guess she had to convince herself she was still attractive to the opposite sex."

"I suppose so."

"What he did was pretty radical at the time," Kate said. "Not to mention illegal. He could have gone to prison."

"Trust you to consider the practicalities," I said, my mind still on the emotional. "But you're right. You tend to forget about all that."

"I'm glad it's not like that now," Louisa said.

"What a waste," I said. "We've lost all those years."

"Are you going to keep in touch?" Kate asked.

Louisa looked at me. "I don't know," she said.

"I think we should. I believe him when he said she threw him out. I see why he couldn't keep in touch. He was protecting us in a way. His actions would have had an impact on all of us if even just a hint of what he'd done had got out."

"I'm not ready for hearts and roses," she said.

"I think Becky would like us to," I persisted. "I've a feeling they're going to be great friends."

Kate had gone all serious. "I think you should," she said. "It would be some compensation for the years of heartache. Seize the day. That's what Iris has taught me. Squeeze every drop out of what life has to offer, while you can … apart from which, I'd like to get to know him better. He intrigues me."

Louisa pulled a face. "Why is he the hero all of a sudden?"

"He's like my lucky charm, Lou. *Electra,* the detective work … he's taken my mind off Iris, helped me to shrink her away."

"You've never been superstitious," I said.

"I'm like everyone else, Genie; any port in a storm. I've made a date for my first sitting with Robbie. I want to get on with the painting now."

"Robbie's a sweetie. I'd like to keep in touch with him," Louisa said.

"How do you think you'll do that without including Papa?" She shrugged and I left it. She was too upset to think rationally. "What are you going to call the portrait, Kate," I asked, "Surely not 'Iris'."

"*The first cut is the deepest,*" she said without hesitation.

Louisa thawed a little. She smiled. "*… When it comes to being lucky he's cursed …*" she trilled.

"*… and when it comes to loving me he's worst …*" I finished off, surprisingly in tune. It must have been all that wine. "That's what I thought, anyway," I said sheepishly.

"He said he's always loved both of us and I'd like to believe that at least," Louisa said. "I want something to hang on to; circumstances, society, life and times … Lettie even, take your pick. They're to blame for keeping us apart, not him. I'll give him that. I just wish he'd had the courage to get in touch sooner. We needed him, Genie and he wasn't there. I can't let that go."

"You've all been there for me," Kate said. "I couldn't have done it without you."

Louisa contemplated her empty wine glass. "Let's crack open another bottle," she said.

"You'll have to go down to the petrol station if you want more," Kate said. "I told you, that's the last one."

"I don't know where you get all your energy," I said. "After the day we've had, I'm ready for sleep." I stood up. "My head's spinning. I'm off to bed."

Kate nodded. "So am I. Sweet dreams everyone."

"Party poopers," Louisa said but she followed us upstairs.

My mind was ticking over and, tired though I was, I couldn't sleep. Seeing my father again after all those years had lent a surreal quality to the evening. His revelations had stunned me. It was as if I had been a bystander in everything; watching from the stalls. It was about a life. Not my life. He'd had little part in that. It was not as if he had told us much about what he had been doing, either, but what he had said had left me wanting more.

All those years of wondering and then as soon as I saw him, they telescoped down to nothing. None of that mattered. He was there and it was as if he had always been there. The past is not as far away as we imagine. It is not a series of photographs in an album to be brought out from time to time and pored over. It cannot be viewed in isolation. Ripples of it spread among us and cling to every fibre like honey to a comb. The past is part of the present and the future. We were all proof of that and now he had come back into our lives, so was he. I had answers to some of the questions I had been asking for ever. My bitterness had gone. Forgiveness was just a whisker away. I hoped Louisa would be able to forgive, in time. She had to or it would eat away at her, day by day, bit by bit, until her peace of mind was as insubstantial as a lace doily.

I decided to try and get some sleep. I turned off the light and I had just re-arranged my pillows when there was a knock on the door. "Genie, are you awake... can I come in?"

"Yes." I said. I sat up again and switched on the bedside lamp. "Come in, Lou."

She was in her nightclothes, her face smothered in cream. "My mind's all over the place," she said.

"Mine, too."

She sat on the bed beside me. "It might have been better if he'd just stayed away and we could have carried on as before. I think it was selfish of him to stir everything up again."

"I can't see it that way. I'm trying to understand his motives," I said. "I want to forgive him. It's the only way I'm going to get any peace." His one indiscretion had cost me a marriage but it had cost him a marriage, too. It could have cost me my life if Kate and Diana had not rallied round. I wanted him to know that. I would tell him eventually.

"He doesn't seem to have a clue how hard it's been for us."

"I still want to forgive him," I said.

"I feel completely let down. He could easily have found us but he didn't bother in all those years. It was cruel. I can't play happy families now."

"I know, but something in me wants to, Lou. Kate said I was soft and maybe I am, but I'm not going to deny myself a relationship with him for what time he has left. Life's too short to bear grudges."

"I guess so, but how do you let them go?"

"I can't tell you that. It's something you have to work out for yourself."

"What if I can't?"

"You will. I believe he's paid the price. He doesn't know us, didn't see us grow up. He hasn't met his grandsons. I'm glad Cerys and Becky will be able to get to know him … and the little one to come. He must have led a lonely life unable to be himself and without a family around him. I suppose I feel sorry for him."

"I don't. I can't imagine how Lettie felt when she found out what he'd done. I almost feel sorry for *her*." She stood up. "I'm not as good as you, Genie. I'm not ready to forgive. I need to talk to Carter. Goodness knows what he'll say."

"Don't you want the boys to meet him?"

She shook her head. "Not until I've worked out what I think about everything."

"You will tell them, though, won't you? You have to."

"Why?"

"If you keep it from them, you'll be starting the secrets all over again. It'll be on your mind day and night eating away at you the whole time; should you, shouldn't you? You know what it's been like for me." My phone buzzed. I had a quick glance at it. "It's a message from Cerys."

"Are they on track now?"

"Yes, thank goodness." I scrolled down the message. "Oh ... they've found out the sex of the baby."

"You said you didn't want to know."

"I didn't but Cerys obviously needs to tell me. It's a boy. Kit wants to call him James after Papa. She's worried I won't approve." I looked up at her. "See? He's back. He's not going away. We've been given another chance."

She frowned. "Do I want one? What if he lets us down again?"

I took her hand in mine. "We have to trust him. There are no guarantees but I'm sure it's the right thing to do, for all of us."

"I need more time, Genie. I'd better let you get some sleep." She bent down to kiss me. I clung to her hand and kissed her back. "Wait for me," she said.

"Always," I said. She slipped her hand away, blew me another kiss and padded off to bed.

Chapter 32

I turned off the lamp and lay back, staring up at the darkened ceiling imagining a sky full of stars. It was sad Louisa was having trouble with Papa's reappearance. I understood why. He had been dead to us for years and, we thought, unable to influence events; unable to give us the support we needed but he had been there all the time, just a step away from our lives. He could have intervened and yet he had chosen to do nothing.

My own attitude surprised me. Had I been asked before his re-appearance, I would have claimed to have wanted nothing to do with him after the heartbreak he had caused. In reality it was not like that. I needed him and whatever Louisa might think I felt her boys had a right to meet him and make up their own minds. They were adults, after all. It was for them to choose if they wanted a relationship with their grandfather or not. He had served his time. We should all be granted a second chance. The children were the future and he had to be a part of it. It would be wrong to airbrush him out.

We could be proud of what we had salvaged from the debris of our shattered relationships with our parents. It had been in his gift to put things right and, although rather late in the day, he had done it. That was very much in his favour as far as I was concerned. It was too painful for her at the

265

moment but perhaps, one day, she would be able to appreciate that.

None of us could forget about the past. Even if it were possible, I knew Becky wouldn't let us. It was not to be feared; it had lost its power to disturb and alarm. There would be no more things left unsaid, no more secrets to be kept unless Louisa refused Papa access to her sons. If she did that, she would be burdening them with her hurt and the whole cycle would begin again.

He should have tried to stay in touch. It was wrong of him not to attempt it. She could not accept the reasoning behind his inability to do so. I could. I did.

The past had been as hostile a place for her as it had been for me. It had been a harsh place over which we had wielded no control and a lot of bad things had happened; a place that had not been safely settled. After this evening it felt less forbidding, safer with the menace gone. I wished Louisa could feel that too and we could all move on.

Kate was moving on. Iris had taught her a valuable lesson. Life is precious. Friends are precious, too. I remembered reading somewhere that the heart of true friendship is a paradox. The more you share the more you have. We were an integral part of each other's lives. We thrived on the mutual support and affection. It was the best sort of family. The only family I had been able to rely on for many years with Lou in America.

I flipped on the bed-side light again and re-read the message. I made my decision. James was a good name. It was fine by me and despite what I had said earlier, I was going to tell Cerys about her grandfather. I was not going to wait until I got home. Kate was right. She needed to know. I had a feeling we might not be home as soon as we had planned and anyway, with my new-found zeal I did not want to be accused of keeping the truth from her.

I pressed 'reply' and I was busy searching for the letters I would need to send my message when I heard a faint scratching on the door and then Becky's voice this time, diffident, no more than a whisper, "Gran ..."

I pushed the duvet out of the way and got up. "What is it?" I opened the door. "Can't you sleep? Don't you feel well?"

She stood there in her nightdress, hair tumbling down her back like a Victorian child waiting for a candle to light her way to bed. "Can I ask you something?"

I urged her in and closed the door as softly as I could so as not to disturb Kate and Louisa. "Come and cuddle up with me for a minute, we don't want to wake the others." She settled down in my bed with her head on my shoulder. I tucked the duvet round us like pastry round an apple pie. "There, snug as two bugs in a rug. What's bothering you?" I said. "Would you like a drink?"

"No, I'm not thirsty. I've been thinking. Where's Lettie gone?"

I had not expected that; quite a question for the early hours of the morning. I did not know if I was up to answering it. "How do you mean?" I asked, buying myself some time.

"Can anyone die and come back to life?"

It was hardly the time for a deep philosophical discussion but I thought I could satisfy her curiosity. "Um … not as a general rule …" I said "... although sometimes it happens in hospital." It was the reply of a lapsed catholic but I hoped it would do.

"Well, Mac died and he's come back to life. Lettie was dead and then she was alive and now she's dead again. Will she come back? Will he go? Are they ghosts?"

Seen from that perspective it was not surprising she was confused. Louisa's ghost hunt must have been preying on her mind. "There are no ghosts," I said firmly. "It's quite simple. Lettie has gone and she's not coming back. It's my fault for not telling you the whole story. I should have explained about her before. I'm really sorry I didn't.

Grown-ups make mistakes and get confused too, you know."

"What about Mac, will he stay?"

"I hope so. He's always been there but I couldn't have told you about him because I didn't know. I was shocked when I found out he was still alive. I hope he'll be here long enough for us to get to know him better. Would you like that?"

"Yes, but ..." she looked at me, her face full of apprehension.

"What is it? What's worrying you now?"

"What's going to happen to me, Gran?"

I put an arm around her shoulders and held her close. "That's easy. You're not going anywhere. You'll grow into a beautiful young woman. You'll find fame and fortune as a writer or a scientist ... or anything else you choose to be; you'll fall for a handsome young man who'll love you more than anything else in the whole wide world ... and you'll be able to explain all this to your little brother so that he'll understand all the things you didn't."

She looked up at me, surprise in those round blue eyes. "A brother ... Mum's having a little boy?"

"She is and she's going to call him, James."

She yawned. "My very own brother ... cool ... just wait till I tell Mia. She's only got two sisters," she said.

I laughed. "Poor Mia; you might change your mind about your brother when he's here. He'll probably want you to play football with him."

"And paper aeroplanes," she said with another yawn. "I won't mind. At lunch time at school the boys are always throwing them around the hall ... Gran ..."

"Yes."

"I was wondering ..."

"Here we go."

"It's nothing bad," she said. "I just wondered if you could tell me about Romulus and Remus now."

268

"Oh ... that. Well, they were twin brothers. Their mother was a princess and their father was Mars, the Roman god of war. When they grew up, they both wanted to be king so they had a fight. Romulus killed Remus with a rock."

"I won't argue with my brother, I promise," she said and yawned once more. "Thanks, Gran, g'night."

"Good night, Becky," I said but I could tell from her breathing that she was already asleep.

Emotionally she had been through a lot in the last few months. I was glad she felt able to talk about things. We had all been tested, one way or another. Kate was dealing with Iris, Cerys and Kit had mended their marriage, Lettie had gone and Papa had come back to us.

The baby was a blessing, a new life, a new start. I couldn't wait for him to arrive, to meet his great grandfather and for Papa to meet his namesake. He had missed out on so much. Sadie had missed out on so much. Her life had been cut short but she had played a vital part in ours. Without her, Louisa would not have made a fuss about the flowers and Papa could have been lost to us for ever.

Becky stirred in my arms. I was lucky to have watched her grow up. I sensed the wholesome fragrance of youth; the sweet scent of tomorrow. I feared Louisa's tomorrows would be difficult until she could find her way through the morass of emotion, the maze of heart-searching, to where she needed to be.

I reached across to the lamp one last time and as the light faded I realised there was no need for the dream dodging any longer. The nightmares had gone. I was calm as I prepared to let the day go, content; ready for the sweet dreams Kate had wished for me and Papa had made possible. The texting could wait until the morning. It was unlikely that Cerys would pick up the message until then anyway.

My journey was over; Louisa's journey was just beginning. There would be no short cuts. It might take her a while to turn the past into a place where she felt safe enough to forgive, a place where she felt settled.

There was no doubt in my mind that I wanted Papa to be a part of our lives from now on. I was looking forward to hearing about his life and sharing mine with him. I had learned how to live without a mother but some small part of me still yearned to be a daddy's girl. I hoped it would not be long before Louisa felt the same. She had said she could not play happy families. I hoped that would change. After all those years in an emotional wilderness, I was ready to play the game. I wanted us to be a proper family once more and however long it took, I would be waiting … we would both be waiting … for Louisa to join us.

Elisabeth Thompson was born in Crosby, Liverpool, but is now resident in West Sussex.

She only found the time to write after a short career at the Foreign Office in London followed by various personal assistant posts in the north-west, after raising her five children, years spent as a foster carer and as a respite carer for children with special needs.

The common theme in all her books is the nature of family relationships and the importance of close friends. Her own core friends are of very long-standing and important to her ... as is her husband and family.

Her favourite quote is from Jane Austen -
'Let other pens dwell on guilt and misery.'

Also available from Elisabeth Thompson

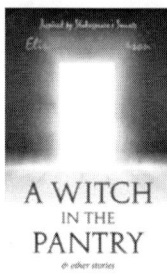